The Unworthy Duke

Charlotte Anne

16pt

Copyright Page from the Original Book

Title: THE UNWORTHY DUKE

Published by
Escape
An imprint of Harlequin Enterprises (Australia) Pty Limited (ABN 47 001 180 918), a subsidiary of HarperCollins Publishers Australia Pty Limited (ABN 36 009 913 517)
Level 13, 201 Elizabeth St
SYDNEY NSW 2000
AUSTRALIA

www.romance.com.au

TABLE OF CONTENTS

The Unworthy Duke
Charlotte Anne

Witty, passionate and fast-paced, this sparkling debut Regency romance is a must-read for any fan of Georgette Heyer.

She's running from her past; he's hiding from his.

Miss Ellen Burney doesn't have a penny to her name. Determined to escape scandal, she flees to London and becomes Miss Smith: spinster and lady's companion. London offers security in anonymity. So long as Ellen can rein in her overactive imagination and become the perfect picture of propriety.

Calum Callaghan spent ten years in the Royal Navy fighting Napoleon and has the scars to prove it. Now he's a duke, but all of London thinks he murdered his brother. Heartbroken and battle weary, he's locked himself away for four long years, a prisoner in his own townhouse.

That is, until Cal's grandmother comes to stay with him for the London Season, her new lady's companion in tow. A lady's companion with a passion for life and love that can hardly be contained by even the most spinsterish of lace caps. She's fooling nobody, especially not this grumpy duke.

About Charlotte Anne

With a degree in archaeology, **CHARLOTTE ANNE** now pens steamy historical romances. She's been writing for as long as she can remember, and in her spare time she climbed to Mt Everest Base Camp and earned her black belt in taekwondo. She's even a pretty good shot with a bow.

Twitter: *@CharlotteABooks*
Website: charlotteannebooks.com

Acknowledgements

The book you're holding would not be in existence today without the help, support and encouragement of so many amazing people. I wish I could thank every single person who has been a part of my writing, but then the acknowledgments would undoubtedly be longer than the book itself. Nevertheless, there are a few I wish to thank by name. My editor, Rachael Donovan, for seeing the potential in my writing the very first time we met more than five years ago (and more than three years before *The Unworthy Duke* was even a twinkle in my eye). Laurie Ormond, for her thoughtful edits, and the rest of the team at Escape Publishing for their support. My beta readers: Jacinta Anderson, Victoria Seymour and Angela Lee. You ladies were honest, insightful and caring. Dr Adrienne White for keeping me company while writing these last ... many years. My wonderful family. My parents and my sister. I could not love you more if I had been given a second heart. My grandparents, especially Little Grandpa, who read the books that came before this one—and who tried to teach a writer how to math. All our puppy dogs and kitty cats, especially Princess and Lizzy, after whom Tzar is fashioned. Myself, for taking my writing seriously. Finally, my readers. This book is dedicated to every free-thinking, romance-loving individual.

Author's note

For anyone who's wondering, I named the Burney family in honour of Frances Burney, a writer from the late 18th and early 19th centuries. She had four novels published. Her work was read and admired by Jane Austen. (And it was from *Evelina* that I borrowed the idea of a night at the fireworks.)

Similarly, the idea for the overall plot came to me when I read a song verse in *Life in London* by Pierce Egan, first published in 1821:

If once to Almack's you belong,
Like Monarchs you can do no wrong;
But banished thence, on Wednesday night,
By Jove you can do nothing right.

As Georgette Heyer wrote in *Arabella*, this novel is a 'Variation on an Original Theme'.

Chapter One

Evendale, Yorkshire
Early spring, 1817

Miss Ellen Burney glanced towards the bedroom door even as she tossed the last of her meagre belongings into her portmanteau. Her heart pounded against her chest so hard and fast she thought it might break free.

Beyond the window, threatening storm clouds were gathering, dampening the last of the sunlight. But Ellen didn't dare light a candle. If her brother returned to a dark house, he would think she was asleep and not notice her disappearance until morning. It was the best she could hope for.

Her bedroom door flew open emitting a gust of cool air. Ellen spun around, but it was only Maggie.

'Everything's organised,' her mother's childhood friend said in her no-nonsense fashion. 'The hired coach is around the back. It will take you as far as the neighbouring village, and from there you'll have to catch the mail coach to London. I've already paid the driver.'

'And Gwen?' As Ellen asked after her, she saw Gwen's face as it had been the day Geoffery had hit her—her wide eyes full of unshed tears, her lips pressed tightly closed against a cry of pain and one side of her face stamped bright red with his handprint.

'Safe. Verity is taking her to my sister-in-law's house, and I'll meet them there as soon as you're on your way, just as we planned.' Maggie smiled, but it looked forced.

Ellen ran a hand over her face, trying to push away her panic. She needed to keep a clear head.

'Have you packed everything you need?' Maggie asked. 'Do you have the marchioness's letter?'

'Yes.' Ellen raised her right hand, indicating the small reticule looped around her wrist. The letter was safe inside. The movement caused the long sleeve of her washed-out gown to slip.

Maggie winced at the sight of the bruises colouring Ellen's wrists. 'We should leave. The sooner, the better.' Maggie clicked the portmanteau shut, lifting one end. Ellen tucked her bandbox under her arm and followed suit.

Together they manoeuvred the portmanteau through the doorway and down the stairs. It was heavier than expected; all she had inside were clothes. Her brother had pawned everything of value Ellen had owned as fuel for his gambling addiction, even their mother's crockery, which had been worth far more to her than the few pounds he'd sold it for.

Yet, like a fool, Ellen had believed Geoffrey when he'd apologised, when he'd said he was sorry. Again and again she'd forgiven him for breaking her heart—and had taken much of the blame for his actions onto her own shoulders. But not any longer. The moment he'd turned his anger towards Gwen was the moment Ellen had vowed never to let a man control their lives again. Gwen was only a child for heaven's sake, and he'd hit her. Just the once, but once was one time too many.

Maggie exhaled in short, determined pants. Her straw bonnet had slipped to one side revealing the frill edge of her mob cap and a strand of prematurely grey hair, while the worn heels of her ankle boots seemed to hit every creaky floorboard. Despite Maggie's fear of Geoffrey, she'd stayed by Ellen's side through all the hardships, and now she would be caring for Gwen when Ellen could not. 'I don't know how I can ever possibly thank you.'

'Nonsense,' Maggie rebuked. 'You and Guinevere safe and sound is all the thanks I need.'

As they came into sight of the back door, Ellen let out a deep breath, a breath it seemed she'd been holding onto for two long years. 'In that case, let's get out of here.'

***

7 Roseworthy Street, Mayfair, London
Two days later

Cal stared out the window. It was going to rain. He could smell it in the air. Clouds hung thick and heavy over London, reminding him of the quiet moments before a battle.

He hated rain! Always had. Always would.

He poured himself another generous glass of good ol' Scottish whisky, glancing suspiciously at the almost empty bottle. Hadn't he just opened it a couple of days ago?

Ignoring the glass, he took a swig straight from the bottle, tipping his head back to drain the last mouthful. He tossed the empty bottle carelessly onto the settee, relishing the fire as it burned its way down his throat. It hit the velvet armrest and bounced onto the floor, rolling out of sight.

Lightning flashed, illuminating the armorial window and chequering the room in heraldic yellow and blue. For a fraction of a second, a great bear, raised high on its hindquarters, marked the far wall, and the family motto stamped itself across Cal's chest.

On we fight.

He yanked the curtains closed, throwing the room into darkness. He'd given up fighting a long time ago.

Thunder cracked, shaking the house until the crystal chandeliers rattled. Cal's heart started racing. *Ye gods.* Why did thunder have to sound so much like canon fire? He fisted his hands to resist the almost overwhelming urge to drop to the ground and cover his head in preparedness for an attack that wasn't coming.

You're safe, ye fool. A bit of rain couldn't hurt him. He forced his legs into action, the familiar ache of his wounded knee slowing his progress. There had to be another bottle around here somewhere. That was one of the few perks of having inherited, amongst other things, his father's distillery.

An inheritance he'd never expected nor wanted.

***

'Are you sure I canna drop you off somewhere else, miss?' The driver raised bushy eyebrows as he reined in the lanky horse drawing his gig. When he'd first collected her off the mail coach, he'd been a little suspicious of a well-spoken woman travelling alone but, thankfully, hadn't refused to carry her. Now, he was apparently having second thoughts about leaving her at the requested address with nothing more than an old portmanteau and a battered bandbox.

He cast a glance towards the house, and Ellen followed his gaze.

Set apart from its neighbours by a great wall, the townhouse sat back from the street front. There was not a single light in any of the blind windows, and a wooden sign hung from the front gates. Someone had crossed out 'Yew Tree House' and scrawled 'Keep Out!' in white paint.

Ellen's stomach churned, whether from apprehension or travel sickness courtesy of the hired hackney, she couldn't tell. Either way, there was a heaviness about the house which its neighbours didn't share. It was almost as if the looming storm clouds shadowed the rusty trellis with intent.

She nodded her thanks to the driver. 'I'm sure, thank you though.' She couldn't delay the inevitable any longer. What was Maggie always saying? Something undoubtedly pragmatic ... *Nothing ventured, nothing gained.*

'All right then, miss.' He helped her down and she paid him with the last of her money—the last pin money her father had ever given her before his death two years before. She'd managed to keep it hidden from her brother by sewing it into the hem of her petticoat.

Depositing her belongings before the front gates, the driver tipped his hat and urged his horse to trot on. A moment later, the clip-clop of hooves had faded into nothingness, leaving Ellen utterly alone.

She let out a shuddering breath.

Thankfully, the gates weren't actually locked, and she pushed them open as far as she could, the hinges creaking in protest. She managed to balance her bandbox on top of her portmanteau and drag them both through the gate, leaving behind two deep scores in the unkempt garden path.

If it could even be called a garden. There were more weeds than flowers, more fallen leaves than grass, more dead plants than living. Her green thumb began to itch. She hated to see a garden in such disrepair. It would be so very satisfying to tame the wayward myrtle hedge, the rambling rose and the prickly holly.

Ellen's trunk hindered her progress, as did the low-hanging branches of an old yew tree, presumably the one after which the house was originally named. But in no time at all the house loomed ahead. It was three storeys high, four including the attic, with rows of symmetrical sash windows and a blanket of overgrown ivy. There was a rather picturesque balcony leading off the first storey but it was in disrepair. In fact, the whole house, like its garden, had seen better days. Even in the half-light of dusk, she could see that the window shutters hung crooked and a few slate tiles had slipped from the roof.

To think this was the house of marchioness!

She glanced down at her reticule. Inside was her letter of employment from none other than Lady Faye. When Verity, one of her mother's two closest childhood friends, had first told Ellen of the dowager marchioness who was seeking a companion for the London Season, Ellen had found out everything she could about her. Without coin for a newspaper to peruse the society pages, Ellen had taken advantage of the circulating library's outdated copy of *Debrett's*.

Accordingly, she knew Lady Faye's husband had been dead these last ten years. Their only child, Grace, had married the Duke of Woodhal, but the duke had died four years ago, about the same time as their only son and heir had also died. Neither the widowed duchess nor Lady Faye had any other close family living in England.

Ellen was no stranger to death herself. At the back of her mind, she had the grand idea that she'd bring a spark of happiness to the elderly dowager's life. They'd bond over their shared losses, and then Lady Faye would adopt

Ellen as a daughter, and Ellen would tell Lady Faye all about her baby sister, and Gwen would come to live with them in London and—

Ellen Burney, that's not how the real world works. She needed to keep tight control of her imagination. Working for the dowager was her new start, and she couldn't say or do or think anything that wasn't completely right and proper for a lady's companion.

As far as Lady Faye was concerned, Ellen *Smith* was the only child of a gentleman who'd died leaving her with little money. It would be better if the dowager knew nothing of Geoffrey, and it would be better if Geoffrey knew nothing of Ellen's whereabouts.

And Gwen ... Well, Gwen had to stay hidden in the country with Maggie. A lady's companion couldn't bring her baby sister to London with her. And coming to London was the only way Ellen could make enough money to start a fresh life for Gwen and herself away from Geoffrey.

Mounting the front steps, she gave the bell chain a tug. The door was not as expected. It was actually two doors, side by side, and they both opened from the right. She could see where some of the bricks had been removed either side to make room for the double doors.

The last echo of the bell died, but nobody came, so she rang again. Still nobody came. She looked up at the house, searching for signs of life. Nothing. Her heart started racing.

She'd been careful to follow the instructions in the dowager's letter—she knew this was the right house and the right evening. But it was quickly growing darker. Soon the last of the light would disappear. Panic bubbled in her stomach—this was definitely worse than feeling a little travel sickness. She had nowhere else to go and no more money.

A large raindrop hit her cheek and rolled down her chin. She glanced skywards. The storm that had chased her from Evendale to London had finally broken. There was a flash of lightning, a rumble of thunder and a great torrent began cascading from the sky. Within a handful of heartbeats, she was drenched through to her chemise. She tried pressing herself against the front door under the shelter of the narrow eaves. White paint peeling from the doorframe glued itself to her wet gloves.

This time she banged on the door with the rusty lion-head knocker. The sound reverberated through the belly of the house, low and deep like the thunder overhead. No answering flicker of light responded.

Even if the dowager was out for the evening, where were all her servants? Abed already? It was extraordinarily improbable.

She couldn't possibly stay outside in this torrent. She'd likely catch her death—or worse, the neighbours might see her and start gossiping. She couldn't risk anything jeopardising her employment. Lady Faye was her last, and only, hope.

***

Cal sat up, grunting in pain as all the blood in his head seemed to rush to the back of his eyes. *Hell!* He lay back down, trying to stretch out his legs, but his feet hit the curved arm of the settee. He cursed again. When was he going to learn drinking himself to sleep was only a good idea when he actually made it to bed?

The storm had finally hit. Rain lashed at the windows.

He rolled onto his side, presenting his back to the storm, startling the dog. Tzar growled his annoyance at being woken, so Cal draped his arm over the edge of the settee, ruffling the wiry fur.

A light breeze tickled his forehead, and he stilled. He hadn't left the window open—had he?

Crash!

Someone had toppled onto the floor by the window and was struggling to their feet in a tangle of curtain. All Cal could see was a slender silhouette.

He crossed the room as quickly as he could manage with his knee seizing. His head thumped with each step. A thief wouldn't be chicken-brained enough to try to steal from him. A bairn then, whose devilish friends had dared them to break into the house of the crippled recluse. Either way, they hadn't heard him, too focused on detangling themselves from the curtain to notice his silent approach.

He caught their elbow in one hand and shook. 'Who the bloody hell are ye?'

Chapter Two

Instinct kicked in and Ellen swung her reticule towards her attacker's face. It hit, and he cursed, his words coloured by a strong Scottish accent.

'Let me go.' She tried to break free, but his fingers dug into her upper arm with painful force. Her heart started stampeding in her chest. 'You're hurting me.'

Pulling her back towards the window, her attacker shoved the heavy curtain aside so the muted light touched her face.

'Not a bairn,' he said, his voice rising slightly in surprise. 'A lass.'

Ellen raised her most ferocious scowl. She could hardly see the bounder's face; her eyes hadn't yet adjusted to the near complete darkness inside, and it was difficult to make out more than the size of him. He was tall—taller than the average Englishman. And wide—his shoulders broad and straight.

The room smelled neglected, like dust and the dark aroma of alcohol.

His grip on her arm wasn't loosening, and she tried to shrug away from him. 'You're still hurting me.'

He released her like she'd burned him, and Ellen scuttled across the room, putting the chaise longue between them. 'I'm not a lass,' she said, rubbing her arm. At the very least, he hadn't grabbed her already bruised wrists. 'I'm the daughter of a respectable gentleman, and I'm expected.'

'Like hell ye're expected.' His voice was rapidly gathering volume. 'Get out!'

She moved back another half step and tripped over something lying on the floor. It was a pair of men's boots, causally abandoned beside a dark mass she guessed could only be the man's jacket and neckcloth. Had he been sleeping here? Most likely he was the footman who was supposed to have opened the door for her. Whatever was the matter with him?

'Her ladyship is expecting me.' She spoke using slow, clear words. Perhaps he was hard of hearing. Across the room he was nothing more than a dark shape against an even darker backdrop of brocade curtain. 'I'm to be the dowager's new companion.'

'Eh?'

'I'm to meet Lady Faye here. She's engaged me for the Season.' A full four months at thirty pounds per annum plus a letter of recommendation. Such a letter would guarantee Ellen long-term employment in another respectable establishment under the safety of her new alias. Such employment would mean Ellen could afford the expense of a boarding school in Bath for Gwen so that she would have a chance at a proper education and a new life. Perhaps they would even be able to spend the holidays together.

'Lady Faye?'

'Yes,' she practically yelled. People who were hard of hearing could often read lips, but there wasn't enough light for him to see her clearly and she most certainly wasn't moving any closer. Not until she knew exactly who this man was and where the dowager was.

She pressed a hand to her chest, trying to steady her racing heart. *You are calm; you are collected; you are a lady's companion of impeccable propriety.* 'When do you expect her ladyship to return? I'm anxious to finally meet her.'

A breeze from the window at his back carried his aroma across the room. A heady mix of peat, heather and smoke. And more than a trace of strong spirits. Had he been drinking? The last thing she needed was a deaf, inebriated footman with a negligent work ethic.

He let out a bark of humourless laugher, limping across the room to the fireplace and throwing more coal onto the burned-out embers.

Ellen circled around the chaise longue, careful to keep the seat between them, and eyed the dark shape of his back as the flames caught light. He wore smart enough breeches, and he'd rolled up his shirtsleeves to show off decidedly muscular forearms.

She was instantly reminded of the illustrations she'd seen of Heracles—a Greek hero with muscles she never would have believed could exist on a human if she hadn't been looking at them with her own eyes. What else was this footman hiding beneath his crumpled shirt?

A lady's companion of impeccable propriety, remember?

As he turned back to face her, he crossed those gloriously muscular arms over his chest. She raised her gaze to scrutinise his face, but now the firelight was behind him she still couldn't make out the finer features of his appearance. She could tell he had a nose, two eyes, a mouth, a rather square jaw and hair much too long for a gentleman of the first order, but that was about all. She couldn't have picked him out of a crowd. Except that he probably towered over most other men.

'Whyever did ye climb through the window?' he demanded, not bothering to mince his words. ''Tis the middle the bloody night.'

He might have the body of a Greek hero, but he had the temper of ... well, the temper of a grumpy Scotsman. It was she who should be demanding answers.

'It isn't the middle of the night; it's barely twilight. And I climbed through the window because you didn't open the front door when I knocked. And it's raining,' she added unnecessarily. She could feel escaped strands of hair plastered to the back of her neck. Her bonnet was a soggy mess, the brim drooping low over her forehead, and her simple muslin day dress, already wearing thin because her brother refused to spare coin for new clothes, clung to her body with indecent familiarity. She didn't even have her threadbare pelisse to cover herself, having left it behind in the mail coach in her distraction.

Perhaps it was providence the dowager wasn't home to see her in such a state. A soaking gown was hardly the way to make a good first impression. She needed to dry off.

She fixed her gaze on the footman. So far he'd demonstrated no inclination towards an obliging manner. If she pleaded with him to help, he might take it as weakness and report it back to Lady Faye. The less the dowager knew of the window incident, the better.

'You should be ashamed of yourself for falling asleep on her ladyship's chaise longue,' she said, giving him her best glower. 'You should count yourself lucky that I've decided not to tell Lady Faye. Now, if you'd show me to my room, I'm rather tired after a long day of travel and wish to change out of these wet clothes. My trunk is outside the window.'

'I don't care if yer trunk is in Edinburgh.' He raked a hand through his long hair. 'Ye're not coming any further into my house.'

'*Your* house?' Did he think she was really going to believe that blatant lie? She was no fool. Silently, she congratulated herself for doing her research. 'You are mistaken, sir. This is the house of the Marchioness of Faye.'

'Lass, 'tis my house. I'm the bloody duke.'

***

She blinked up at him as though Cal had fired a cannonball at her.

He crossed his arms, waiting for his words to sink in. There was a lass in his front room where a lass should not be. A rather mutton-headed one as it was transpiring.

'Your house?'

'Aye.' Of course this was his damn house. 'It certainly ain't Buckingham Palace.' He shot her a sardonic look.

'I don't understand. Is her ladyship renting this house from you?'

'Nay. Her ladyship certainly is not. Her ladyship is my grandmother.' His busybody grandmother. She'd written him letter after letter, inviting him to stay at her country estate, but he'd ignored every one. What was she up to now? She hated London.

The lass shook her head, her eyes flashing with conviction. 'That, sir, is a Banbury tale, and don't try to tell me otherwise. I know Lady Faye doesn't have any living grandchildren. *Debrett's* told me so.' She scrunched up her nose. 'Admittedly, my copy was a little out of date, but not—' she waved an elegant hand in his general direction '—by thirty years.'

'I don't give a damn about your book.' If she took her information from the gossip rags like everybody else, they wouldn't be having this waste-of-a-time conversation. In fact, if she'd read the gossip rags, she wouldn't have dared climb through his front window in the first place.

Echoes of old headlines seemed to swirl about his head.

The new duke ... publicly humiliated by his stepmother ... Is the duchess right? ... Did he really kill his own half-brother?

The wee lass was either brave or foolish. Or just foolishly brave.

She raised her petite nose even further into the air. Though so much shorter she somehow still managed to talk down to him. Considering the state of her attire, it made the entire experience all that more bizarre. She couldn't have been wetter if she'd been swimming in a loch.

Dry, her gown could probably be more accurately described as a sack. Wet, it was a masterpiece. Practically scandalous. A gentleman would have offered her his jacket. Cal's jacket was bundled on the floor along with the dust and the dog hair, and there it was going to stay.

She pressed hands to hips. She really wasn't going to make this easy, for either of them. 'If you don't tell me who you really are this instant, I'll call the Bow Street Runners.'

'Ye're ruining my rug,' he said shortly. Of course he couldn't see her legs through the settee, but he could hear the steady drip of water. When Tzar actually bothered to wake up again, he wouldn't be happy to find his favourite sleeping spot damp.

'Your carpet!' She let out a contemptuous laugh but gave herself away by running her hands self-consciously down her soaking dress. His eyes followed their descent from shoulder to midriff. The fabric clung to every curve, leaving little to the imagination. This shapely but sodden lass was anything but intimidating. If his head wasn't thumping so loudly he might have been able to think of the word opposite to intimidating.

Infuriating?

'Aye, lass. 'Tis my rug. 'Tis my whole damn house.' He scowled at her, determined not to let his admiration of her finer qualities distract him.

She glanced towards the open window but otherwise stayed put. 'I'm not leaving. I'm waiting right here for her ladyship to return.'

'And why should I believe Lady Faye is expecting ye? Last I heard my grandmother was still in Gloucester, where she's been for the last four years.'

Four years since Cal had returned from sea without his half-brother by his side. Four years since Pierce's funeral, though they hadn't even had a body to bury.

The lass spluttered with indignation. Pulling a folded piece of paper from the tiny bag hanging at her wrist, she waved it at him. 'Here's my proof, sir. Which is more than I can say for your claims.' She waved the dratted paper again, moving it too fast for him to get a good look.

Her hands were shaking. She was more nervous than she was pretending to be. Cal felt a stab of admiration but pushed it aside. His eyes had started watering, and there were about fifty other things he would prefer to be doing right now. Like attempting to drink away his bad memories.

'Give over.' He limped closer and snatched the letter from her grasp before she could stop him. He opened out the single page, moving to the fire to read it by the flicking flames.

A low groan rumbled up his chest. There was no denying his grandmother's bold hand. She was indeed coming to Town. And, from the sound of it, she was expecting to stay in his house, with him.

One thing he knew for sure: she wasn't coming all the way to London just because he'd ignored a couple of letters. She hardly ever left her precious country estate, and she absolutely didn't come to Town without an ulterior motive.

'I should have known ye weren't lying, Miss Ellen Smith,' he conceded, reading her name from the letter. It was an altogether boring and very English name. 'Ye're exactly the type of impetuous lass my grandmother would employ.' He cast the letter into the fire.

'No!' The window adventuress dived around the chaise longue, reaching for the paper even as it caught light.

He wrapped an arm about her waist, pulling her back. Easy, considering how small she was. She was more wisp than woman. Yet he couldn't fail to notice how her perfect little backside pressed against him as she leaned forward, trying to struggle free of his hold. Quickly tossing her onto the chaise longue before he started noticing anything more, he watched her bounce, the old springs squeaking.

Why did a shapely arse have to be his greatest weakness?

'What did you do that for? It wasn't yours to burn.' She leaped to her feet, crossing her arms over her chest. The movement tightened the already indecently clingy fabric of her damp gown.

Intriguing, that was the word he'd been search for. *Dangerously intriguing.*

***

'You're staring.' Ellen plucked at her bodice, trying to pry the clinging fabric loose. It was he who should be embarrassed. Fancy telling lies about being the dowager's grandson, about being a duke! Surely that was a criminal offence. 'That's it, I'm fetching the Runners.' Exactly how one did that, she wasn't precisely sure, this being her first time in London. But the Runners he deserved.

'Hold yer horses, lass.' He raised his hands as if imploring the heavens to give him patience. 'I'll get ye proof.' He limped to the desk in the far corner and started riffling through one of the drawers.

Ellen tapped her foot, the heel of her half boot clicking with satisfactory impatience against the floorboards. There was nothing he could pull out of that desk that could possibly persuade her he'd been telling the truth.

The wretched Scotsman withdrew a fumble of documents and shoved them into her hands. 'I am the duke, and this is my house.'

He'd handed her some very official looking paperwork. She couldn't quite make it all out in the half-dark and she started towards the fire but realised that would bring her closer to him. Changing direction, she moved closer to the darkening window and quickly scanned their contents. They seemed to be the entitlement deeds to the Woodhal privilege.

Calum Callaghan ... eldest son of Hammond, late duke of Woodhal ... ducal heir...

But that meant ... Her stomach dropped. No. It couldn't be. The duke's son had died. *Debrett's* had told her so.

But the document in her hand was irrefutable. The man before her was...

Had *Debrett's* really gotten it so wrong? People lived their entire lives by that book.

'But that makes you...' A duke. A peer. One of the Upper Ten Thousand. Maybe even a friend of the Prince Regent himself. In short, Society!

She looked back down at the papers in her hand.

The Most Noble Calum McKenna Callaghan: Duke of Woodhal, Marquess of Holliway, Earl of Eyles, Baron Summerhayes and Gleeson.

'Son to the devil himself,' he finished aggressively. 'Aye, lass, that I am.'

'But...' She examined the documents more closely, searching for any clue that this was all a big mistake. Aside from this London townhouse, he'd also inherited his family's vast country estate and a number of smaller country properties scattered throughout England. She turned the page to find the former duke, Hammond Callaghan's personal will, bequeathing his son and heir an additional hunting lodge in Gloucester and a small but profitable distillery in Scotland.

That at least explained the smell of whisky permeating the air as if it were engrained into the very walls of the house.

'I concede I may have jumped to conclusions rather too quickly,' she said, the words catching in her throat. 'But this bequest doesn't prove *you're* the duke. You could be an impostor.' An impostor who knew exactly where the deeds were kept?

Why wasn't he dead? Hammond's son had died. *Debrett's* had said so!

She cast a desperate eye down his form. A flicker of light from the fire momentarily chased the shadows from his face. She caught a glimpse of a prickly scatting of unshaven beard over cheek and chin, and a faint shadow that might have been a scar cutting through his left temple and disappearing into his hairline.

Calum. A Scottish name. It rather suited him, she admitted to herself reluctantly. But *Duke? Your Grace?*

'Duke of Woodhal? Are you quite sure?'

'Aye, last time I checked.' He scowled down at her. Despite his distinctly dishevelled appearance, he cut a rather fine figure.

And then he bowed. It was the most on-point, elegant, self-righteous, disdainful bow she'd ever seen a gentleman make. How he managed to look both respectable and disgruntled, she couldn't comprehend. It absolutely wasn't the bow of a footman.

Oh lordy. Forget butterflies, an army of frogs leaped around her stomach. 'It appears I may have made a small mistake.'

'An understatement if ever I heard one,' he sneered.

'I beg your pardon.' It was a mistake anyone could have made. For goodness' sake, he wasn't even wearing a cravat. 'It was a mistake not entirely of my construction,' she hastened to remind him. 'You should have made yourself known the moment I climbed through your window.'

'I should have made myself known when you *climbed through my window?*' His skepticism was almost palpable. 'Now you know the truth, what are you going to do about it?'

She probably couldn't call the Bow Street Runners on a peer of the realm. Could she?

'Well,' she said, thinking fast. 'I'm still going to wait for Lady Faye. She's expecting me, even if she didn't tell you of my employ.' Was that a bad sign? Why hadn't the dowager told her grandson?

Ellen just had to hope for the best. Returning to Evendale was not an option. There was no knowing what Geoffrey would do to her.

'Ye're not waiting inside my house.'

'But this is the drawing room. It's where the guests wait.' When it wasn't being used as a duke's bedroom, apparently. 'Besides, it's still storming outside. I could catch my death out there.'

'Ye should have thought of that before ye barged into my house.'

She baulked. 'That's not very gentlemanly, Your Grace.'

'Lass, I might be a duke, but I'm certainly no gentleman.'

'I see that now. I'll have you know that, if you make me leave, my death will forever be on your conscience.'

He laughed—a single, humourless grunt of laugher. 'If ye actually read the gossip rags like everyone else, ye'd already know I don't have a conscience.'

'Well...' She floundered for a second, startled by his response. 'If that's the case ... if you make me leave, I promise my spirit will haunt you for the rest of your life. And I have to warn you, Your Grace: I'm very persistent.'

Chapter Three

Cal was not intrigued by the lass who'd climbed through his front window. Absolutely, irrefutably not. He didn't want her in his house. It was best he be left alone. It was no more than he deserved. Dammit, it would be better for the both of them if she just left!

'Did you hear me, Your G-Grace?' She faltered over his title as though she still didn't quite believe him. A small part of him hated her for it, though a bigger part didn't blame her. Hadn't he heard enough times from his stepmother that he wasn't worthy of his father's title and property? That his brother should have inherited instead? That Cal didn't act like a duke or speak like one—or even look like one?

And the gossip rags had wasted no time agreeing with her. What was it they'd written about him when his father and brother had died four years ago? Who was he fooling? He could recite all the articles by heart.

Nothing more than a rough-and-tumble Scotsman ... The man who has prospered from the bad fortune that has haunted his family ... Murderer...

'Aye, I heard ye, lass. Doesn't mean I'm going to let ye stay just because ye're threatening a temper tantrum.' A flash of lightning momentarily lit up the sky behind her, casting a bright light around her head like a halo. Cal almost laughed. Like hell she was an angel. Angels didn't have plain old English names like Ellen Smith. Companions to elderly grandmothers did. Spinsters did.

He shuddered. God forbid there should be a spinster in his house, even a pretty, curvaceous one. Crazy, bossy things, spinsters were.

As if to prove his point, the wee devil marched back to the chaise longue and sat down. 'Temper tantrum,' she repeated. 'Hardly!' Swishing her skirts into place as much as she could in their sodden state, she crossed her hands in her lap, looking exactly like a respectable lady who'd come to call during visiting hours.

He crossed the room in three mismatched steps, stopping before her knees. Despite the wear and tear of her clothes, she was very well put together. Before her, he suddenly felt cumbersome, like his body was too big for the room. A lummox of a man.

She didn't acknowledge him. Instead, she examined one gloved hand as if she had nothing in the world to worry about. And that miniature bag of hers hung innocently from her wrist as if he hadn't been hit over the head with it less than a quarter hour ago.

What did she even keep in there? More to the point, however did she fit anything in there? It was positively tiny. Like herself.

'I'll throw ye out,' he threatened.

Still she didn't bother looking up at him. 'Empty threats, Your Grace.'

Anger boiled in the pit of his stomach. He was many things, but a liar wasn't one of them. Yet she was right, damn her. Unless he was going to drag her bodily from the room, he didn't think there was any way he could get her off that chaise longue. She was like a terrier with a bone—stubborn and self-bloody-righteous. So much for her being in awe of him because he was a duke. That had lasted all of three short seconds.

Hellfire and damnation. Bossy spinsters. Give him a choice and he'd never go near them. He limped back to the fireplace, accidentally kicking the empty whisky bottle as he went. It skidded across the floor away from him. What he wouldn't do for a drink right now.

***

Footsteps sounded as the Scotsman retreated back across the room, and Ellen let out an inaudible sigh. For a second she'd thought he'd actually toss her over his shoulder and march her out the front door like a sack of flour at a mill.

Now he stood before the fire with his hands tucked into his pockets and his feet firmly planted like a solid, immovable mountain of a man. He had none of the fine airs her brother was forever trying to exude but had never obtained. What he did have was the confidence that came with years of giving orders that were obeyed and never questioned.

Of course he was no footman. She should have realised that at once.

Behind him hung a portrait of another man whose features she could see more clearly in the flicking firelight than the duke's own. It was probably one of Lord Woodhal's long-dead ancestors. He had something of the fair-haired, sweet-faced Hermes about him for all that he was dressed in elaborate turn-of-the-century frills. She was hard-pressed to see how anyone could have taken him seriously.

Ellen dropped her gaze back to the man standing before her. His hair was more ordinary brown than gold, and he didn't strike her as someone who'd wear the colour asparagus even if his eyes turned out to be green as his ancestor's.

Ellen wriggled on the chaise longue. She was hungry, cold and wet. Her backside ached after two long days sitting on the wooden bench of the mail coach and all she really wanted to do was sleep. She glanced towards the clock on the writing desk: a quarter to seven. Was that all?

Her body longed to move to the fireside where the warmth would chase away the chill creeping into her bones. Not that she would ever give His Grace the satisfaction of knowing just how tired and cold she really was. If she had to, she'd sit here all night.

A dark shape by her foot snuffled. Ellen jumped. It was an old dog, sound asleep. His fur was decidedly scruffy and there was a crinkle in his tail like it had been broken and healed crooked.

Ellen shifted an inch or two further away. He was the ugliest dog she'd ever seen. Mr Walter back in Evendale had dogs that were more pleasing to the eye and they were notoriously bad tempered. The one sleeping at her feet had scars on his snout and one of his ears was missing a chunk as if something had taken a bite out of it. If the saying about dogs being like their masters was true, this one would probably attack if she got too close.

'He's deaf,' grunted the duke, as if that explained everything.

She looked away. Thank goodness the dog hadn't been able to hear her tumble through the window. An angry Scotsman was more than enough to deal with.

Before her, said Scotsman swayed on the spot.

'I do believe you're drunk,' she said. 'I can smell the whisky from here.' Perhaps the alcohol went some way to explaining his behaviour tonight. Perhaps he wasn't normally this ...much.

'Drunk?' He shoved a hand through his too-long mane of dark hair, looking startlingly like a wild man. 'Lass, I'm not even sure I'm awake.'

She narrowed her eyes. 'This is certainly no dream, Your Grace.' If anything, it was a nightmare.

Unbidden, Geoffrey surfaced to the front of her thoughts. He'd be looking for her by now, although there was no way he'd be able to find her in London. The city was too big. Verity and Maggie were the only two who knew exactly where she was, and they'd never tell her secret.

'You're shaking.' The duke sounded decidedly unimpressed.

'Yes, well...' He could not know of Geoffrey or Gwen. If he found out about them, he'd surely tell his grandmother, and Ellen couldn't risk anyone knowing. She needed this position. 'Don't think I didn't see you kick that empty bottle across the room a few moments ago,' she snapped, on the defensive. 'And this.' She'd caught sight of something that had been pushed haphazardly between the back of the golden chaise longue and an embroidered cushion and pulled it out. It was an empty crystal glass. 'At least you were sober enough at the beginning of the evening to pour yourself a drink.'

'Lass, that's been there since last week. Tonight I drank straight from the bottle.'

'I don't doubt that, Your Grace.' She placed the glass on the small table by the settee.

What would it be like to be so wealthy that you could treat a crystal glass in such a fashion? She didn't doubt the set was worth more than a year's pin money.

His attention had settled on something over her shoulder and with a decisive nod he started towards the window.

'What are you doing?' Her eyes widened in alarm.

'Don't want anyone else climbing in. Ye're enough trouble to last me a lifetime.'

'But my luggage is still outside.'

'So?'

'So, unless you're going to give me the key to the front door, it's going to have to be brought in through the window.'

'No key,' he said predictably. Reaching up, he grasped the sash window.

She rushed to his side. 'My portmanteau!' They couldn't leave it outside. All her remaining worldly goods were in that truck. Her clothes, Gwen's first baby tooth, a fragment of her father's handwriting, a lock of her mother's hair. Nothing of her brother's.

'I don't care. It cannot come inside.' And he turned his head to glare down at her.

Ellen's breath caught in her chest. This close to the window she could see his face: straight nose, proud forehead, strong chin and ... It was a scar, as she'd suspected. It slashed down the left side of his face, cutting through his eyebrow and cheekbone.

A warning rumble reverberated up his chest, but Ellen couldn't take her eyes off his face. It wasn't just one scar. It was many scars, all twisted together, heedless of pattern or shape, contorting the left side of his face. It was as though someone had whipped his cheek again and again until his skin had split and bled.

He looked nothing like the ancestor hanging over the fireplace. Where the man in the painting was pale and insipid, Lord Woodhal was dark and stormy like the rain outside.

'Do ye always stare?' His voice was dangerously low.

'N-no, Your Grace. I'm sorry.' She tore her gaze from his face but almost immediately she was looking at him again. His scars were wild. They ran any which way, with no distinction between cheek or forehead or chin. He was lucky to have escaped with his eye.

Lucky? Balderdash!

'What happened to you?'

'Nothing.' Brusque. Abrupt. End-of-conversation style. And this time he really meant business. He was watching her through hooded eyes, the lines tight around his mouth. He looked ... ashamed? Yes. That was it. And tired. Like he hadn't slept in years and years.

'Crazy Calum,' he grunted into the silence.

'I beg your pardon?'

'The bastard with the bad leg and the scars ugly enough to give children nightmares.' The self-mocking tone was undeniable.

'Who told you that?' Her words were barely more than a whisper, but they were standing so close there was no way he couldn't have heard, even though he didn't reply.

Was this the reason he didn't want her in his house—because he didn't want her to see his face? Was this why she'd found him asleep on the settee at twilight, an empty bottle of whisky on the ground? She had so many questions. When had it happened? Was it an accident or had someone done this to him?

Without thinking, she brushed her fingertips down his cheek. He flinched but didn't pull back.

His skin was hot; his whole body radiated heat. She could feel it seeping into her hands, warming her chilled fingers.

His gaze was locked on her slightly parted lips. She snapped her mouth shut and snatched her hand back. As she moved, her reticule swung back and forth, still dangling from her wrist.

He cleared his throat. 'What do ye even have in there? Rocks?'

She raised her chin, defensibly. 'Maybe.'

'Rocks,' he repeated, his eyebrows raising and a hand jumping to his head where she'd hit him. 'Ye've got to be fooling me!'

She shrugged, clutching the reticule to her chest. She couldn't very well tell him that she'd starting carrying pebbles in her bag to use as a weapon to protect herself the day Geoffrey had first hit her. She couldn't possibly tell him that she'd never been brave enough to actually defend herself against her brother's fists. That when he'd finally turned his attention towards Gwen, the only thing she managed to do was scream and beg, and that the instant he'd left the house, she'd packed their bags and sent that beautiful, sweet little girl off with Maggie and run away to London.

'I'm unchaperoned,' she said instead. It was all she could think to say. 'I don't want anyone thinking they can take advantage of me.'

He pulled back half an inch to examine her expression more closely, and that was all the cue she needed. Knocking his hand out of the way, Ellen reached through the window to feel for the portmanteau that she had dragged with her along to the window. Unfortunately this would be a whole lot easier if she could climb outside and lift her portmanteau in that way—assuming she could even lift it by herself—but she was sure the duke would take the opportunity to lock the window behind her.

'Give over!' he demanded, his voice back to its usual loud and angry resonance.

She ignored him. Her fingertips brushed the top of her portmanteau. Thankfully, the eaves overhead had protected it from the worst of the rain. If she just leaned a little further, she should be able to reach the side handle. She raised herself up onto her tippy toes. And then something wet touched the back of her leg.

She startled in surprise and her feet left the floor as she pitched forward.

Chapter Four

For the second time that evening, Cal found himself with his hands around Miss Smith's slim waist. He'd caught her before he even realised he'd moved. Turning her to face him, he set her before the hearth, a safe distance from the window. She clutched at the front of his wrinkled shirt, her face pale.

Her hold sent sparks skittering over his chest.

The top of her head was scarcely level with his shoulders. He could have tucked her under his arm for a perfect fit.

She was uncommonly pretty, even though her soaking bonnet had sagged low and a wet strand of hair had glued itself to her cheek. It was difficult to be sure when she was so wet, but the darkness of her hair, eyebrows and eyelashes made him think she had some Mediterranean heritage—Italian, most likely. And she had a rather sharp jaw with a small chin that drew attention to the curve of her mouth. She was also older than he'd first supposed, maybe four and twenty.

And her lips, he realised with a start, were the same colour as his favourite strawberry jam. Delicious. And distinctly ... irresistible.

He gave his head a shake to dislodge such rogue thoughts. 'T'was just the dog nosing the back of yer leg that frightened ye.'

Tzar had finally decided to show a little interest in the lass, and she'd almost fallen out the window in surprise. Finding the whole event entirely satisfying, Tzar was now staring up at Miss Smith as though hoping she'd do something else to entertain.

'I was startled, not frightened.'

There was barely an inch of space between them. He could feel her chest move with each breath, and when he looked down he saw where her damp gown had stuck to his shirt.

Following the direction of his gaze, she tensed. 'You can let go of me now, Your Grace.'

'I will,' he countered, 'if ye let go of me first.'

A deep blush crept up her throat to stain her cheeks, and she snatched her hands back.

He released her, immediately hating himself for wanting to pull her closer. It had been more than four long years since he'd held a woman. Four years since the fire; four years since his brave, kind half-brother had died, leaving Cal the sole heir to an estate and title he neither desired nor deserved.

Pierce shouldn't have died. Not like he had. Not when Cal had survived.

He shoved his hands under his arms. He deserved nothing more than to be left alone in this empty house with his memories and guilt, his drink and his father's old books as his only companions. His gaze fixed on the woman standing before him, the woman who should not have been there. 'Leave. Me. Alone!'

Silence met his shout. Then she turned on her heel and darted from the room. Her footsteps echoed down the hallway, in the opposite direction to the entrance. An inner door opened and closed.

'Nay! Don't go further inside.' He looked down at Tzar, who'd been watching the drama unfold, and the tip of his tail waged. 'Women,' scoffed Cal.

The dog just blinked up at him, as if to say, 'Well, what are you waiting for?'

'Reinforcements.' *Ha!* If only that were true. He limped down the dark, narrow hallway. The sound of his mismatched footsteps echoed like the beat of a regimental drum. Behind him came the sharp clicks of Tzar's nails on the floorboards as the old dog laboriously followed.

The next room down was the library. The curtains were closed. He couldn't see anything but the dark outline of the bookshelves. He crossed the room intending to rip the curtains open, but a quick intake of breath stopped him mid-stride.

'I know ye're in here, wee lass. Ye canna hide from me.' At least she hadn't gotten very far. If she'd run upstairs, he'd would have been searching half a dozen empty bedrooms. And downstairs was a maze of cold, dank cellars rarely used.

'I'm not hiding,' she snapped. 'I vacated the front parlour in favour of leaving your ungentlemanly presence.'

'Ungentlemanly?' Back to that already, were they? Well, he'd heard worse insults. A hundred of them. 'Would a gentleman have let ye fall to your death?'

'I wouldn't have died. It was only a few feet.'

'Ye would have hit yer head on the edge of yer trunk.' He turned towards her voice. She must be standing behind his father's desk, closer to the towering bookshelves lining the far wall than to the door he'd just entered through.

He stepped over the red-velvet footrest he couldn't see but knew was there. His wounded knee throbbed like an old man's.

'Don't come any closer.'

''Tis my own library. I can come and go as I please.'

Ignoring the incessant thumping in his head, he lit the candles standing sentry on either corner of the mantel. He was right: she was standing just a few feet from the window, with her back to the books. Stepping before her, he pulled out a small bundle of bank notes from the top drawer of the desk.

'Here.' He pushed them into her hand. 'This should be more than enough to cover the fee Lady F promised ye. Take it and go back to wherever ye came from. Go home.'

***

Home. She blinked. What did that even mean?

Geoffrey? Gwen? Maggie? Her parents' graveside?

No. She didn't have a home to go back to. There was nothing for her in Evendale but pain and misery and fear. London, working for Lady Faye—there was hope for her in this great city, where nobody knew who she was or anything of her family's past.

Ellen glanced at the bank notes he'd stuffed into her fist. It was a lot of money. More than she'd seen in a very long time. She and Gwen could live off this money for a few months. And she could pay Maggie back for the coach ticket.

Then what? She'd be without shelter and employment. Gwen was relying on Ellen providing a future for the two of them away from

Geoffrey, and she could only start building that future if she could earn some money. And without a new character reference, she was unlikely to find another position. It was a miracle she'd been accepted into Lady Faye's household in the first place. What the duke was offering was only a temporary solution.

She opened her fist, and the notes fluttered to the floor.

'You can't get rid of me that easily, Your Grace. I'm the daughter of a gentleman. I accepted a position with your grandmother and I intend to keep it, so long as she wants me. I won't go back on my word.'

'Of course ye won't.' He scowled down at her.

The room was small for a library. The old, heavy books lining three of the walls from floor to ceiling seemed to bear down on her.

She'd stumbled into this corner of the room because it had been the furthest from the door. Now she felt trapped. He was standing uncomfortably close. And the dog was sitting on the rug just inside the door, as though barring her escape.

She stepped to the side but bumped into the large desk. Something fluttered to the floor, and she glanced down.

Newsletter cuttings littered the desk top. They were a couple of years old, the pages yellowing and the corners curling. She skimmed her hand over the sheets, catching glimpses of headlines. *Shipping Intelligence. Lloyd's Marine List. Births, Deaths and Marriages.* As well as an etching of a ship. According to the caption it was HMS *Surus*, a fully rigged 80-gun warship.

'Can't ye mind yer own business for one damn second?' the duke growled. 'Get away from my things.' He took hold of her wrist as though to guide her to the door, and Ellen let out an involuntary cry of pain as his fingers dug into her bruises despite his light hold. She flinched away from him, and he pulled back, startled.

'I hardly touched ye.'

She wrapped her arms around herself even as the sharp pain faded. 'But it hurt.'

'Ellen.' A concerned crease appeared between his brows. 'Has someone hurt ye?'

She startled. It was too intimate, the way her name sounded on his tongue. More exotic with his Scottish accent.

'Show me yer arms.'

She looked about the room again but there was nowhere to run. Where would she go anyway? So Ellen did the only thing she could think of. Straightening her spine to her full height, she filled her voice with as much of Maggie's forthrightness as she could muster. 'Of all the ungentlemanly things to demand of a lady, that has to be scrapping the bottom of the barrel, Your Grace.'

'I thought we'd established that I'm no gentleman.' He sounded considerably less put out than she'd hoped. 'If ye don't show me, I'll pull yer sleeves up myself.'

'You wouldn't dare.' She took a step back, bumping up against one of the bookcases.

'Wait a minute.' His voice deepened with new suspicion. 'Ye've run away. Why else would ye be so determined to stay here with me if ye weren't already in trouble?' His eyes narrowed. They weren't green as she'd predicted, but a deep, dark copper, like the colour of a dying fire, or a sunset right before darkness fell.

'No.' Ellen tried to laugh it off.

He looked utterly unconvinced. 'It's the only reasonable explanation. Well, ye canna stay here. Ye'll find no sympathy from me, whatever yer problems are.'

Her eyes darted to his scars. Day-old stubble littered his uninjured cheek and chin but the other side was bare, the skin too damaged. 'This is ridiculous.' She heard the quiver in her own voice. 'I'm not hiding from anyone. Mrs Verity Nott was kind enough to contact Lady Faye on my behalf as she'd heard that your grandmother was looking for help. Lady Faye agreed to employ me for the upcoming Season. I was to meet her here today.'

'Lass.' He sighed, sounding for the first time since they'd met less than angry. 'Show me.'

Her secret shame. She'd tried so hard to keep the bruises hidden. Even among the gossips and busybodies of Evendale, not one person suspected just how cruel her brother was. Nobody knew that he'd spent the last two years since her father had died constantly grabbing at her wrists, pushing and pulling her, trying to control her every move. Trying to control her every thought. When that hadn't worked, he'd hit her. Again and again. Nobody knew but Maggie and Verity, and little Gwen, God help her. And now this bad-tempered Scotsman who lived in this big old empty townhouse with crystal glasses and velvet settees and who wasn't even willing to let her wait for his grandmother out of the rain for fear of them being within sight of each other.

Well, if Lord Woodhal thought he was the only one who'd suffered just because he had the scars to show for it, he was sorely mistaken. She pressed her lips together, determined not to make a sound as she slowly pulled up the long sleeves of her gown to expose her wrist.

'Who did that to ye, wee lass?' He spoke through clenched teeth.

'As you said yourself when I asked about your scars,' she replied curtly, 'it's nothing.'

He remained motionless, his gaze fixed on her bruises. The ticking of the desk clock was the only indication of passing time.

Ellen too remained motionless, even as humiliation turned her cheeks hot and beads of sweat began to gather on her forehead. Was she daring him to demand more answers or to apologise? She didn't know. All she knew was that if she tried to move while his eyes were locked on her like that, staring at her as though he couldn't believe someone had hit her, she might just start crying.

His expression said it all: disbelief, distress, anger. Seeing his disgusted reaction, she knew this man would never hit her. Then he raised his gaze to meet her eyes and his emotions were abruptly shuttered. 'This changes nothing.' And he turned his back on her to pour himself another generous glass of whisky straight from the bottle on the desk.

***

It changed everything.

A dreadful stillness came over Cal. He clenched his jaw until his mouth ached. The lassie's wrists were black and blue. He should never have grabbed her like he had.

He downed his drink in one, quickly pouring himself another. Without turning back around to face her, he raised the glass in a salute. 'Want one?'

'No, thank you.' Her contemptuous tone had returned. She was back to her old self and clearly refusing to talk about what had just happened.

Ellen Smith as she tried to present herself to the world: a tight-laced pernickety spinster, and thus the perfect lady's companion. Ellen Smith as he was beginning to suspect she really was: impetuous and decidedly stubborn. And someone clearly held a grudge against her. His mouth turned dry at the thought of someone grabbed at her as they clearly had. Was this the real reason she carried rocks in that wee bag of hers? To ward off unwanted attention?

No wonder she'd hit him when he'd first caught her.

'Ye should try it sometime.' The whisky slipped down effortlessly. 'It really takes the edge off.'

She clicked her tongue disapprovingly. 'Just so we're completely clear, Your Grace: if you drink yourself into a stupor, I'll not hesitate to drag your unconscious body out the front door and lock it behind you.'

'I'm too heavy.' Glancing over his shoulder, he saw that she'd covered her arms again and was tapping her foot on the old red rug. A few loose strands of her damp hair unglued themselves from her neck to dangle over her shoulder in a way that made a man wonder what it would be like to see her without her bonnet, her hair freed of its pins and set loose down her back...

She tipped her head to one side, contemplating him and then the rug. It was clear as day she was planning to use it as some sort of sled to move his unconscious body.

He shot her a peevish look then wrenched his gaze away. If anyone was going to be determined enough to drag him through his own house and toss him outside like nothing more than a vagabond, it was surely the woman standing before him.

'It's no more than you deserve,' she said. 'And you would do the same to me. Admit it.'

'Ye're...' He spluttered. His house, his rules. 'Insufferable.' Admitting defeat—albeit temporarily—he slammed the glass back onto the table. It shattered.

Tzar scrambled to his feet as fast as his old bones could manage, making a beeline for the shards of glass, undoubtedly searching for spilled food.

Cal nudged him away with his boot. Tzar gave him a reproachful look before settling down between the lass's feet.

Taking sides now, was he? *Mangy dog.*

'I'm Crazy Calum,' he reminded her. 'The creature nightmares are made of.'

The rest of London believed that particularly juicy piece of gossip so whyever shouldn't she? Anything to get her out of his house and away from him. She deserved better. The maddening spinster with lips like strawberry jam.

A long silence. He could almost believe himself to be alone except he hadn't heard her leave.

'I don't know, Your Grace. You're not scary enough to haunt my dreams. In fact, I'm beginning to doubt there are any rumours about you at all. You're just trying to scare me away from Lady Faye.'

'Ye don't get it.' How could she not understand? How could she not see the anguish in his eyes? The guilt? The pain? The rest of the world had—and it had turned its back on him. He tugged his shirt over his head, tearing off a couple of buttons, and stood before the oh-so prim and proper spinster naked from the waist up.

She moved to turn away from him but he growled a warning. 'Look. Look at me.' He turned on the spot so she would take in all the damage. So she could begin to understand just how lonely he deserved to be.

***

Ellen pressed her hands over her mouth. The duke was rippled with muscles—lean and strong. Not an inch of fat to be seen. And scars. His entire left side, from his shoulder, down his arm and chest, was covered in scars. Burns: that's what they looked like.

'Who did this to you?' She reached out a hand. Like before, his skin was hot to the touch, and she could feel every one of his scars—jagged, raised. Savage. They weren't new, probably years old. And completely healed. Although he must be in constant pain because the skin was pulled tight, particularly around his shoulder and neck.

'There was a fire.' He pulled back. Her hand hung in the empty air between them.

She tried to pull her thoughts together. He must be in pain. Every time he turned his head. Every time he talked or ate. She could barely comprehend it. No wonder he moved slowly, turned carefully. Each step was calculated and precise. 'Your limp. Does it, ah, extend all the way down?' Her eyes dropped to the waist of his breeches. The scars continued down and out of sight.

'Nay, not so far. Though my knee was damaged also. Hit by a piece of shrapnel. Do ye understand now?' he asked, softly. 'Do ye understand why ye canna stay here?'

'Shrapnel?' She looked back at the newspaper clippings scattered over his desk. Every one of them about the Navy, about the war. 'Were you fighting the French? Was that your ship?' She pointed to HMS *Surus*.

Just two years ago Napoleon had been exiled to St Helena. But before that the war had raged for twelve long years, with countless lives lost. So many mothers and wives of Evendale were now without their sons and husbands. Mourning dress was a common sight.

The duke made a non-committal sound.

Even at this distance, she could feel the heat of him seeping through the layers of her clothes. He was like fire, burning hot and wild. He was still bare-chested, and the sight was doing funny things to her knees. She gripped a bookshelf behind her to keep herself upright.

'Ye're staring again,' he said roughly. He spoke with intense feeling, craggy and raw like the scars on his face and chest.

He turned his head to the side, looking out the window, obviously trying to hide the damaged side of his face.

'Why did you show me?'

'Ye need to understand what type of man I am.'

'No.' She glared at him, a maelstrom of feelings warring for her attention. Chief contenders were anger and attraction. She settled on anger, resolutely ignoring the way his muscles tightened as he crossed his arms. 'Your scars don't tell me anything more about who you are than the bruises on my arms. We both know you're trying to scare me away. But if you thought making me scared of you or making me pity you would get me out of your house, you thought wrong. Nothing and nobody but Lady Faye is going to move me from this library.'

'I could easily carry ye out.'

'You didn't earlier, and I don't think you're going to now.' Despite his muscular frame, it was unlikely his left arm or even his knee would be quite up to the task of tossing her over his shoulder. It was an ever-so-slightly comforting thought.

He spluttered for a second, clearly used to giving orders and having people obey him without question. That, more than anything else, confirmed in her mind once and for all that he was indeed a duke. Hammond's son hadn't died after all.

'Insufferable woman,' he said at last. 'I don't want yer pity.'

'Then what do you want?' she demanded. It seemed she was developing a habit for overstepping the mark. Lady's companions didn't normally argue with dukes.

But it was his own fault. Lord Woodhal was pushing her to it. She had to fight fire with fire. Gwen's safety was her first priority.

'I want ye to understand that this isn't going to work. Ye being here; none of this is.'

'I understand now that this is your house, but your grandmother invited me here for the duration of the Season. That isn't so long. Before you know it I'll be out of your house and out of your life. It's not as if the two of us are about to be wed or anything so dramatic.' She determinately kept her gaze locked on his face, refusing to turn away. If she gave him an inch, he'd take a yard.

'I'm half Scottish,' he scoffed. 'The Scots are a lot more cantankerous than any wee England lassie.'

'We'll see about that.' She glared. He didn't look away. She could feel the tension in him, hear each breath and see the rise and fall of his great chest. Awareness raced along her nerve endings. She wanted to feel the ridges of his scars and his muscles. She wanted to circle the tip of her finger around one of his nipples.

Oh no. That was definitely something a lady's companion didn't do.

'Lass...' he began.

'I'm not moving. Not until I've spoken with her ladyship.' He might not want houseguests, but she had so much more to lose than he did. And she wasn't giving up. Not after everything she and Maggie and Verity had been through to get her here.

He fell silent again, his copper coloured eyes narrowing even further. He didn't even look away a when a key rattled in the front door. A second later someone was traipsing down the passage. Two someones.

They stopped by the open library door.

A man's voice sounded: 'What the devil is going on here?'

Ellen didn't break eye contact. Instead, she smiled up at the duke. 'I do believe your visitors are referring to the fact that you're still shirtless, Your Grace.'

He swore.

Chapter Five

'Damn, Tattershall.' Cal broke eye contact with the fearless woman still glaring at him, and groped around for his discarded shirt. His cousin leaned against the doorframe as he studied Cal and his newly acquired spinster. Cal could only imagine how it looked: a half-naked man towering over a small and rather moist lass. 'Didn't anyone ever teach you to knock?'

'We did.' His grandmother, Lady Faye, the dowager marchioness, pushed her way into the library, practically toppling Owen over on her way through the door. 'Nobody answered. Don't you have *any* servants?'

Reaching just over five foot, his grandmother was shorter even than Miss Smith—and round. While she'd always been pale, now her eyelashes were almost invisible and he could see small, broken veins on the side of her nose where her skin had turned almost translucent.

'Don't just stand there,' she snapped at Owen. 'Light more candles. I refuse to conduct any sort of conversation in the half-dark. Barbarous!'

Her voice, of course, hadn't faded. She had a pair of lungs on her that could fan a forge. And it was a voice she put to constant and steady use. A veritable dragon was his grandmother. Any man—soldier, sailor or shoemaker—would quake in their boots if she had a mind to make them.

Hell, she probably could have won the whole damn war in a single afternoon.

And now she had in her employ an equally determined companion, a feisty drone to do her bidding. Cal shuddered. He was quickly becoming outnumbered and out manoeuvred, and in his own house of all places.

'Your ladyship.' The drone curtseyed. 'I assure you, this isn't what it looks like.' She tossed Cal's bare chest an accusatory glower.

'None other than the glorious ducal warrior in the flesh,' mocked Owen with an exaggerated bow.

Cal pulled on his shirt, his fingers fumbling with the remaining buttons. 'None other than the family's black sheep in an overabundance of Chinese silk,' he retorted.

'You must be Miss Smith.' Lady F interrupted the men, giving Ellen the once-over. She tugged aggressively at the fingers of her kidskin gloves until they came free. 'Mrs Nott provided me with an excellent character reference, but I have to say that I'm still not completely convinced.' She slapped her gloves against her other palm.

Miss Smith blanched. 'Oh, your ladyship, I assure you I'm a diligent worker. Not quick to temper. I can sew and draw and sing a little. I love to garden and can arrange flowers tolerably well. I can relate all the Greek myths and dance a full country set,' she said hastily, clearly reciting a prepared speech. 'I promise I'll do everything in my power to be the perfect companion. You'll not regret—'

'How do you take your tea?'

'My tea?' Miss Smith blinked, glancing at Cal again as if he were going to help. She was on her own. He moved back a step, seeking refuge in the shadows even as Owen lit more candles.

'Yes,' demanded his grandmother. 'How do you take your tea?'

'B-black. With sugar.'

'What do you think of afternoon naps?'

'Not enough time in the day.'

'Town or country hours?'

'Country. I'm a light sleeper.'

'And the gossip columns?'

'Never read them.'

'Hmm.' Lady F paused as though ticking off a mental list. 'And before, when my grandson wasn't wearing his shirt: what *was* that all about?'

'It wasn't what it looked like, your ladyship,' Miss Smith repeated. He could practically hear her thoughts as she silently cursed him into oblivion. Using only the most respectable language, of course. Spinsters didn't actually curse.

'I see.' Lady F paused again with another suspicious look, then a smile broke across her face. She clapped her hands. 'It looked a lot like you were putting my grandson back in his place, as I'm sure he rightly deserved.' She tossed her gloves at him, quickly followed by her travelling cloak and bonnet.

'I most certainly deserved nothing of the sort,' he scowled, dropping her outerwear onto the footstool without ceremony.

This abrupt change had Miss Smith blinking in confusion, and Cal's eyes were drawn to the enchanting rose blush creeping out from under her modest neckline.

Enchanting? When did he ever use words like enchanting?

'Your shock is a perfectly natural response to meeting Lizzy for the first time,' Owen assured her, with a bright smile. He tossed his greatcoat at Cal too, but Cal tucked his hands in his pockets, letting Owen's coat drop to the ground at his feet. With a frown at Cal, Owen bowed over Miss Smith's hand, raising it to his lips in an over-exaggerated show of appreciation. 'It's a pleasure to make your acquaintance.'

Owen Tattershall: never one to do anything by halves.

Miss Smith curtsied in response, looking even more baffled as she managed to extract her hand from Owen's fervent clutches. Owen was ... a handful. This evening he was looking dapper with a three-green waistcoat. He was also clutching the most ridiculous-looking walking cane Cal had ever seen. It had a large porcelain handle on the top, like a spherical doorknob. He used the end of the cane to hook his jacket up off the floor and ran a hand over it to brush away the dog hair that had already began to transfer from the rug.

Cal turned his attention back to his grandmother, looking down at her with the most formidable scowl he could muster at such short notice. 'Now that you've both finished scaring the woman half witless, would you care to explain exactly what you're doing in my library at this god-forsaken hour?'

'Is that any way to greet your most beloved grandmother?' Lady F raised a hand to her forehead in a show of dramatics that would be more welcome on a stage than a ducal library. 'I'm nearly eighty years old and I've been travelling all day. Surely I at least deserve a welcoming kiss.' She presented him with a papery cheek.

'You're only sixty-eight.'

She gave his chest a light slap with the back of her hand, and he quickly pressed a kiss to her cheek. An overabundance of sensibility in an elderly relative was never a good sign. Like he'd said: a veritable dragon.

'It was your choice to travel to London,' he reminded her. 'And you didn't even bother to write ahead. I didn't know you were coming to Town until...' He gestured towards Miss Smith. Enough said.

Miss Smith's gaze flickered between him and Lady F as though she were watching a game of shuttlecock. Her eyes were wide and her mouth slightly open. She was staring. Again.

He tapped a finger to the underside of her chin. Her mouth snapped shut.

'I shouldn't have to write begging permission to visit my only living grandson,' Lady F was saying. She bent down to scratch Tzar under the chin. The old dog lifted his head as high as it would go, granting her full access. 'You should be absolutely delighted to see me and welcome me into your home with open arms.'

'Of course I'm happy to see you,' he ground out between clenched teeth. 'But you can't stay here, which you would have known if you'd bothered writing ahead.' She'd written to him constantly these last four years, but she couldn't put nib to paper for a quick warning? Years had passed since her last visit, so what had changed to send her scampering to London now?

Ignoring him entirely, the dowager glided across the room towards her new companion. 'Miss Smith, it really is a pleasure to meet you at last. I've been excited all day. I've never had a companion before.' Only then did she seem to register the state of Miss Smith's damp gown, which was still clinging indecently to her curves. 'Didn't you have an umbrella, gel?'

Unfortunately, Owen had long since noticed Miss Smith's curves. His gaze was firmly fixed on her flushed décolletage, his eyes as wide as cart wheels.

Cal grunted a warning. *The randy dandy.*

Owen completely ignored him, so Cal grabbed the knee blanket from the armchair, folded it in half to form a triangle and wrapped it around Miss Smith's shoulders like a shawl.

He knew that look in Owen's eye. It was the same look Cal would have given her had it been four years ago. He scowled again and felt the left side of his mouth pull uncomfortably tight. He could always feel his scars; they were never far from his thoughts.

Miss Smith clutched the blanket tighter and for the first time all night Cal realised she was shivering. If he hadn't been trying so desperately to make her leave, he might have realised sooner she was on the verge of catching her death of cold, for all that she'd warned him.

Conflicting feelings warred inside him but most of all he felt guilty. Guilty she was so cold. Guilty she was still under his roof.

His grandmother was still talking. '...running rather late, but it wasn't my fault. Owen did insist we stop at each and every posting-house for tea as though I'm some sort of invalid. Oh, aren't you a pretty young thing.' She took both of Miss Smith's hands in her own. 'I'm sure we're going to have a lot of fun together.'

Miss Smith still looked rather startled, but then she smiled a smile that could have felled a whole regiment of battle-hardened soldiers. 'I do hope so, my lady.'

He quickly averted his gaze.

'Excellent,' cried Lady F. 'Now, how about some supper? I've barely eaten anything all day.' She picked up a candle, pushed her way back past Owen and hurried down the passage towards the kitchen stairs.

Miss Smith followed. Of course she followed.

Am I ever going to get that lass out of my house?

'Cal.' Lady F called so loudly she could have still been standing in the library. 'Be a dear and bring Miss Smith's and my trunks inside before it gets any wetter.'

Apparently not any time soon.

'You could have warned me she was coming,' he hissed at Owen.

'Where would the fun be in that?' Owen smirked. 'Besides, I know you wouldn't have let us in if I'd warned you.'

'I didn't let you in,' Cal reminded him.

'No need, old man. I have a key.' He patted his waistcoat pocket, flashing Cal a full mouth of straight teeth.

'What key? I never gave you a key.' He lunged towards his cousin, but Owen ducked easily out of the way, using his cane as leverage. They weren't actually cousins; there was no blood connection, but Owen's parents had died when he'd still been in leading strings and Lady F had taken him in. Now Owen and Lady F were almost inseparable. Except, of course, when Owen was gallivanting around Town, chasing beautiful married women left, right and centre. His reputation was almost as bad as Cal's, though for entirely different reasons. 'What's the dammed stick for?' Even as he spoke, Cal knew he was going to regret asking.

'Upon my honour! It's *dernier cri*.' Owen gave Tzar a pat and the little turncoat wagged his tail. It thumped against the rug almost as loudly as the thunder rumbled outside.

Cal looked towards the window. It was still storming. Apparently, the one and only upshot of having Miss Smith barge into his house was that she'd proved herself to be a worthy distraction from the rain. Not that he'd ever tell her that.

'...matches the waistcoat,' Owen concluded with a flourish.

And there it was: regret for asking about the cane. 'It bloody well doesn't.' How could a cane possibly match a waistcoat? Owen might as well have been speaking Mandarin for all Cal understood.

His cousin gasped in exaggerated shock. 'Didn't you hear me? It's the height of fashion. And, if you ever bothered to leave this dank house anymore, you'd know that too.'

'It's not dank.' More regret. Owen was much too cheerful. How could anyone be cheerful when their head was pounding so hard it might actually split in two? 'Don't insult my house. I don't see you for years, and then you just show up—'

'I called in a few months ago, but you wouldn't open the damn door.'

Cal shut his mouth and shrugged. Had that only been a few months? The days tended to blend all together like the faded colours of over-washed clothes.

'That's why I dug out my old key.'

'Which I'll have back now, thank you very much.' Cal held out his hand.

Owen made a show of checking his pockets and coming up short. 'Sorry, old man, must have misplaced it.'

'Moonshine!' He could see the shape of the key through the silk of Owen's waistcoat. But his knee started aching just thinking about tackling him for it, so he limped from the room to follow the women, resolutely ignoring all their trunks.

He'd deal with Owen later. Preferably when he had a glass of whisky in hand. Preferably when his eyes had stopped watering.

The women's voices were coming from the back of the house where the kitchen was. It was easily the largest room in the house; situated at the end of the long hallway, it was as long as the house was wide. It was also his favourite room and the only one he spent any time caring for.

Though, apparently with the storm, he'd completely forgotten to bank the fire and it had burned itself out, because Miss Smith was kneeling on the flagstone hearth, coaxing life back into his large cast-iron range. He pressed hands to his hips and glared at her back, hoping she could feel his angry eyes prickling her skin, as well she deserved.

She'd wrapped two corners of the blanket right around her waist and tied them off behind her back to form something similar to a hands-free sontag. Practicality in a woman was never something to be admired. It usually resulted in a tireless need to 'improve' other people's lives and a plethora of decidedly displeasing lace caps.

His narrowed gaze moved to the back of her head. She'd finally removed her dishevelled bonnet to reveal, not a tumble of luscious brown hair any man would want to run his hands through, as Cal had hoped, but a mob cap, just as he'd suspected. White and lacy with an excess of frills.

A chit and a spinster Miss Ellen Smith may be, but there was a revolting lace cap on her head where a revolting lace cap should not be. A pretty face and a fine figure such as she possessed should not be sullied by an ugly cap.

There was a commotion coming from the other end of his kitchen. He turned his attention to his grandmother lest she create too much mayhem in his pantry while his thoughts were preoccupied with a pair of fine eyes and a shapely arse. He looked in behind Lady F but had to quickly limp out of the way as she emerged carrying a large cake tin and a couple of biscuit tins.

'Even as a child, you always did hide the best at the back,' she told him, placing the tins on the battered kitchen table.

'You can't eat that for dinner,' he chastised, for all the good that it did. If ignoring other people's advice were an art, Elizabeth Debelle would be a master craftswoman. Her head was a much more appropriate place for a frivolous lace cap—a head which was suspiciously bare. If he hadn't caught Miss Smith climbing through his front window, he'd have thought she the sensible old biddy and his grandmother, who was this very minute ogling cake, the green girl.

'Plates,' she instructed Miss Smith, whose handiwork had a cheerful fire illuminating the room. A moment later, the two women had loaded four plates with fruit cake and sweetmeats—and stale tea biscuits which he'd forgotten about weeks ago.

'I'll never understand why you refuse to keep servants,' Lady F chided, taking his place at the head of the table, completely disregarding the fact that this was the kitchen and not the dining room.

'They just get in my way.' He leaned down, resting the heels of his hands on the table beside her plate until they were almost eye level. 'You can't stay here. You know I don't receive visitors.'

'Cal, dear, stop being so tiresome and eat your cake.' Standing for a moment, Lady F reached across the table to take a scoop of marmalade from a cooling stockpot and lavished it onto her slice of cake. The sweet and tangy smell of orange permeated the room and made his nose tingle. It smelled clean and fresh like the beginning of spring. Clean and fresh like Ellen Smith.

'I don't want cake.' He sounded like a child even to his own ears.

'Of course you do. You baked it.'

Baking: just another thing he liked doing that dukes weren't supposed to.

'He did?' Miss Smith looked up. She sat to the right of Lady F and was digging into her cake with almost as much enthusiasm.

He did a double take. Spinsters were certainly not supposed to enjoy cake quite that much. Crumbs had caught at the corners of her delectable lips. And he had a sudden urge to lick them clean.

'That must be why it tastes suspiciously like whisky,' she concluded.

'I like it.' Owen had taken the seat beside Ellen even though there were five other perfectly functional chairs at the table he could have chosen. He flashed her a roguish grin, pushing his spectacles further up his nose all the better to see.

'Tattershall,' Cal warned again. He was sitting much too close for anyone's comfort. But Owen completely ignored him. Following Lady F's lead, he leaned forward to take a scoop of marmalade, brushing his arm lightly, and completely purposefully, against Ellen's shoulder.

'So, Grandmother, why are you here?' Cal asked the dowager for what felt like the tenth time. She couldn't avoid answering forever.

'Dinner is not the time for philosophical conundrums, dearest.'

'I mean: why are you here, in London, in my kitchen, eating my food, *dearest*?'

'I like London.'

He grunted his disbelief. Lady F liked London about as much as he did.

Beneath the table, Tzar was moving from person to person, giving each his largest, most pathetic hungry puppy dog eyes. Quite an achievement considering he was so old most of his fur had turned grey and wiry.

'Still up to your old tricks.' Lady F reached under the table to pat his head.

Cal didn't bother keeping the anger and frustration from this voice. 'Don't try to change the subject, Elizabeth Debelle. I want it out with you: why are you here?'

'Phiff. You sound just like my mother. She was the only one who ever called me Elizabeth.' She fidgeted beneath his stare, then let out an exasperated sigh. 'If you must know, I'm not here to interrupt your sulking. You needn't worry on that front. I've come to enjoy the Season.' She rolled her eyes. 'Isn't that what people of the *ton* do?'

'Not you.' He knew his grandmother. Since her husband's death, she'd been running Faye Park in place of the new marquess, a distant cousin, who'd moved to Canton as a child and apparently wasn't in a hurry to return to England despite his large inheritance. Cal couldn't help but envy the man. 'You're up to something.'

'I'm up to nothing of the sort.' She rapped his knuckles with the back of her fork, and he pulled away. 'What a ridiculously provincial idea.'

He threw another questioning look at his cousin, but Owen simply smiled back at him. He was feeding cake crumbs to Tzar. The dog had clearly decided Owen was the chink in the armour and had parked himself firmly at Owen's feet.

'You haven't been to London since...' Cal faulted.

'Since Pierce's funeral,' she finished for him matter-of-factly. 'That was four years ago. When are you going to stop mourning your brother?'

'Brother?' Miss Smith looked up.

'I'm not—' Memories flashed before his eyes. Pierce. The ship. The fire. The screaming. Napoleon might have packed up but there was still a war raging—a war inside Cal's own head. 'He shouldn't have died,' was all he could say.

'No. But he did.' Lady F's expression softened, her hand touching the gold and pearl mourning brooch she wore. 'Come now, you needn't worry about me interrupting your private time. I have Miss Smith to look after me, and Owen. You'll hardly notice the three of us at all.'

He looked from one to the other. His grandmother blinked innocently up at him. Miss Smith was deliberately avoiding his gaze. Owen was staring at Miss Smith as if he hadn't seen a pretty companion with lips the colour of strawberries before.

'Tattershall!' Cal marched around the table, took hold of his cousin's chair and dragged him away from Miss Smith. Owen grabbed at the table with a yelp, but Cal didn't relent until Owen was at the other end. Then he turned back to Lady F. 'You can finish your dinner'—if you could call cake dinner—'but then you have to leave. You absolutely cannot stay here.'

'Yes, my darling,' said his grandmother in soothing tones that suggested she was going to do nothing of the sort. Turning in her seat, she gave her full attention to her new companion-in-arms. 'Do you like fireworks, Miss Smith?'

***

'Fireworks?' Ellen paused, a forkful of cake halfway to her mouth. The marchioness was absolutely nothing like she'd imagined. Then again, she'd never have imagined a duke quite like Calum Callaghan. *Had anyone?* 'I've never actually seen any fireworks, my lady.'

'Dear me.' Lady Faye touched her arm in condolence. 'We must fix that immediately. The fireworks at Vauxhall are always spectacular this time of year.'

'You hate fireworks,' said His Grace. The only one still standing, he was glowering over the table at Mr Tattershall. His hands were crossed over his chest again and his brows were low over his eyes. Arguing with his grandmother had brought a red, angry flush to his face, and his Scottish accent had completely disappeared.

Now she thought on it, his Scottish accent had disappeared as soon as his family had come bursting into the library. On purpose or not, she wasn't sure. Whatever the reason, she didn't much care for his English voice—his Oxbridge drawl. It did not suit.

'I've changed my mind,' Lady Faye responded lightly. 'How does that saying go?' She drummed her fingers on the table.

'It's a lady's prerogative to change her mind,' Ellen suggested.

'That's the one.' Lady Faye turned her radiant smile on Ellen. 'How was your journey into Town? Mrs Nott wrote to me to say you're from ... Evendale? I haven't been out that way in years and years.'

'Nobody's been out that way,' Lord Woodhal interjected, sulkily.

Lady Faye laughed. 'Whatever did you do to him, gel?'

'I'm not sure what you mean.'

'I'm sure he was already like that when she found him,' teased Mr Tattershall.

'Arghh! Owen, why can't they stay with you?' Outside, the storm raged on; inside, Lord Woodhal raged on.

'My place simply isn't big enough, old man.' He was completely unaffected by the duke's temper. The way he was acting put Ellen in mind of a brother or a cousin but he looked nothing like either the marchioness or the duke. Where the duke had dark hair, Mr Tattershall was blond, and where Lady Faye had an aquiline nose, Mr Tattershall was blessed with a button.

'I'm not staying with Owen. He has a dog.' Lady Faye had finished off her plate of sweets in record time.

'So do I!' The duke pressed a fist to his solar plexus as though to release some tension in his chest.

The dowager shook her head, waving a hand haphazardly in Ellen's direction, which she took as her cue.

'It's a lady's prerogative to change her mind,' she repeated.

'Perfect.' The old lady beamed at her, a twinkle in her eyes. 'We're going to get along handsomely.'

'Not perfect.' Lord Woodhal ran a hand down his face. There was a strange beauty in his scars. They spoke of hardship and loss.

If she kissed his cheek, would his scars be rough like sand or soft life feathers? Rough, hopefully. Rough suited him—made him somehow larger and stronger.

Kiss? Wherever had that idea come from?

He caught her looking. There was a kind of cowardliness in turning away, so she kept looking, drinking him in. She was suddenly hot under the collar, her dress too tight, the blanket about her shoulders too warm.

'I need a drink.' As abrupt as ever, he turned on his heel and stalked towards the door. 'This isn't over, Elizabeth. There's no way in hell you're all staying here.'

'The trunks!' was her only response.

Ellen watched Lord Woodhal's retreating back. Drawing rooms hadn't been designed for men of his stature. Only in the kitchen did his sheer size not look out of place. The muscles in his neck and shoulders jumped as though he could feel her watching him. A second later, he was out of sight.

'Ever the gentleman,' chucked Mr Tattershall, returning his chair to its original location and flashing her a toothy grin.

'Is he always so ... disagreeable?'

The smile slipped from Lady Faye's face. Even Mr Tattershall looked halfway serious. Her question had touched a nerve.

'I'm feeling rather tired all of a sudden. Ellen, gel, could you show me to my room?'

'Of course.' Ellen jumped to her feet. She had absolutely no idea where the bedrooms were or even where the staircase was, but that didn't seem to matter because the dowager took the lead. As the old lady passed Owen, she pressed a kiss to the top of his head. 'Do help him with the trunks, dear. And don't be too hard on him.'

'Me?' He feigned surprise. 'Never!'

Ellen curtsied her goodbye to Mr Tattershall whoever-he-was and hurried to follow. She adopted a brisk step to impress upon her ladyship just how superior a companion she was going to be and just how seriously she was taking her employment.

The passage was narrower than she'd first noticed, and there were doors down only one side. Ellen looked ahead and saw a single front door where there had been two doors on the outside. Where the second door would have been, there was a wall, which presumably meant the house had been divided in half.

Whoever had heard of such a thing?

'This way.' Her ladyship led Ellen into another room. Most of the ceiling had been removed to make way for a narrow staircase. It was dark and miserable, and she had to light the three-arm candelabra on the small table by the door.

They climbed on past the first storey, stopping at the second, where there was another long and narrow passage with doors down only one side, echoing the passage on the ground floor.

'I don't suppose Cal told you about the house?' Lady Faye asked, opening a bedroom door. Ellen hurried to hold it for her.

'No, my lady. He said nothing.' Nothing about the house, although he'd probably revealed more about himself than he'd have liked in an effort to scare her away.

The guest bedchamber was the picture of neglect. There was a musty four-poster bed with heavy curtains, a dressing table with a cracked mirror, a chest of drawers missing two handles and a porcelain washstand with faded bluebells painted on the inside.

A middle-aged woman was waiting for them. She curtsied as they entered. Judging by her dress and manner, she was Lady Faye's abigail. 'I've laid out your nightdress, my lady, although the rest of your luggage is still outside. And I'm afraid the bedding is quite dusty. I tried shaking it out, but it really should be thrown straight into the fire. I don't think anyone's been in this room since we were here last.'

'You've done excellent work, Pamela. Miss Smith will help me change this evening. There's cake in the pantry for your supper. And remember to take no notice of His Grace.'

'Thank you, my lady.' Pamela curtseyed again, gave Ellen a friendly smile and left, closing the door behind her.

'I don't know what I'd do without that gel.'

Ellen helped the dowager change into her nightgown and climb into bed. The musty mattress sagged in the middle.

'You and I are going to have to take this house into our own hands,' Lady Faye said. She removed her white wig and started pulling pins from her hair. Wispy strands dropped to frame her face like cobwebs—silver in the light from the gently crackling fire Pamela must have lit. 'Cal can bake a scrumptious cake, but we really need a proper cook. Not to mention a butler, two footmen and a small army of maids.'

'Won't that just make him angrier?' His Grace clearly valued his solitude. Although, as Ellen had learned these last few years, valuing solitude and actually being happy were two entirely different matters.

'His ranting and raving does nothing to scare me.' Lady Faye patted the bed, indicating Ellen should make herself comfortable.

Emboldened, Ellen asked the question she'd been dying to ask all evening. 'What happened to Lord Woodhal? He showed me the scars on his chest and back, but he said nothing more than that there'd been a fire.'

The dowager sighed. 'There was a fire, yes. At sea. Pierce died. Calum didn't.' She patted Ellen's cheek affectionately which Ellen took to mean Lady Faye wasn't unset by the question and she was free to keep talking.

'Pierce. His brother?' The son *Debrett's* had said had died the same month as their father, the old duke.

The dowager nodded. 'Younger half-brother.'

'I see.' Almost. 'What did you mean when you asked if His Grace had told me about the house?' She asked an easier question.

'Oh, that.' Lady Faye settled back against her pillows. 'Well, I guess the story starts a good few years ago, when my daughter married a very handsome young man.'

'Hammond Callaghan, the fifth Duke of Woodhal.' *Debrett's* had gotten that bit right at least.

'Yes. Hammond had been married previously, but his bride, Finella, wasn't happy in England, and soon after their wedding she ran back to Scotland. Hammond went looking for her, but by the time he found her she'd already died in a carriage accident.'

'Back to Scotland...' Ellen frowned.

'Calum's mother,' Lady Faye confirmed. 'Finella McKenna. The thing is, nobody told Hammond that she'd given birth to a son before her death. I think her family thought if Hammond knew there was a son, he'd take the child back to London with him, which I suppose he would have done. Finella's parents had already lost their daughter. I cannot really blame them for not wanting to lose their grandson as well.'

'The old duke didn't know Her Grace was expecting before she ran away?'

'Finella never said a word. And I've been told Cal was a particularly small newborn.'

They shared an amused smile.

'Hammond knew nothing of Cal until he was ten,' the dowager continued. 'His grandparents died of consumption, and their lawyers contacted Hammond. By that stage, of course, Hammond had been married to Grace for eight years, and Pierce had been born.'

Ellen could see where the story was going. Everyone would have believed Pierce to be the Woodhal heir. But Calum was—she quickly counted—close on three years older and a legitimate son. Assuming, of course, there was proof Calum really was Hammond's progeny.

'There's a portrait hanging over the fireplace in the drawing room of a fair-haired gentleman,' Ellen remembered.

'That's Hammond's father; Cal's grandfather. They don't much look alike, if that's what you're thinking,' said Lady Faye perceptively. 'Cal looks a lot like his mother. But Hammond believed Calum was his son, without a doubt.' She gave a forced smile. 'Grace wasn't happy.'

A shout echoed through the house. Downstairs somewhere Lord Woodhal and Mr Tattershall were arguing, although it was impossible to make out their words.

Clearing her throat, Lady Faye continued. Nothing seemed to faze her when it came to those two. 'Grace blamed Hammond for not knowing about Calum. She was very angry ... heartbroken. She wanted a divorce but didn't want the scandal, so instead she divided the house in half.'

'And that's why the corridors are so narrow.' And why there were two front doors.

'Pierce lived on the other side of the house with Grace, and Calum lived with Hammond on this side.'

'Does your daughter still live next door?'

'Goodness, no. Grace moved out the month Hammond died. Less than a sennight after we received news of Pierce's death. He was a first lieutenant, you know.' She took one of Ellen's hands in both of hers. Her skin was lovely and soft but wrinkled and marked with age. 'Does all this talk make you want to run away from us?'

'Of course not, my lady.' *Both my parents are dead, my brother beats me and I'm hiding little Gwen away in the country. Maggie is risking my brother's wrath by helping keep Gwen safe, and*

Verity lied about my identity in her recommendation letter so you would employ me. 'Every family has their own story. Do you know why Lord Woodhal hasn't taken down the dividing wall now your daughter has moved out?' After all, as he kept reminding everyone, this was his house.

'I guess because he still believes the other half is Grace's. And Grace isn't his mother.' She rubbed a hand over her eyes. 'My daughter is ... heartbroken. She won't have anything to do with Cal, even though he provides her a generous allowance.' Her shoulders drooped and she seemed to shrink in on herself.

The dowager duchess wasn't the only one with a broken heart. Lady Faye's family was divided and the thought clearly distressed her. Ellen searched for a change of topic. 'Who exactly is Mr Tattershall?' The man downstairs currently arguing with the duke was a breath of fresh air. He had a ready grin, which she was quickly coming to think of as 'the Tattershall Twinkle'. And she'd had the distinct impression he'd been flirting with her at dinner.

He could not have been more different from the stern and grumpy Lord Woodhal if he'd lived on the moon.

'Ahh.' Lady Faye straightening, looking instantly happier. 'He believes himself to be a veritable Bond Street beau, but in my opinion his waistcoats are a little too magnificent to be considered entirely fashionable. Don't you ever tell him I said that though!' She nudged Ellen with an elbow. 'What you really want to know is that he's my ward. Owen's mother was a good friend of mine although she was close to twenty years my junior. In fact, I'm surprised you haven't heard of the Tattershalls. I don't mean the Tattersalls of Tattersall's London horses,' she added quickly as though that was exactly what Ellen had been thinking, despite being only newly arrived to London. 'Owen's family is also from Evendale.'

'No, I haven't heard of his family.' She was surprised. There were only seven and twenty families in Evendale. Although, as Mr Tattershall was an orphan, it was quite possible his parents had died before Ellen had been born. By the looks of it, he was a year or so older than herself—and a couple of years younger than Lord Woodhal. Probably about the same age as her brother. Or even Lieutenant Callaghan, had he not died.

One reclusive grandson, one dead grandson, one heartbroken daughter and one sweet-talking ward. The Woodhal-Faye clan was a peculiar bevy indeed. 'This is all very personal, my lady. If you don't mind my asking, why did you tell me? We've only just met.'

'To be frank, gel. We may be a family of dukes and marquesses, but that doesn't put us above reproach.' Lady Faye squeezed her hand. 'I'd prefer you heard all of this from me rather than the London gossips.'

Chapter Six

'You're following me,' Cal said as he limped into the library. 'Isn't it time you were heading home?'

'Miss Smith's a bit of an armful.' Owen slumped into the old wing-back armchair. Dinner had finished and the ladies had headed upstairs for an early night. All Cal wanted was another whisky, not more company.

'Quite the belle of the ball,' Owen continued. 'You must have noticed.' Propping his cane against the side of the chair, he stretched his legs out before him. With his arms behind his head, he cupped the back of his neck with interlaced fingers, looking for all the world like this were his library.

Of course Cal had noticed. He'd been trying not to notice for the last few hours. Companions to elderly grandmothers were not supposed to raise the blood. He stuffed his hands into his pockets, pursing his lips to stop himself saying something he'd regret.

'Of course you did, don't try to deny it.' Owen chuckled. 'Her style could do with a bit of an intervention though.' He picked up the closest book, flicked through without interest and let it slide to the floor. 'Whyever do you think she was so moist?' he asked with a smirk. 'Her dress was positively clinging to—'

'It's raining.' Cal stalked across the room and back again. Something crunched underfoot, and he swore. He'd forgotten about the broken glass. That was perfectly good whisky soaking into his Persian rug.

'Oh, lark. You didn't make her wait outside, did you, Wood?'

'No.' *Not for lack of trying.* 'It was her own fault.' He quickly related the events of the evening, leaving out the bit where he'd bullied her into showing him her bruises. Even he could admit that hadn't been his most chivalrous moment.

'Wood!' Owen laughed. 'Bested by a slip of a girl. I have so many questions. Why—'

'I don't want to talk about it anymore.' His head ached. Everything ached. He looked around the library, searching for another glass. No such luck. He took a swing straight from the bottle.

'All right. All right. Just one quick question. Whyever were you shirtless?' Owen laughed again, banging his knee with the palm of his hand.

'Stop being such an arse.' Cal pinched the bridge of his nose. How had he ended up in this mess? A few hours earlier he'd been blissfully alone. 'Couldn't you have suggested Lady F rent a house of her own? She listens to you.'

'No, she does not. Besides, you should know by now that when she gets an idea into her head, nobody and nothing can stop her.' Owen lifted Tzar onto his lap, and the old dog pressed his nose into the crook of Owen's neck. As though Owen was the one who fed him and groomed him and let him sleep on the bed and took him outside every few hours for a piss and a shit.

Little traitor.

'Wait a moment.' Cal's thoughts suddenly caught up with Owen's words. 'What do you mean "an idea" What's she planning?' He glared at his cousin. 'What's she doing in London?'

'She's planning to enjoy the Season,' Owen said, gently rubbing one of Tzar's ears between two fingers. A couple of stray dog hairs clung to his otherwise perfectly black lapel.

'Like hell. I can count the times she's come to Town on the fingers of one hand, and not once has it ever been to enjoy the Season.'

Twenty-three years ago, she'd come into Town announcing her intention to 'enjoy the Season' when she'd really come to meet him for the first time. That was back when Cal had only been ten, and his father had brought him to live in London after his grandparents had died. Nineteen years ago 'enjoy the Season' had translated to attempting to mediate peace between his father and Grace. They'd barely been speaking by then. Fourteen years ago she'd come to see him off to sea, back when he'd thought it was going to be a great adventure. Four years ago it was for Pierce's funeral. Not that they'd had a body to bury. Sailors who died at sea were left at sea. Even first lieutenants.

What a poor replacement for a grandson Cal must be. He and Lady F weren't even related by blood, just marriage, and even that connection was dubious considering Grace loathed the very sight of him.

He stopped before Owen and kicked lightly at the soles of the other man's shoes. 'You know more than you're letting on.'

'You don't scare me.' Owen straightened, drawing his legs in close to the chair, one arm still around the dog. 'I've known you for too long. I remember you in leading strings.'

'Nay, I remember you in leading strings.' He suddenly felt very tired. 'It's been a long evening, Owen. I don't have the patience for this conversation.'

'It's only early, old man.'

'For fuck's sake, just get out of my house.'

Owen blanched, his smile finally disappearing. 'You can't stay locked in here forever. Pierce wouldn't have wanted—'

'You don't know what Pierce would've wanted. Nobody knows what he would have wanted because he's rotting at the bottom on the sea.' He turned his back on his cousin. He was breathing as though he'd just run a race, and he could hear the blood pumping in his ears. He wanted to hit something so much it was like an ache in his arm.

He heard Owen put the dog down and stand up. 'It wasn't your fault.'

'What did you say?' Dread, like ice, turned him cold.

'I've read the inquisition report, Cal. Your name was cleared of all suspicion. Nobody on that ship, nobody with half a brain, believes you lit that fire. It was very clearly an accident.'

'And yet I was suspended under investigation.' He turned back around to face Owen. His cousin wasn't as tall as him nor was he a fighter. But he was younger, and he wasn't wounded or scarred.

'It was only because—'

'What would you know? You didn't even have the balls to join up,' he yelled, the words out of his mouth before he could stop himself.

Owen flinched. But Cal didn't take it back. He didn't even apologise. It would be better if Owen hated him, if Owen stopped trying to make him feel better.

'Nobody cares anymore, Wood. You're the only one who thinks it still matters.' The pity in Owen's gaze was like a brick wall between them.

'Grace—The newspapers—'

'Grace didn't know what she was on about. Her son died; she was grief-stricken. And the newspapers haven't printed a word about you in almost three years. Most of London has forgotten you even exist.' Moving to the table, Owen swept his hand over the yellowing newspaper clippings, scattering them to the floor. 'You're a grumpy old hermit and you're barely more than thirty.' He finally turned his back on Cal, heading for the door.

Tzar let out a low cry, following Owen.

'I'll see myself out,' Owen called from the passage. 'Tell Lizzy I'll be back in a few days once they've settled in. I'm taking the ladies shopping.' And he left, his footsteps fading as he traipsed down the passage towards the front door. Even the click of his cane against the floorboards soon disappeared, leaving Cal completely and exceedingly alone.

***

By the time Ellen departed Lady Faye's chamber, the dowager was snoring softly. She suppressed a yawn of her own, moving down the passage to the next door. The knot between her shoulders eased a little—a difficult day was over finally over. She'd survived the wrath of a duke and been accepted by Lady Faye.

As if summoned by her very thoughts, His Grace came padding down the passage towards her. His stockinged feet made barely a sound; his boots were slung over one shoulder.

'Your Grace.' She dipped a curtsy.

'Miss Smith, everywhere I turn, there you are.' His voice was tinted with the residue of anger. Whatever he'd been arguing about with Mr Tattershall had left him waspish.

'Not by design,' she quickly assured him. Spots of light and shadow cast by the three-arm candelabra she held threw his scars into sharp relief. She could easily see the ridges and hollows where they pulled at the skin on the left side of his face.

'Why exactly are you lurking in the shadows?'

'I have to argue against your choice of words. I am not lurking. I just saw your grandmother to her bed." She paused, steeling herself. "I would like to thank you for not telling her ladyship about the window and our earlier ... misunderstanding.'

'If you think that enough to turn Lady F against you, you're in for a surprise. My grandmother delights in the absurd. If I'd told her, she probably would have adopted you as her own. Not telling her was most definitely to my own benefit.' He was frowning again—or perhaps that was just his resting face.

'Thank you all the same. This opportunity is very important to me.' More than he could ever know.

'Just because you and Lady F have managed to browbeat your way into my home for an evening, doesn't mean I've admitted defeat. The two of you might have won the battle, but the war has just begun.'

Ellen eyed the obstinate man before her. He had the potential to make the next few months of her life very difficult. 'Wouldn't it be easier for the both of us if we simply called a truce?' And she held out her hand for him to shake.

He scrutinised her offering disdainfully. She taken off her gloves when they'd sat down to dine, but she doubted that was the source of his displeasure. More likely it was the thought of having to be civil for four months—four excruciatingly long months.

His own appearance was less than perfect. He'd haphazardly shrugged on his crumpled jacket over his crumpled shirt. It was the one she'd seen abandoned on the floor of the drawing room earlier that evening. Despite the impressive breadth of his shoulders, the jacket was clearly a little too large, as though he'd recently lost weight. That, along with his too-long hair, gave the impression he hadn't been looking after himself. In fact, close up, he looked positively exhausted.

She felt a peculiar urge to start feeding him cream and raspberry trifle.

Or ravish him.

Whoa! Where did that thought come from? Yes, he was devilishly attractive in a dangerous sort of way, but she didn't even like him. He was an insufferable old grump. *And lady's companions most definitely do not have indecent thoughts about members of their employer's family.* She gave her head a small shake, trying to settle her wayward thoughts. What had they been talking about? She'd just offered him a truce. That was it. 'Do you accept?'

'Absolutely not.'

'You haven't even heard my terms and conditions,' she insisted, entirely unsurprised by his refusal. 'It would be well worth your while.'

His already thinly pressed mouth pressed into an even thinner line. Understanding this to be the only indication of his consent to listen, she hurried on. 'What I mean is, if her ladyship asks me to do anything that will have the potential to interfere with your life, I promise to do as little interfering as possible without disobeying her direct order, if you promise—'

'I will not make such a vow. Thank you very much, Miss Smith, but I'm perfectly capable of looking after myself.' He shifted uncomfortably. His wounded knee must have been paining him again. It was a wonder he didn't need a walking stick, but maybe that had more to do with this self-sacrificing quest he seemed to be on. Or just sheer stubbornness.

Ellen silently cursed. Now she was fighting the urge not only to feed him but also to rub cooling lotion on his scars and massage the tightness from his leg.

Or ravish him.

Oh, no.

***

Miss Smith was watching him with a curious expression on her face. What was that expression? Attraction? Nay. It had been so long since anyone had looked at him with interest that he must be mistaken.

Lady F: concern.

Owen: pity.

Grace: hatred.

The rest of the world: unmistakable suspicion.

She blinked, and there it was again: attraction. And now she was actually smiling at him. How the deuce was he supposed to conduct a rational conversation when she was smiling at him? His body began to respond.

He brushed past her, limped into his chamber and slammed the door in her surprised face.

Hell and damnation. He wanted her.

He rested his forehead on one post of his four-poster bed, his forearms above his head. In the passage, he heard as she huffed her indignation, and he could easily imagine her glaring at his closed door. A moment later, she retreated down the passage, taking herself off to bed in the guest room furthest from his own.

Miss Smith in bed. In his bed. Naked and beneath him, sweaty and quivering.

Then again, she was a feisty one. Perhaps she'd take charge, toss him onto the bed and take him in hand.

He tried to sink that foolish notion, but already his cock-stand was straining against his breeches, demanding to be taken care of, to no longer be ignored.

Back there in the corridor, his younger self wouldn't have hesitated to kiss her senseless. His younger self had been untouched by war and loss, his ego controlled entirely by his innocent confidence, his sense of propriety governed only by his desires.

He banged his forehead against the post, and the whole bed shook. He'd been living the life of a hermit for four years, cutting himself off from almost all company, denying himself pleasure; living only with pain and heartbreak.

That's all I deserve. Because his brother was dead, and it was his fault.

But this sudden need for Ellen driving through his body tonight was like a kind of pain too. So forceful was it. He ground his teeth. What was she doing to him? Just one look and he was ready to melt before her feet.

He unbuttoned his breeches, taking himself in hand.

He didn't deserve to feel like this. Maybe he was drunker than he'd realised? But his head wasn't even pounding anymore; all his blood had rushed south.

He tugged, clenching his hand tighter, making himself wince. It was a kind of half torture touching himself like this when he knew no-one else would ever want to, least of all the prim and proper miss just a couple of doors down. A sore reminder that he was alone and would be alone for the rest of his life.

He stuffed his other hand into his mouth, stifling his grunts.

That look she'd given him—not of disgust, not of judgement, not of anger. That look was exactly why he needed her gone from his life.

When his release came, it was anything but freeing.

Chapter Seven

Calum Callaghan, the new Duke of Woodhal and once notorious rake, lately returned from sea, last night was rejected by every eligible debutante at the Hunt's private ball. It was his first social outing since being acquitted of lighting the fire that killed his half-brother. How will he dare show his scarred face in public again?
—*The Daily Tatler*, 15 April 1813

'Why is there a butler, a cook and two maids in my kitchen?'

Ellen put down her sewing as the duke marched into the dining room. He was scowling. Surprise, surprise.

She, on the other hand, was calm. She was serene. She was the perfect lady's companion. Her new No. 1 rule: *to behave, even when being provoked by a vexatious, self-righteous duke.*

Rising to her feet, she bestowed upon him her most gracious curtsy. A curtsy that clearly said: 'I work for your grandmother and don't answer to you, especially as you didn't accept my very chivalrous offer of a truce.'

'Good morning, Your Grace.'

It was the first time she'd seen him since that first night three days ago. He'd locked himself in his bedchamber, refusing to admit even his personal secretary. He'd also ignored the trays of food they'd left by his door, raiding the kitchen during the night when everyone was sleeping.

'Don't "good morning" me, Miss Smith. I want to know why there's a cook in *my* kitchen.'

Even the tone of his voice was a scowl. It was no wonder Lady Faye had made herself scarce the moment they'd heard the duke's mismatched footsteps on the stairs. Ellen wished she'd run away too but she hadn't been quick enough to realise what was happening, and now there was a six-foot-something Scotsman who'd clearly woken up on the wrong side of the bed blocking the only exit.

She regained her seat, taking a sip of near-cold tea as she collected her thoughts. The pause only angered him further. If His Grace were a kettle, he'd have steam billowing from his ears.

'Her ladyship thought it a good idea to employ more staff for the duration of her stay in London.' Unwittingly, her gaze flickered to his scars. Light against his otherwise tanned skin, some so fine they could have been the threads of a spider's web but others so deep they twisted and pulled at the left side of his face.

This morning he was actually wearing a waistcoat, cravat and jacket. He'd also tied his shoulder-length hair back in a simple queue at the nape of his neck, similar in style to the look favoured by men of the militia. Her gaze travelled down to his footwear—black topped boots with brown bonding and worn-down heels. Unlike Mr Owen Tattershall's shoes, which she'd describe as shoes fit for a dandy, Lord Woodhal's were scuffed and scraped and perfectly practical.

In fact, Calum Callaghan looked halfway decent.

Not that it was any concern of hers how he looked.

'Are ye trying to imply ye had naught to do with it?'

'I suppose, mayhaps, it might have been me who hired the servants. But her ladyship instructed me to,' she said, deciding on the spot not to mention the two downstairs maids he obviously hadn't yet encountered. That would be a pleasant surprise for another time.

Ellen had paid a call to Miss Steele's Respectable Household Servants registry before breakfast two days ago with a missive in Lady Faye's own hand setting out exacting instructions. The servants had arrived that afternoon and had been hard at work ever since, trying to return the duke's house to some sort of order.

It was a wonder Lord Woodhal hadn't noticed earlier. Even locked in his room, it would have been impossible not to hear the hustle and bustle of cleaning. Unless, of course, he'd had another bottle of whisky in his room and had drunk himself into his cups.

She eyed him suspiciously, but there was no look of the sloshed about his person this morning.

There was a suspicious look of his upon his face. 'Wait a moment...' He turned a full circle, scanning the room. 'Where are all my papers? The estate papers I had laid out on the table?'

She glanced down at the ten-seat table, empty save for her stitching and tea. 'I'm not sure. I believe her ladyship moved some things out of this room.' Lady Faye had been working just as hard as the rest of them. For a woman of advanced years, she didn't hold back. 'She might have moved them when I was out.' *Hiring the servants,* she added silently. She placed her hands on the table, intending to rise. 'Would you like me to ask her?'

'Nay, you've caused enough trouble as it is.' His mouth pursed into another one of his thin frowns. He had so many frowns. Angry frowns. Disapproving frowns. Sulking frowns. About-to-start-yelling frowns. Now he was giving her one of his displeased frowns.

Moving to one of the mahogany dressers, he started searching. This brought him closer to where she was sitting, and she suddenly caught his scent. It definitely wasn't whisky, but he still smelled of heather. Like a breath of fresh air after a long and stuffy carriage ride.

She returned to her tea and stitching, determinedly ignoring the impressive framework of muscles beneath his suit. His jacket might be a little too large, but that did nothing to hide the power of his arms.

She made another small stitch. Her hands trembled. His nearness was unnerving. She could hear the tap, thump, tap, thump of his limp as he slowly moved down the length of the dresser and the rustle of his plain grey jacket as he slid open another drawer.

She peeked at him from under her lashes. There were wrinkles in the back of his carelessly tired cravat. He pushed the drawer shut and bent at the waist to open the cupboard below, one hand resting on the top of the dresser to take a little weight off his wounded knee.

Her gaze locked on the taut stretch of his breeches over his muscular thighs and backside. Not that a lady's companion would notice such a thing. Certainly not! She tried to look away, to focus on her work, but her gaze felt paralysed. He was like every improper fantasy she'd imagined in her lonely bed after dark.

Slamming the cupboard shut, he opened another. There was tension in his movements. He was worried. And still sulking. 'How, pray, did ye manage to find any servants willing to work for me?' he inquired, without bothering to glance her way.

She wrinkled her nose. Another question he wasn't going to like the answer to. 'They aren't exactly working for you.' Lady Faye was the one paying their wages.

He straightened, turning to face her. 'And?'

'And...' Was she really that obvious? Or did he really think so little of himself? 'I made a couple of concessions. Chakrabarti used to be a footman but I promoted him to butler.' She stumbled a little over his unfamiliar name but was determined to get it right. 'Adelynn is the new housemaid, but Pamela is teaching her to be a lady's maid so after this she'll be able to find an elevated position.' And the two downstairs maids didn't yet have character references so were unable to find work anywhere else half so respectable.

She blinked at him innocently, daring him to say something, to object. He didn't, just drummed his fingers on the dresser, glaring over her shoulder at the open bay windows, which were letting in the glorious rays of spring sunshine, as if they'd done him a personal injury.

With a disgruntled grunt, he moved towards the matching dresser on the other side of the room, pulling open more drawers and cupboards.

Ellen turned in her chair slightly, presenting him with her shoulder and hoping he'd take it as an indication of her need to concentrate on the work at hand. It was slow going and she was taking more care than usual, hoping the dowager would admire her neat work.

Suddenly his shadow was blocking her light. He'd abandoned the second dresser as a lost cause and moved to stand behind her. Her heart started racing. How was it possible to be more aware of his presence now she couldn't see him? She heard his breathing as clearly as if he stood by her ear. She smelled him as clearly as if he kneeled under her nose. And she felt the ghost of his touch on the back of her neck as clearly as if he'd actually brushed his lips against her skin.

The hairs on the back of her neck rose as if in anticipation.

Concentrate on your sewing.

She bowed her head, conscious she was exposing more skin at the back of her neck to him. What would it be like to kiss the back of his neck, to slip her fingers beneath the collar of his shirt?

To ravish him?

Her fingers shook and she crossed her ankles, locking her legs together. *Concentrate on anything but that!* She lifted her head slightly and searched the room, desperate to distract herself with something else, anything else. It was clear this space hadn't always been a dining room. It had probably been converted into one when the duchess had the wall built down the centre of the house. Judging by the green and white wallpaper with its border of hibiscus flowers in faded pastels, it used to be a lady's morning room.

Now it was cramped with dark furniture that overpowered the small space. Sunlight bounced off the crystals in the dusty chandelier, sending little rainbows dancing over the papered walls.

She heard him shuffle from foot to foot and looked at him over her shoulder. She couldn't have stopped herself from looking no matter how hard she tried.

He wasn't facing her at all. He had his back to the room and was staring out the open window again.

A knock echoed down the passage from the back door, and he turned towards the sound.

He moved like a predator—alert and wary. 'What was that?'

'I heard nothing.'

The glare he threw suggested he didn't believe one word.

'Or mayhaps it's a delivery of extra food from the market or the new linens your grandmother ordered. I really couldn't say.'

'Och, ye couldn't, could ye?' He made the sound at the back of this throat that only the Scottish-born seemed able to do justice. 'I don't need new linen or a butler or a cook.'

'Which is exactly why her ladyship didn't have me employ a valet for you.'

'I should be grateful? If I'd known ye were going to be this tyrannical, I really would have tossed ye over my shoulder and thrown ye out the front door the instant ye climbed through my window.'

'Well, Your Grace, you missed your chance. Your grandmother has set up home here, and I don't think anything will persuade her to leave now she's decided to stay for the Season. Eat something for goodness' sake.' She pushed the tea things in his direction, including butter sandwiches courtesy of the new cook.

'Is there anything else ye need to tell me?' he demanded. 'Did ye manage to clear out my pantry of all the good cake or are ye saving that task for this afternoon?'

'Don't be ridiculous, Your Grace,' she scoffed in mock offence, but unable to stop herself glancing out the window. From here it was impossible to see where she'd been working earlier that morning, thankfully.

Lady Faye chose that moment to dignify them with her presence. She strolled into the dining room as though she hadn't vacated it moments before her grandson's arrival less than a quarter of an hour ago. 'Morning, morning,' she trilled.

'About the servants—' Lord Woodhal began.

'Keep up, dearest. That was absolutely days ago. Miss Smith and I have been working very hard.' Her ladyship practically waltzed her way around the table. Today she was wearing a burgundy morning gown with an empire waistline. It was a stunning gown; one designed to draw the eye and complement her curves.

Ellen touched a hand to her own dowdy mob cap. Maggie had given it to her before she'd left Evendale. It was the perfect accessory for an unmarried lady's companion. It only piqued her vanity a little to have to wear it.

What vanity? she scoffed silently. *Beggars can't be choosers.*

'What did you do with my estate papers?' demanded His Grace. Just like magic, his Scottish accent had disappeared again.

'I moved them to the library where they should have been in the first place.' Lady Faye paused right behind Ellen's chair, looking completely unfazed by his rudish manner. She had one hand behind her back, hiding something from sight.

'I have a system—'

'Your system is all wrong. Whyever are you keeping all those old newspaper clippings? If you tossed them away, you could actually do your work at your desk like a normal man of business.' She clicked her tongue in disapproval. 'Not that dukes normally run their country estates without stepping outside their London townhouses.'

He opened his mouth to respond, but like the expert she was Lady Faye pressed on without pause. 'Now, dearest, are you coming with Miss Smith and me to the fireworks tomorrow evening?'

'We've already talked about this.'

'Just remind me...'

'No.'

'Sulking, are we?' She rested her free hand on Ellen's shoulder, squeezing lightly as if to share her amusement.

'No!' Lord Woodhal straightened his already straight shoulders as though to add gravitas to his words.

'So you are coming, good. Although you'll need to get a haircut if you're to be seen in polite company. It's far too long at the moment.'

'I'm not getting a haircut, and I'm not leaving this house.'

'But you don't have to leave the house. Miss Smith will cut your hair for you.' And she produced a pair of shears from behind her back.

'What? My lady, I've never cut anyone's hair before.' Ellen scrambled to her feet.

'No. No. No.' The duke was practically breathing steam now.

'Then you'll be coming to the fireworks. The choice is yours.' Lady Faye's voice darkened, taking on a threatening edge. She watched her grandson closely. A smile still played with her lips but her eyes were suddenly serious. She meant business. 'Stop being such a milksop, Cal, and make up your mind.'

Ellen glanced between them. Apparently it wasn't his Scottish ancestors who he'd inherited his stubbornness from. It was his five-foot, sixty-eight-year-old English grandmother.

Facing down Lady Faye was like facing down a bull. A very determined, very tenacious bull. With horns. And it seemed Lord Woodhal was beginning to realise this too. He backed up a step, suddenly looking like a man on the run. His eyes locked on his grandmother's face, begging her to leave him be.

'There's absolutely no point running. I'll just follow you. And now I have help.' She waved the shears towards Ellen.

'My lady, I've never—'

Lady Faye silenced her with a look then motioned for her grandson to take a seat. For a moment Ellen was sure he'd push his way out of the room, threat or no threat, but he sat back down with a grunt, crossing his gloriously muscular arms before his chest.

Her breath hitched.

She determinately ignored it.

'See, that wasn't so bad,' the dowager cooed, delighted to be getting her own way again. She handed the shears to Ellen, nodding towards His Grace's too-long hair.

Seeing the danger, he turned his gaze towards Ellen, bestowing her with the full brunt of his gaze. His expression said, 'touch my hair and I'll never forgive you.'

Lady Faye clicked her tongue impatiently. 'Get on with it, gel.'

She was trapped between a rock and a hard place, as the saying went. Taking the shears from Lady Faye, she moved around the table to stand behind Lord Woodhal. Even seated, he was so tall his head was level with her shoulders. His neck was corded with muscles and the odd scar that disappeared beneath his cravat.

He sat perfectly still. The tension in shoulders was almost catching.

How hard could cutting the hair of an annoyingly obstinate yet tantalisingly irresistible duke possibly be?

Oh lordy!

***

Cal stiffened as Ellen stopped behind him. He could hear her shifting from foot to foot, her breathing a little fast. Nervous or flustered at having to stand so near him? He bit the inside of his cheek as a growing sense of unease churned in his stomach like waves rushing towards the shoreline.

She smelled of soap and sugar and ... And something he couldn't quite put his finger on. Something uniquely Ellen. How strange he hadn't noticed the other night. Then again he'd been a little foxed.

He frowned at this own thoughts. *When had she become Ellen and not simply Miss Smith?*

Turning his head slightly, he watched her reflection in the old cracked mirror over the sideboard. She was wearing another one of those shapeless gowns she favoured and the same lace cap as the first night they'd met, though a few loose curls had escaped. One grazed her collarbone as though tempting his gaze downwards. Their eyes met in the mirror, and he quickly looked away.

Before him, Lady F was wearing the smile of a well-pleased cat. He could practically feel her gaze on his twisted, scarred face. Expectant. Waiting. He wanted to turn his head and present her with his good side, his untouched side. But that would be showing weakness, and he'd already lost one battle today.

'Would you just start already!' His heart was racing and his forehead felt a little clammy. He'd come face to face with Napoleon's troops at the Battle of Trafalgar when he'd been just twenty-one, and yet he couldn't even say no to his pocket-sized grandmother and her impetuous companion.

The sooner Ellen started, the sooner this hell would be over.

A moment later, the tie in his hair was pulled free and Ellen's fingertips brushed his neck so softly it was like the touch of a wisp.

It didn't take her long to cut his hair. The snip of the shears and her breath heavy with concentration the only sounds to scare away the silence. Her touch was gentle but firm as she sectioned pieces of hair, cutting until it was short enough she was running her fingers over his scalp, testing the length from various angles.

The touch of her fingers sent vibrations down his entire body—his traitorous body, which was quickly beginning to ignore all the common sense he'd just managed to talk himself into.

The deep insatiable hunger of the other night returned, clawing its way up his throat and through his blood. His cock jumped to attention in his breeches like a soldier, eager and ready to please.

A hand in his hair: was that really all it took? He'd never been so grateful for a table in his life. It was doing a fine job of keeping his unruly body hidden from prying eyes.

Prying eyes. He looked around but Lady F was nowhere in sight. When she'd left the room, he couldn't have said.

He ran his hand up and down his thighs, feeling unbearably restless. If Ellen wasn't holding a pair of shears to his head, he would have jumped up and starting walking circles around the dining table. He needed to put some space between them, needed a moment to breathe, to clear his mind.

He clenched his fists. And then her fingers brushed against his scalp, sending another wave of desire rushing through his body. He was behaving no better than an untried youth.

She's a gentleman's daughter, for goodness sake! A country lass, who's probably never even been kissed in her life. She deserved to be pampered. To be wooed by a proper gentleman, not a damaged hermit with half a body of scars.

She was too good for him. Ellen Smith, in all her spinsterish ways and wearing that revolting lace cap: too bloody good for the likes of him. *And a hundred times too good for the brute who'd laid his hands on her, turning her wrists black and blue.*

He pinched his leg, focusing on the pain, wanting to feel anything but the urgent hunger racing through his body like a fire through the undergrowth. Right now he felt as though he was two people. One of those men couldn't turn his back on Pierce, on everything his brother's death meant and everything his scars represented. The other man had been alone for so long he wanted nothing more than to pull the feisty, intelligent, window-climbing adventuress into his arms and bury himself so deeply inside her it was impossible to tell where he ended and she began.

'I've finished.'

He heard her back away and tuck the shears into one of the dresser drawers—probably afraid of what his reaction would be.

Instantly suspicious, he stood up, all the better to see his reflection in the mirror. He kept his gaze diverted from his scars, looking only at his hair—or what was left of it. She'd obviously been attempting a style similar to Owen's—short on the sides and back, slightly longer on the top. What she'd actually achieved was, hands down, the worst haircut he'd ever seen, as though she'd put a bucket on his head and cut a circle. He ground his teeth. Absolutely bloody perfect. Just what he needed: a haircut as hideous as half his face.

'I never professed to knowing what I was doing,' she said.

His eyes settled on the crack in the looking glass. It radiated out from a centre point, like a spider's web. He'd thrown a knife at it a couple of years ago. The mirror had broken but hadn't fallen from its frame. Ellen shifted from foot to foot, and his gaze focused on her reflection. A dozen or so freckles spotted her nose, so faint he'd missed them until now. Her lips were pressed firmly closed and her eyes danced.

'You're laughing at me!' He turned to face her.

'I'm not. I swear.' A giggle escaped her strawberry lips. A blush, the colour high on her cheeks. 'I'm sorry.' An apologetic hand on his arm. A flash of surprise in her grey eyes at her own audacity. And, in that instant, for the briefest second, he saw his own hunger reflected back at him. He hadn't imagined it the other night. She wanted him, as he wanted her.

Cal's self-resolve died instantaneously. His hand was on her waist, the other behind her neck before he could draw breath or form another coherent thought.

And then *she* was kissing him.

He blinked in surprise, then surrendered. Pulling her closer, he claimed her mouth just as she was claiming his. She tasted sweet, like the sugary tea she favoured. It should have been too sweet. He'd always preferred a savoury palette, but he suddenly couldn't get enough.

He kept his eyes open, not wanting to miss a moment of it. Her hands were on either side of his face, pulling him down to her level. Her eyes were pressed closed, her lashes incredibly long. Her back arched and her breasts strained towards him.

His blood was on fire with need more powerful than anything he'd felt these last four years, even as his mind tried to stop him, tried to tell him that he shouldn't be doing this, that she was off limits. Hell, she was his grandmother's companion.

With a rip, the top button of his shirt bounced to the floor. His collar opened, letting in cool fingers of air to stroke his burning skin. He staggered to the left a little, his wounded knee giving way, but she held him up, her slight form offering him the stability he craved. He couldn't stop. He didn't want to stop.

She broke away, trailing kissing down his cheek, over his scars.

Cal wrenched back, stumbling on his own two feet until he hit the dresser. He wiped his mouth with a trembling hand. How could he have done that? How could he have lost control like that? Drawing a shaky breath, he yelled with all his might. 'Get out!'

Verity

Evendale, Yorkshire

Mrs Verity Nott, once of Hornsby Manor House, now of a small cottage in Evendale, opened her front door to find herself face to face with the man she'd been dreading meeting for the last few days.

He stood with his hands tucked into his suspenders, his hips thrust forward and his feet firmly planted on her top step. He eyed Verity with open distrust. The eldest Burney child had inherited his family's grey eyes, but there was nothing of the warmth and kindness of his late parents in them.

'Geoffrey, I don't often see you at my threshold.' She took a step forward, even though this brought them closer, so that she could close the door behind her. She wasn't about to let Geoffrey into her house; she didn't want to be in a confined space with him.

'It's "my lord" to you,' Geoffrey snarled.

'Of course, Lord Blackford. My mistake.' Verity had been friends with Geoffrey's mother since girlhood. That was why she'd chosen to resettle in Evendale after her husband's death many years ago. She'd known Geoffrey his whole life, but never had she suspected he'd grow into such a man as this.

'Ellen's missing,' he grunted.

'Missing?' She feigned surprise.

'Missing. You know: gone, lost, run away.' The young baron glared at her.

'Why would you think Ellen ran away?' She chose her words with care.

'Because, you fool, she's not at home where she's supposed to be. And neither is the mute.'

Verity took a calming breath, determined not to let her emotions get the better of her, lest she say something that betrayed her role in all of this. 'Ellen's a grown woman. She has as much right—'

'She's a whore!'

Verity grit her teeth. To call any woman a whore was despicable. To call your own sister one was unforgivable. 'I'm more worried about what you've become, Geoffrey.'

'It's "my lord"! I know you're somehow involved. You tell me where she is.' He pressed a hand to the doorframe, crowding her, which would have worked better had Verity not been over a head taller.

Verity raised her hands before her chest, trying to create some distance. Over his shoulder she could see early morning shoppers at the street market. If she shouted, they would hear.

Geoffrey was a coward at heart. He wouldn't hit her when there was a chance someone would intervene. He only picked fights with those who were weaker than himself or more vulnerable. Why else would he hit a six-year-old?

She looked him full in the face. Her husband had been a boxer back at university. Verity—well, she'd been taught to embroider slippers and paint screens. But that didn't mean she wouldn't fight him with every breath in her body. She'd picked up a thing or two watching her husband. Anything to keep Ellen and Gwen and Maggie safe.

There was fire in Geoffrey's eyes, but something in her expression must have given him pause for thought. He took a step back. 'I know Maggie's cottage has been empty for as long as Ellen's been missing. You've always had a soft spot for Maggie, everyone knows.' He hissed his words as though her feelings were a dirty secret that could be used to punish Verity. 'I will find them. Mark my words.' He turned on his heel, his pocket jingling, and sauntered away, kicking the garden gate as he passed.

Verity's heart started racing as the fight gave way to fright. Where had Geoffrey gotten money? Had his luck at the gambling tables finally turned?

She pressed a hand to her hammering chest, massaging the knot that seemed to have taken up permanent residence beneath her ribcage. Geoffrey with no coin was a worry; Geoffrey with coin was a serious concern. How long would it be before he remembered Maggie had a sister-in-law living within walking distance of Evendale?

Little Gwen and Maggie weren't safe.

With shaking fingers, she pulled on her travelling cloak, locked her front door and hurried down the lane in the opposite direction to Geoffrey. She had to do something. She had to protect the people she loved most in this world.

Chapter Eight

Of all the ridiculously idiotic things she could have done in her first week of employ, kissing Mr Obnoxious was right at the top of the list.

Ellen clenched her hands in her lap. What in heaven's name had come over her? She'd long ago learned that kissing men was a bad idea. She should never have gone near him. Nor should she spend a moment longer recalling the delicious sense of wonder that had unfurled inside her when Calum—Lord Woodhal!—had swept her into his arms. Because lady's companions didn't kiss their employer's grandsons. Lady's companions were supposed to be beyond reproach. Women who knew when to keep their mouths shut and their hands to themselves. They certainly didn't flirt with dangerous dukes with sad eyes. Even if the deep brogue of his voice did strange things to her nether regions. His Scottish voice, not his schooled Oxbridge one.

It absolutely, positively, categorically could never happen again. She gave a terse nod. Rule No. 2: *No kissing Calum Callaghan ever again.*

A carriage horn sounded, jerking Ellen from her thoughts.

'Are you feeling all right, gel?'

Both Lady Faye and Mr Tattershall were staring at her, brows furrowed.

'Carriage travel doesn't sit well with my stomach, I'm afraid.' Ellen forced a smile, before turning her face towards the cooling breeze. The half hood of the barouche had been pushed down despite the biting spring chill as the dowager had declared the weather to be 'charming'. Owen didn't look too impressed. He clutched his beaver hat to his head while strands of his blond hair were whipped into his eyes.

'We're almost there.' Owen caught her eye and flashed her another one of his 'Tattershall Twinkles'. This morning he was sporting a particularly spectacular waistcoat of royal blue and a pair of black Hessian boots with gold tassels—footwear not for the faint of heart. Thankfully, his immaculately starched collar points were not so high as to obscure his vision or impede the movement of his head left to right as Ellen understood was the fashion in London. A pair of spectacles completed the ensemble, adding an air of intelligence to an otherwise rather blue-ribbon appearance. He would be a welcome addition to any lady's evening soiree, despite not being titled.

A veritable Bond Street beau Lady Faye had called him.

She glanced towards the dowager. What would Lady Faye think of her if she knew about the kiss? More to the point, what did Calum think of her? She'd practically strangled him in her desperation to pull closer. No lady of quality would have acted as she had.

Heaven above, what was wrong with her today? His name was Lord Woodhal. Lord Woodhal. Lord Woodhal! She discreetly wiped her mouth with the back of her gloved hand. At least the cool breeze was tempering her burning cheeks.

The barouche juddered to a stop. The driver opened the door, and Mr Tattershall handed them down. The street was awash with people; there were not half so many people in Evendale as there were shopping on that one London street.

'Welcome, Miss Smith, to the best dressmaker's in all of London.' Lady Faye flung open her arms with dramatic flair.

Unlike the shop next door, with its floor-to-ceiling window displaying a range of English muslin with a sign reading 'Two Shillings In a Yard Cheaper than Any Other Shop in London', the shop Lady Faye indicated looked rather ... drab. Old paint was peeling off the rafters and the weathered sign over the door was almost unintelligible. As if guessing the direction of Ellen's thoughts, the dowager hurried on. 'It doesn't look like much from out here, but I promise you Mademoiselle Bond of House of Bond *knows* gowns. You can't go wrong with her.'

'I can't go wrong?'

Without a reply, Lady Faye bounced into the shop, and the bell over the door tinkled to announce her spirited arrival.

'Sacré bleu!' Mademoiselle Bond of House of Bond, Bond Street, rushed over and pressed kisses to Lady Faye's cheeks. 'Bonjour, madame. Mon amie.'

Dismissing further introductions entirely, the two women began rushing around the shop like whirlwinds, collecting bolts of fabric from every which way to hold up against Ellen's face, umming and ahing.

Ellen looked around the shop, clutching her reticule to her chest. Fabric was packed into every corner; it was more a maze than a place of business—an unusual combination of drapers, dressmakers and haberdashery. There were certainly no signs in here advertising low prices. There was no way she could afford any of the fabrics the two women were discussing, let alone pay a dressmaker to sew her a new gown. Any money she earned working for Lady Faye, she planned to save for Gwen.

As Lady Faye came flying back past her, a bolt of sprigged muslin in one hand and the latest copy of *La Belle Assembleé* in the other, Ellen managed to catch her arm. She leaned in close, heat burning her face, her humiliation all the greater for knowing Owen and Mademoiselle Bond could hear every word. 'I'm sorry, my lady, but I can't afford any of this. I don't have any money.'

'Nonsense,' boomed Lady Faye. 'You're working for me now, and I can't have you going about Town in your old clothes, can I?'

'But—' She looked down at her faded gown.

'I purchased Chakrabarti a new suit so he'd look smart for when we have callers,' finished the dowager as though that was the only argument she needed. Her expression read: dispute me at your own risk. 'While we're on the subject of fashion, you're not to wear that mob cap for another second. You're much too young.' She hurried off across the shop again, heading straight for the lace trims.

There would be no changing the dowager's mind, and an argument would only make Ellen look ungrateful and embarrass her ladyship, so Ellen closed her mouth, biting back another objection. Owen patted her shoulder. 'Wise choice, sweetheart. You're a quick study.'

***

They were staring at him. Cal could feel their beady little eyes on his face as he staggered around the kitchen table.

The butler. The cook. A couple of blurry maids. *Wait a moment.* Where had those two scullery lasses come from? Were they multiplying now?

'Your Grace, are you quite well?' The butler's Indian accent suggested he hadn't begun his career in service in England.

'Course I'm well.' He frowned. Where had his Scottish accent come from? He tried again. 'Vera well.' *There it was again* ... 'Vera. Well.' *Damn and blast!* He took another swig of whisky—drinking straight from the bottle just to spite Ellen. 'Haven't ye ever seen a duke in a kitchen before...' What was his name?

'Carrying a chain and padlock, no, Your Grace.' The butler nodded towards Cal's other hand.

Cal swung it up, bringing it closer to his face. So he was. 'I'm doing something vera important.' At least he was pretty sure he was doing something important. It had been important a moment ago when he'd collected the chain and padlock from the front gate. If only he could remember what...

'You're not going to lock us up, are you, Your Grace?' asked his grandmother's abigail. Her eyes were as wide as saucers. The cook and the maids all moved further back. Even the butler cast a furtive glance towards the door.

'What? Nay!' He wasn't that sort of monster. Just the sort who accosted gentleman's daughters in his own dining room. The sort of monster with a haircut that would give any man the horrors.

Too damn pretty. Too damn bossy. And too damn tempting. Ellen was more dangerous than anyone he'd ever met. More dangerous than all of Napoleon's troops stuffed aboard one stinking ship.

Something about her made him want to forget all about the Navy and the war and the fire. When she'd kissed him with reckless enthusiasm, he'd lost his finely-tuned control. But he was thinking much clearer now that the temptress was out of his house. Much clearer. He was ... *Ha!* He remembered. He was heading towards the pantry.

If Lady F and Ellen thought he was going to sit idly around and let them run amok with his life, they were very much mistaken. He was going to do what any gentlemen would do when faced with a pride of dominant lionesses: he was going undercover to make their lives wretched. At least until they learned their lesson and moved out.

The butler made another brave half-hearted attempt to stop him. One of the maids squealed and made a run for the back door. The cook raised her rolling pin, as if actually considering hitting a fully-fledged duke.

Good for her.

He stepped around the servants, paying them absolutely no heed. Lady F should have known better. He'd been perfectly miserable before she'd turned up with Ellen Bossy Smith, the not-so-spinstery spinster. With her bruises and her secrets and her strawberry-lipped smile.

Because if there was one thing he was absolutely certain of it was that, for all Ellen tried to look like a spinster, she was no green girl. A green girl didn't throw her arms around a man's neck and sink into a kiss the way Ellen had. A green girl didn't nip at his bottom lip until she could slip her tongue into his mouth to caress him and taste him until his blood surged with possessive need as Ellen had.

That most certainly had not been her first kiss.

***

Three exhausting hours later, Lady Faye declared their shopping adventure 'a jolly-good success'. She had eight gowns on order for herself and another two for Ellen. Luckily, Ellen had been able to persuade the dowager to allow her long sleeves, rather than the short sleeves which were currently all the fashion in London. Her bruises were beginning to fade, but they probably wouldn't completely disappear for a few weeks yet. Tired, but pleased with themselves, they allowed Owen to escort them back to Roseworthy Street.

By the crashing and cursing coming from the drawing room, it seemed safe to assume the duke had been drinking again, probably to ensure, once and for all, that Lady Faye couldn't bully him into attending the fireworks.

The servants wouldn't go near the drawing room, and even Tzar seemed unimpressed with His Grace's behaviour. The old dog had laboriously climbed two flights of stairs and fallen asleep under Ellen's bed.

Long after the sun had set, Lady Faye threw a disgusted look at the closed drawing room door and marched down the front steps to clamber into the waiting carriage. Ellen followed suit, not glancing towards the offending door herself. Lady's companions paid no heed to ranting and raving dukes, even ranting and raving dukes whose kisses sparked delicious tingles between her legs.

Rule No. 3: *No encouraging temper tantrums of any variety.*

***

Another hired barouche carried them safely across Westminster Bridge to Vauxhall. Owen flashed their silver tickets at the main entrance, and they were bowed in. Rows of elms lined their passage down the colonnade, their shadowy branches illuminated by thousands of globe lamps. They strolled towards the grassy downs at the far end.

It was already some time after ten and most of the visitors were either in the Rotunda enjoying the concert or settled into their supper boxes partaking of the sliced ham Vauxhall was so famous for. Nonetheless, their small party was soon sighted, and Lady Faye started receiving countless offers from every direction to join some box or other.

One portly gentleman went so far as to abandon his companions and approach the dowager, offering his arm. 'Let me be your protector tonight, my lady. They let in all sorts into the Vauxhall these days.' With his free hand, he raised a quizzing glass to his eye, all the better to survey the darkness, as though 'all sorts' lurked in the shadows just beyond sight. 'They really should increase the ticket price, as they've done at Ranelagh. To keep the riff-raff out, you know.'

His collar points were immaculately starched and so high they actually touched his cheeks. If he wanted to look one way or the other, he had to turn his whole person for his neck was barricaded in.

'But, Sir Kefford,' Lady Faye said with a light laugh, 'raising the price would do nothing to dissuade you from coming.'

The elderly lord forced a laugh. 'As droll as ever, Lady Faye.' Then he bowed and slunk back to his dinner, shame-faced.

'You don't appear to be enjoying yourself, my lady,' said Ellen. 'Is there anything I can do?'

'No, no. I'm just beginning to remember why I never come to London. Disgusting, judgemental folk, the lot of them.' The dowager tucked Ellen's hand into the crook of her elbow, pulling her closer.

'You don't enjoy Society?'

'Gel, nobody is supposed to enjoy the *beau monde*. That's not what it's for.'

'Then why come to Vauxhall?'

'Because Cal was so worried I'd come to London expressly to see him. Which I have, of course. But I don't want him to think that, else I'll never hear the end of it.'

'I see. Well, the *ton* certainly seem to enjoy your company. Everyone is simpering to please you.'

'I'm the wealthy widow of a marquess. My daughter's the widow of a duke and my grandson, however surly and unlikeable he may be, is an actual duke. Gel, I am the *bon ton*. I can be as indelicate as I please and nobody will dare take offence.'

'Here, try this.' Owen wiggled his way between them, holding three cups in two hands. 'It's a lively drop of arrack-punch. Upon my honour, Miss Smith, you'll enjoy it.'

'Thank you.' It smelled of rum and, after a tentative taste, the rest went down a treat.

'It's mixed with sugar,' Owen explained, his grin widening. 'I noticed you had a sweet tooth.'

Lady Faye swallowed hers in one go. 'Goodness, I needed that.'

Owen returned their empty cups, hastily returning to their side. 'The first set-piece should be starting soon.'

As though responding to his words, the orchestra began to play and a loud bang reverberated through the grounds. In an explosion of bright light, sparks filled the air. Ellen jumped, and Lady Faye grinned up at her.

More explosions of yellow stars and Catherine wheels illuminated the pavilions, the kiosks and the firework tower itself. Ellen's mouth dropped open at the lights dancing before her eyes. With a final bang, everything faded back into darkness.

'Pleased we came now?' Lady Faye asked with a genuine smile.

'Absolutely, my lady.' Ellen rubbed a hand over her face. Before she had barely rubbed the spots from her blurry vision, the second set began. Gwen would not have liked the fireworks for all their excellence. She hated loud noises. In fact, they sounded much like Ellen imagined canon fire to sound. Perhaps that was why Calum had not attended.

As the second set faded away, Lady Faye tugged on her arm. 'I rather think it's time to leave. Quickly, before anyone else sees us.'

They started back the way they'd come, the lingering smell of gunpowder settling over their clothes and in their hair. Grey smoke, the aftermath of the fireworks, wafted amongst the trees and over the grove, tainting everything it touched.

As they stepped off the grass, passing under a small pavilion, somebody bumped into Ellen's shoulder, knocking her hand from Lady Faye's elbow.

'I'm so sorry.' The woman bobbed a curtsy.

'It's wasn't your fault.' Ellen made to move on, but the women pressed an unguarded hand to Ellen's shoulder.

'Wait a moment, don't I know you?' She frowned at Ellen from under the brim of her straw hat. A faded navy ribbon was tied around the bonnet and under her chin, partially blocking her face from view, despite the many lamps hanging from the pillars of the pavilion.

'I don't think so.'

Neither Lady Faye nor Owen had noticed she wasn't following and had continued on down the colonnade. Ellen raised a hand to hail them, but the woman moved closer.

'I could have sworn I recognise your face.' She wore a simple dress with a muddied hem and a linsey apron, the original colour of which Ellen couldn't guess at. While they were of a similar age, it would have been impossible for Ellen to forget someone with such hair. Curls of red peeked out from under the rim of her tatty bonnet, framing her face and trailing down the back of her neck. It was a beautiful colour, for all it wasn't fashionable.

'I really don't know you.' Ellen winced in a silent apology, trying to detach the woman's hand from her shoulder. 'I've been in London barely a sennight.' Lady Faye and Owen had completely disappeared into shadow. Ellen clutched her reticule to her chest. If they left without her, she could not afford a hackney back to Yew Tree House. 'You must have me mistaken with somebody else.' Ellen tried to step around the woman but her fingers were biting into Ellen's shoulder with surprising strength.

'My name is Sophy. Sophy Calder. Maybe you remember my brother, Sherborne Calder. He's a sailor—' Her voice was rising in desperation, drawing the eyes of passersby.

'I don't know any sailors,' Ellen interjected, trying to quieten her. 'I've never even travelled as far London before now. I'm from Evendale.' Even as the words left her mouth, Ellen realised her mistake.

Sophy's eyes widened. 'Evendale?'

'I'm sorry, but Lady Faye has moved on and I really must catch up before her party leaves without me.' She pushed her advantage, this time persistently ignoring the stranger's attempts to block her, and hurried after the dowager.

Dew seeped into the worn soles of her half-boots until her stockings were soaked and her feet began to freeze. Ellen stumbled on the uneven path but didn't slow as she hurried to the entrance. The dowager and Owen were nowhere to be seen. She glanced over her shoulder, searching for Miss Calder in the shadows.

Why had she told her about Evendale? It had been a silly slip of the tongue. *You won't ever see her again. There's no way she could know who you really are—who your brother is.* Her heart started racing.

'Miss Smith!' Someone grabbed her arm, and Ellen swung around, flinging her reticule towards their face.

Owen ducked easily out of the way. For a man who insisted on carrying a cane, he moved like a dancer.

'Mr Tattershall!' She let out a shuddering breath. 'I'm sorry. I got lost and then—' There she was. Sophy had been following her.

'Lady Faye is waiting in the carriage. We worried when we realised you were no longer with us.' Owen ducked his head to bring their faces more to a level. 'What happened? You're as white as a ghost.'

'I couldn't find you.' She linked arms with Owen before he even offered. He preened, and, like the gentleman he was, graciously guided her to the waiting carriage. Ellen sped up, putting as much smoke and darkness as possible between herself and the mysterious woman.

Chapter Nine

Ellen barely slept that night. She dreamed of Gwen and Maggie and a great looming shadow that had chased them around the garden to the sound of firing canons until her counterpane was so tangled around her legs she could barely clamber out of bed.

She pushed open the curtains and window, breathing in the morning air. It smelled of smog and grit. Of course that woman she'd met last night wasn't a spy for Geoffrey. The idea was ridiculously absurd in the light of a new day. There was no way he could have followed her to London—or hired someone to follow her. For starters, he didn't have that kind of money. What money his crumbling estate did make went straight to covering his gambling debts and bribes.

She gripped the windowsill.

Gwen was safe. Maggie was safe. Even Verity was safe. Everything was going according to plan.

She repeated it to herself like a mantra.

Gwen is safe.

Geoffrey mightn't come to London, but Gwen wasn't in London, said that niggling voice at the back of her mind. Gwen was much closer to home. Much closer to Geoffrey.

Maggie is safe.

Her sister-in-law's cottage was almost impossible to find unless you already knew where it was. And it had been years and years since Geoffrey had even spared a thought for Maggie's family. He would not think to look there.

Unless, of course, someone else reminded him. Evendale was a small community and people liked to talk.

They're safe!

For now.

She took a shaky breath. The best thing she could do for Gwen was to concentrate on her position with Lady Faye.

Church bells sounded the hour, carrying their cries across the city. It was still very early, even the servants would only just be rising. But Ellen couldn't bear the idea of climbing back under the suffocating counterpane, so, after tending to her personal needs, she wandered outside into the mess of a garden.

By the far wall, overgrown gooseberries, ivy and honeysuckle had tangled themselves into one big mass. Using a pair of only slightly rusty shears she'd found in a spider-ridden shed, she rolled up her sleeves and set to work. It filled her chest with a happy buzz. Her mother had taught her to garden, although Ellen hadn't really had a chance to get her hands dirty these last few years.

She redoubled her efforts, humming softly under her breath even as the gooseberry bushes caught at her skirts. With the high walls completely surrounding the house, she could almost imagine she was back in the country. It was almost as though the rest of London didn't exist just a few feet away.

In no time at all, she had a satisfyingly large pile of clippings at her feet. Looking up, she caught sight of Calum watching her through one of the first-storey windows. Her stomach backflipped.

She had yet to explore that part of the house, having only seen the ground floor and the second-storey guest bedrooms where she and Lady Faye were staying. It had taken them days just to get those two floors into some semblance of order; she hadn't had any free time to explore.

Fustian! She should have hidden around the side of the house like she had the other mornings. Out of sight, out of mind.

He tucked his hands behind his back, staring unashamedly. She raised a hand to her forehead, shielding her eyes from the morning sun.

His hair hadn't looked half that good last night. Either she was better at hairdressing than she'd realised or someone had fixed it for him. Her gaze flickered to his burn scars, and her heart skipped a beat. They were even more visible now his hair was short. The twisted side of his face, the slight turn to the corner of his mouth. How close he'd come to losing his left eye! There was something so very unique about his scars. They added an air of wildness, of untamed danger. A man not to be taken lightly.

Whyever did he have to be so very handsome? In a dark and brooding sort of way. For all he claimed to be no gentleman, he certainly looked the part. She could remember the feel of his arms; the hardness of him. Something resembling a statue, but not cold like marble. His skin always burned hot.

Oh lordy, he was the last man on earth about whom she should be having such ideas.

Remember Rule No 2. Remember Rule No. 2! No kissing Calum Callaghan ever again.

Don't even think about kissing Calum ever again. That should be Rule No. 4 ... Or maybe she was up to five?

Either way, no kissing and no thinking about kissing.

He still wore yesterday's wrinkled clothes. Her eyes lingered on the inch of flesh just below his crumpled cravat where the button was missing from his shirt. Heat flushed her cheeks. She'd done that. For just a few moments, he'd responded in kind. And then he'd pulled back and yelled at her.

She dropped her gaze and caught sight of the *Keep Out!* sign he was wearing around his neck. It was the sign from the front gates.

Maybe he looked a little less like a gentleman than she'd first thought...

***

Tzar was sleeping on the middle of Cal's bed, snoring as loud as a racing curricle. The cook was in the kitchen, reorganising *his* cupboards. The butler was milling around the front door as through expecting actual visitors to come calling here, of all places. And Lady F's abigail was bustling up and down the stairs with the new housemaid, airing out the guest bedrooms and chattering in high-pitched over-excited voices that had the thumping in Cal's head redoubling its efforts to make his life miserable. He shuffled from room to room, trying to find somewhere quiet to work, lamenting, for the first time, that his house was half-sized.

'Calum!'

He winced. Lady F's voice was getting louder and louder, demanding the attention of everyone within a twenty-foot radius. He hurriedly limped out the kitchen door and ducked behind a particularly vicious looking rosebush that had seen better days.

'Returning the sign to the gate, Your Grace? I thought it rather suited you.'

He jumped sky high, spinning around to find Ellen watching him from the other side of what used to be a small lawn but which was now knee-high weeds.

She curtseyed in greeting. He eyed her suspiciously. How had he forgotten she was out here? She'd rolled up the sleeves of her faded dress to her elbows. The bruises on her wrists were beginning to fade but it would still be many days, maybe weeks, before they'd disappear completely.

Noticing the direction of his gaze, she tugged her sleeves back down with jerky movements. 'Your Grace.' Her greeting was cooling.

There was a smudge of dirt on her cheek as through she'd wiped her hand across her face. She'd also abandoned her bonnet; it hung hostage in a rather determined but frazzled honeysuckle, as though lady's companion and climbing plant had been waging war.

He pitied the honeysuckle. It didn't stand a chance.

Neither did he if Lady F found out he was hiding from her.

'Go away before someone sees you,' he hissed, glancing back around the rosebush and through the kitchen window.

He'd been right. Lady F was on a rampage. She was now rushing around the kitchen, the servants at her heels. If he'd taken a second longer, he wouldn't have made it out in time.

'What are you doing?' Ellen stepped in front of him and bent at the waist so she could lean around the rosebush for a better view. 'Ah, you're hiding.'

He glanced down. It was a most improved view. The curve from waist to hip was exaggerated, despite the drab, spinsterish gown she was wearing. She'd also—thankfully!—abandoned her self-righteous lace cap, and he had his first real look at her uncovered hair. It wasn't light enough to be called brown or dark enough to be called black. It was ... Och, he couldn't quite put his finger on the right word.

She shuffled from foot to foot. Her skirts swished around her ankles, and his eyes were drawn to her arse as though they had a mind of their own. His cock stirred. Apparently it had a mind of its own as well, one that was all too aware of Ellen's curves.

He pressed his eyes closed, willing himself not to close the small distance between them. It didn't help. His imagination was suddenly running wild. *Hellfire!* With her leaning over like that he could close the distance between them with a single step and they'd be—

'Cal!' Lady F's screech could not be contained by the four walls of Yew Tree House. 'Calum McKenna Callaghan, get in here this instant!'

Well, that was certainly one very effectively way to kill the mood. He grabbed Ellen by her waist, tugging her further behind the rosebush and out of sight. Thank goodness it was so overgrown; it provided the perfect cover.

She was so close now her scent infiltrated his every breath. A heady combination of soap and honeysuckle and damp earth.

Ye gods he wanted to sink into her hot, slick centre. But it was more than that. He wanted to rub her back and massage the tension from her shoulders. He wanted to learn the shape of her face with his lips and memorise the curves of her body with his hands.

She turned to face him, but he pressed a finger to her lips before she could speak. 'If you so much as think about giving me up, I'll...' He faltered, his thoughts unable to think of a single punishment worthy of such a despicable crime.

'You'll hang that sign about my neck?' she suggested lightly, brushing his hand away. 'My earlier idea for a truce doesn't seem so ridiculous now does it, Your Grace?'

That damned sign. He took it off and tossed it to the ground. 'That's a rather long bow to draw,' he snapped, attempting to save face. God only knew what he'd been doing with it yesterday. The latter part of the afternoon was completely hazy. Something about the kitchen and the dark bitter taste of whisky. Whatever he'd done, he could distinctly remember feeling particularly cunning. Now, with this proper little miss standing before him, hands on hips as if preparing to wage war with him, he wasn't so sure.

He glared down at her. She was so petite. Her head was barely level with his shoulder. He would have to bow his head to kiss her again.

Or perhaps she could stand on a stool...

Better yet, he could toss her onto the damp earth she seemed to love so much. And then he could see if her scent was as good when mingled with the sugary taste of her lips.

Nay! Yesterday he'd proven once and for all kissing Miss Ellen Smith was a spectacularly bad idea. It led to dangerous feelings of desire and need and—*shudder!*—self-worth.

Kissing Ellen couldn't happen again. He couldn't open that door, not when he'd spent so many years desperately keeping it locked firmly behind him.

His cock was less inclined to agree.

Ellen brushed a wayward strand of hair from her face, leaving behind another trail of dirt. The light scattering of freckles adorned her nose and cheeks had darkened somewhat—a secret only sunlight revealed. He reached out, brushing the pad of his thumb down her cheek. Her skin was beautifully soft.

Her mouth opened in surprise. He snatched his hand back. What was he doing?

Every part of Cal, his very being, wanted the woman standing before him, his hands were practically twitching with the need to take hold of her. He shoved them deep into his pockets.

'Your Grace.' She raised her own hands, trying to put a little space between them, although with the rosebush at her back she couldn't move away. 'I've been thinking about yesterday, and I've decided that I really, really shouldn't have kissed you. I'm your grandmother's companion. I have a reputation to uphold. And I can't go around kissing dukes. It's not right, and it certainly isn't proper. What if we were seen? Or what if...'

She was lecturing him. Him! Calum McKenna Callaghan, the stuff of nightmares. Just like the other night when she'd tried to make a truce with him, she didn't seem repulsed by his nearness or scared or even particularly angry, not that he'd blame her if she was. She just did seem determined to finish her speech, like she'd planned it ahead of time.

She pressed her hands to her hips and stood straighter. The movement pulled the fabric of her dress tighter across her chest, further revealing the flush creeping up from the milky-cream flesh of her neck.

She looked like nothing less than a soldier on a battlefield. Resolute and courageous. If about a thousand times more attractive.

Deadly to behold.

He glanced around, seeking an escape route. But if he moved from behind the rosebush Lady F was sure to see. He was stuck between a rock and hard place.

Not that Ellen was hard. Hot blood rushed through his veins. He'd held her in his arms for long enough to know that she absolutely wasn't hard. 'Curvaceous' was more the word he'd use. If he had paper and ink, he'd have written that word down, right next to 'intriguing'.

His *List of Everything Ellen Smith* was growing momentum.

'...proper. I don't know what you were thinking yesterday. I know I wasn't thinking, but

I've thought about it since then, and I know what we did was wrong...'

Wrong ... not proper ... He didn't give two figs about 'proper'. Proper wasn't the reason he'd sworn off kissing lady's companions. Yesterday he'd listed every reason under the sun why kissing Ellen Smith was a bad idea, and propriety wasn't one of them.

He focused on that list now to keep his attention from her curves.

1. She was too good for him.

2. He owed Pierce.

3. She was hiding from someone and very determined to keep her own secrets. Family, enemy, lover ... husband. It didn't bear thinking about.

4. And ... something ... about something else...

Hell, she was biting that bottom lip of hers. And then she was off again, waving her arms in the air, chattering away at full speed. He supposed whatever she was saying was important. And he was probably supposed to be listening. There was a mad glint in her eyes.

'...a duke and a lady's companion. That's not how the world works—'

'How the world works?' He clenched his teeth, forcing himself to keep his voice to a low whisper even as his temper flared. 'Ellie, nothing about this is how the world is supposed to work.' Pierce wasn't supposed to have died. Cal wasn't supposed to be a duke. He glanced around, grappling for another example and his gaze caught on her arms.

'Yer bruises,' he said harshly, accidently slipping back into his Scottish accent in his temper. 'Nobody should hit a woman. Not ever. There isn't an excuse for it. That's not the way the world is supposed to work.'

'Hush, please.' Ellen's confidence slipped from her face, and she wrapped her arms around herself.

His voice had risen in anger despite his efforts.

'Are ye ashamed, wee lass?' He whispered the question though his voice still sounded harsh. Or perhaps it was the question that was harsh. 'The person who did this to ye should be ashamed.' *The coward.* 'Not ye.'

'Is that your argument?' She was still scared but her confidence was quickly returning. 'Tell me about your scars if everything is so black and white.'

He stumbled back a step, his wounded leg buckling at little under his weight.

Her mouth opened in surprise, and she reached out towards him. 'I didn't mean ... I'm sorry, Calum. I shouldn't have said that.'

There was a long moment of silence. The confines of the garden seemed to grow smaller. And then he caught sight of the look in her eye.

Turning on his heel, he limped through the long grass to retrieve her bonnet. Anything to get away from her pity. He had to stretch above his head to reach it. Hell only knew how she'd managed to get it tangled so high.

She followed him cautiously to the boundary wall, her hands tucked behind her back and keeping more than a respectable distance between them.

'Your hair looks different,' she said, eventually breaking the stilted silence.

He handed over her bonnet. 'The butler's father was a barber back in Calcutta, so he fixed it for me.' Before Cal had gotten sloshed.

'Then I wish Lady Faye had asked him to cut it for you last night.'

'Me too.' His gaze lingered hungrily on her lips.

***

'Can you believe what that grandson of mine's been up to?' demanded Lady Faye as Ellen entered the kitchen a few moments later, bonnet safely in hand and Calum's words spinning around her head.

'Look at this!' Lady Faye pushed a cake tin into her free hand. It was the one that housed the whisky infused fruit cake. Only now it was wrapped in a chain and padlocked shut.

Suddenly the *Keep Out!* sign Calum had been wearing made sense. She was absolutely not impressed by his creativity. Well, maybe a tiny, eensy bit. 'Surely we can find the key.' She glanced around the kitchen. How difficult could it be to find a key hidden by a man deep in his cups?

'We've looked,' huffed the dowager, waving a hand towards the small gathering of servants standing behind her. 'It's not in the kitchen. If I know my grandson at all, he's probably hidden it somewhere quite devious.' With a glint in her eye, Lady Faye rushed into the passage. 'We'll search the whole house. Forces, divide and conquer! Posthaste!' She raised her fist into the air like a captain commanding a warship into battle.

Ellen caught Pamela's eye, and the lady's maid winked before taking hold of Adelynn's hand. Boldly, both women set forth up the stairs on the quest for the hidden key, and Chakrabarti marched gallantly into the dining room.

'To me,' called Lady Faye, and Ellen followed her into the front room.

The drawing room was a little worse for wear after the duke's drunken sulk last night. There were no fewer than three crystal glasses scattered around the room, while the dartboard on the back of the door was lopsided and a suspicious scattering of small holes marked the architraves.

In the end they searched for half an hour to no avail.

The dowager flopped onto the settee. 'Imagine, locking up a cake! Preposterous!'

'Why don't we do something else, to keep your mind off the cake?'

'Like what?' Lady Faye sat up a little straighter, watching Ellen in anticipation.

'Well...' She racked her brain for an activity appropriate for a gentlelady and her companion. The dowager had already admitted to not enjoying London society and since the fireworks hadn't mentioned them leaving the house for another similar activity. After all, she'd clearly come to London to see her family, not to partake in London entertainment. 'How about I read to you? Lord Woodhal has a whole library just down the hall.'

'Goodness, no. Hammond only collected boring books on agriculture and distilleries and ... and bedbugs.'

'Bedbugs?'

'I'm sure I once saw a book about bedbugs.' Lady Faye leaned against the back of the chaise longue. 'I don't like bedbugs.'

'There must be a lending library or a bookshop somewhere in this great city of London Town. Why don't I find us something a little more exciting to read?'

'Oh, an excellent idea.' The dowager's smile creased the corners of her eyes. 'Take Chakrabarti with you. And make sure it's an absolutely shocking novel. Something to make us blush!'

Verity

Verity tugged the collar of her travelling cloak tighter around her throat and glanced over her shoulder for what seemed like the hundredth time to check she wasn't being followed. Satisfied, she veered right, down a narrow country lane lined high with hedgerows.

It seemed unbelievable in the sunshine of a bright, crisp day that she was on a mission of stealth. Then again, she reminded herself, not all monsters hid in the shadows.

Another two miles and the cottage was in sight. Framed by two spring kissed sycamore trees, the small two-room cottage blended seamlessly into the countryside.

Little Gwen was playing in the kitchen garden, industriously poking something with a stick. She watched Verity warily. She looked so much like her mother. Verity waved her welcome, but Gwen only stared.

Maggie appeared in doorway. The corners of her mouth naturally turned down, giving her a permanently thoughtful expression. She raised a hand in greeting—they'd known each other long enough to have dispensed with more formal ways.

'Is everything well?' Maggie hurried closer. 'Have you heard from Ellen?' Her concern was marked in the pitch of her voice. She looked older than when Verity had last seen her, as though the weight of the world lay heavy on her slim shoulders. Verity wished she bore happier tidings.

'Everything's well with Ellen, At least, I haven't heard otherwise.' She cast a glance towards the girl.

Understanding, Maggie led Verity a little ways from the child.

'She still doesn't speak?'

'I've never heard a single word pass her lips in six years. Ellen tells me she can talk, but...' Maggie shrugged.

'Geoffrey should be locked away for what he's done to those two girls.' Verity fisted her hands. She knew Geoffrey had only hit Gwen once. Ellen had taken the brunt of his anger to protect the child. 'Speaking of Geoffrey—' She relayed the story of Geoffrey's threat. 'I know we hoped that you and Gwen would be safe here but I think we underestimated just how determined he'd be,' Verity finished. 'Now he actually has some coin, I don't think there's anything stopping him from finding this cottage.'

'He's never been here before.'

'But others in Evendale have.' Why had she ever thought hiding Gwen with Maggie's sister-in-law would be good enough? *Because we were desperate.* Desperate to get Ellen and Gwen away from Geoffrey as fast as possible.

Maggie touched her arm reassuringly. Her fingers were cold but warmth curled around Verity's arm. Their eyes were almost level. Verity liked not having to look down to meet Maggie's gaze, as she did with so many other people. Maggie was as tall as she was, an inch or two taller even, with long skinny arms. Some might call her lanky or ungainly but those words did nothing to recognise her tempered personality or her nurturing disposition.

She'd helped her friends escape an abusive household. She was the strongest woman Verity knew. A loving, kind, nurturing woman. A woman with a backbone of steel.

'You're not safe here. I can't stand back and let something happen to you ... to all of you.'

'I fear you're right. We need to devise a better hiding place. Trust never an old enemy,' Maggie quoted. She ran a hand over her head, tucking a loose strand of greying hair back into her tight chignon. 'At all costs, we must keep the girls safe.'

Chapter Ten

The Dowager Marchioness of Faye was yesterday evening sighted at Vauxhall Gardens enjoying the fireworks with her ward, Mr Owen Tattershall, and her new lady's companion, a Miss Smith of whom nobody who's anybody seems to know anything. A mystery indeed.

—*The Ladies' Gazette*

New plan: avoid Miss Ellen Smith at all costs.

Just to be on the safe side, Cal thought he'd better continue avoiding Lady F as well.

In fact, avoid everyone. The Season couldn't last forever. As soon as July began to roll towards August and the true heat of summer hit Lady F would leave London, and so too would all the servants and, most importantly, the window adventuress, who he didn't want to kiss and who wasn't slowly but persistently pulling down the walls he'd built around his damaged heart for the last four years. All in just over a week, dammit!

He didn't want to see Ellie. He didn't want to think about Ellie. And he definitely didn't want to strangle the person who'd struck her wrists black and blue.

Cal clenched his fists. Her secrets were her secrets. And he wanted nothing to do with them. Nothing to do with whatever she was keeping from him and the rest of the world.

He was standing by the front window in first-storey ballroom. In its heyday it had been a grand space with a moulded ceiling and a set of matching doors that led out onto a balcony. Now there was a wall down the centre, leaving Cal with half the space, half a window, and one of a pair of doors that had been boarded over since before he'd joined the Navy. It had been a long time since this ballroom had seen any dancing.

Nonetheless, the half-window offered a partially decent view of the front garden and the street beyond.

Tzar sat at his feet. He wagged his tail each time Cal glanced down at him. Relenting, Cal took the last treat from his pocket and tossed it down to him. Tzar gobbled it up without even tasting it. The only time he ever moved faster than the pace of a snail was when there was food.

'Good pup.'

With one last tail wag, Tzar lay down, his head on his front paws. Cal could practically hear his old joints groaning. The poor beggar. When Pierce had rescued Tzar from the streets, he'd seemed old then, and that had been many years ago. Now Tzar was positively decrepit. Yet tough as old nails. He'd probably outlive them all. Well, except for Lady F, who'd probably live forever just from sheer force of will.

As though in mockery of his new plan, the front door opened and Ellie stepped outside, right into his line of sight. She was clearly heading out. There was a small reticule around her wrist again and her bonnet had been returned to its rightful place, looking no worse for wear after its encounter with the honeysuckle. She was chatting amicably to someone just out of his sight.

A moment later, the young butler followed her down the steps.

Cal had spent some time in India with the Navy. There they didn't have to suffer through these wishy-washy springs. It had just been bloody hot.

Chakrabarti was wearing the new suit Lady F had bought him. The dark fabric suited his brown skin, and the overall effect of the dark on dark made the white of his necktie so startlingly crisp even the great leader of fashion, Beau Brummell, would be hard put not to be envious—that is, had Brummell not escaped to Paris to avoid paying his debts. Cal had no time for wealthy men who lived beyond their means nor those who gambled away their fortunes.

Ellen spoke, her voice muted to Cal by the closed window, and Chakrabarti laughed.

Jealousy reared its ugly head, sending pain spiking through Cal's stomach with the thought of another man touching, kissing ... loving Ellie.

Hellfire. What was happening to him?

More to the point, what was Ellie doing to him? It was bad enough he was lusting after her. Now he was jealous?

'...told me how you locked up the cake. Wait, are you even listening to anything I'm saying?' Owen pushed his way in between Cal and the dividing wall to claim the best view out the half-window, careful not to step on Tzar.

Cal ignored his cousin, resolutely not moving away even though Owen was standing much too close. Chakrabarti said something that caught Ellen's attention for she turned back to look at him. The smile slipped from her face as the butler handed her a missive.

'She doesn't look happy,' Owen commented. Ellen tucked the correspondence into her minuscule bag without breaking the seal. Then they moved through the unlocked gate and started down the street. 'Maybe it's bad news from her family.' Owen pressed his cheek to the glass, trying to watch the two of them for as long as possible.

'Not happy' was an understatement. Ellie had looked downright terrified when she'd seen the letter. Her eyes had widened and her features had frozen. He'd practically heard the breath catch in her throat.

Not that it's any of my business.

Owen's spectacles tapped against the window. He looked ridiculous with his face scrunched up against the glass. Hell, he looked ridiculous in his bright orange waistcoat.

'Did you bring that cane with you just because you know it annoys me?'

'Of course.' Owen flashed him a classic Tattershall grin—genuine happiness with a sparkle of disarmingly white teeth.

'And the orange waistcoat?' Cal couldn't help himself.

Owen's smile faltered. He pressed a hand to his chest. 'You don't like the waistcoat? It cost me five guineas. It's silk. Here, feel it.' And he puffed out his chest.

Cal didn't move.

Owen straightened with a shrug. 'You're no fun anymore. I don't know why I bother coming to visit you.'

'Neither do I.' Cal strode away from the window, wanting to put as much distance as he could between himself and Ellie, even though she was well out of sight. 'Can you hurry up and get this visit over and done with? I've got work to do.'

'Actually, today I came to see Lizzy. She wanted to talk to me about Grace.'

'What about Grace?'

Owen gave him a startled look. 'You do know Grace hasn't spoken to Lizzy since Pierce's funeral.' He shook his head. 'Of course you didn't.'

'What's that supposed to mean? Grace hates me. It's not like we've kept in touch.' These days contact between himself and his stepmother was strictly through their lawyers, who ensured Grace was provided with a generous allowance, part of the proceeds of the ducal estates.

'It means in the last four years have you ever bothered asking Lizzy how she's coping?'

Guilt tasted bitter. 'She's a tough old bird, and she's coping just fine.'

'You're so caught up in your own world you can't see what's right in front of your eyes, Wood. She's not fine. She stood up for you when everyone else thought you were responsible for that fire. And Grace has never forgiven her for it.'

Cal blinked. It took a moment for Owen's words to sink in. 'They're fighting because of me?' *Fan-bloody-tastic!* Just another nail in his coffin.

'They're fighting because they're both heartbroken and because Grace isn't thinking straight.'

'Elizabeth shouldn't have taken my side.'

'Of course she should have.' Owen raised his voice. 'You didn't start that fire. You didn't kill Pierce. She did what was right and what she knew to be true.' He sighed. 'If only Grace would forgive her.'

If only he'd never been promoted to Captain.

If only he'd never joined the Navy.

If only his father had never brought him to London.

If only his mother had never run back to Scotland.

If only—If only—It was a dangerous game to play.

He turned his back on Owen. 'Maybe I did kill Pierce.'

'Don't start that again.'

Even without looking, Cal knew Owen had just rolled his eyes. 'Pierce died helping *me* put out the fire, on *my* ship.' He hit his fist to his chest, relishing the second of pain.

'You didn't start the fire. I read the report. I know it was an accident.'

'He should never have joined the Navy. This should all be his!' He threw out his arm, waving at his house, at his title—his entire inheritance.

'You're the first born.'

'Am I?' The question burst out. It was the first time he'd even spoken his worry aloud. It was like a boulder on his chest, slowly crushing the breath out of him. 'I don't look anything like Hammond.'

'Lizzy says you look like your mother.'

'My mother,' Cal spat. He couldn't remember a thing about her, but he was acutely aware of the decision she'd made to abandon her husband and return to Scotland. A decision he didn't have the luxury of making.

'Hammond loved—'

'But she didn't love him. Not enough to stay. We all know there's a possibility she lied about me. We all know there's a possibility I'm living a lie. But Pierce wouldn't have been.' Pierce had unmistakably been Hammond's son. They could have been brothers, they'd looked so alike. He raked a hand through his dark hair, such a contrast to Pierce and Hammond's blond hair.

'He wanted to join up.' Owen squeezed his shoulder again. 'I was there, remember? You bought your commission, and Pierce was so excited by the idea of an adventure he decided to come along too. You never pushed him into it.' His voice dropped to a whisper. 'If only I'd joined up too. Maybe...'

Cal turned back to face him. 'You were much too young.'

'Younger men than I was joined.'

'It would have broken Elizabeth's heart.' He'd been at sea for ten years—and Pierce for eight. Eight long years of their family not knowing if they were alive or dead. If Owen had gone too ... if Owen had died ... Thank goodness one of them had sense enough to have stayed behind.

'Hammond was an extraordinary man,' Cal continued. 'He donated to countless charities, raised money for numerations organisations. And he was smart. He knew how to look after his tenants and manage his investments. Everyone loved him. And Pierce...' He could barely form his thoughts into words. 'He would have outshone even Hammond. Now, look at me.' Cal waved a hand at himself. 'I'm not half the man Pierce was. I don't look like a duke. I don't sound like a duke. And I certainly don't behave like one.'

'I disagree. What about all the documents I moved off the dining table the other day? They looked like estate papers, and you've clearly been working hard.'

'*You* moved them?'

'And from what I hear, the Woodhal empire is as prosperous as ever, for all that you run it from the comfort of your London dining room. Imagine how successful you could be if you actually stepped outside your front door once in a while.'

'Tried that. It didn't work.' A while after Pierce's death he'd made a gallant effort to rejoin Society. He'd attended the opera and more than his fair share of boring music recitals and dreary theatre performances. That was until he realised the *ton* would never again welcome the Duke of Woodhal into their company without remarking on his scars or his limp or his possible illegitimacy.

He might hold one of the most powerful titles short of royalty, but he'd quickly learned even his ducal inheritance wasn't enough to save him from the vultures of Society, not when he presented them with so much to gossip about.

***

Ellen tucked the book more firmly under her arm as Chakrabarti opened the front door. He stepped aside, letting her enter first.

Lady Faye had requested scandalous, and Ellen had taken the dowager at her word. She now held a rather explicit romance the bookseller had slipped to her from behind his counter. She was pretty sure it was banned book, or at least it would be banned if the authorities ever got their hands on a copy.

She also had a letter that was burning a hole through her reticule. For the umpteenth time, she glanced down at the small bag looped securely around her wrist. Why had Verity written when they'd agreed it would be safest to keep correspondence to an absolute minimum? If Geoffrey had laid a finger on Gwen ... She ground her teeth. He would live to regret the day he decided to bully an innocent child.

'Miss Smith,' Lady Faye stuck her head around the door of the drawing room as Ellen and Chakrabarti entered the hall. 'My lawyer has just arrived. Apparently we have much to talk about.' She rolled her eyes.

'My lady,' came a harrowed voice from the room behind her. 'This is your first visit to London in four years. Excuse my impertinence, but I intend to use this time wisely.'

'He's always going on about leases and payments and whatnot.' She rolled her eyes again, indicating that she considered his presence more hindrance than help. Ellen put the book on the small table by the front door and started shedding her gloves, bonnet and borrowed pelisse.

The dowager's eyes lingered on the leather-bound book. 'My toes are tingling in anticipation. Unfortunately they're going to have to wait a few minutes.'

'At least an hour,' called the lawyer. 'Or three!'

'As you wish, my lady.' Ellen curtsied, trying not to look relieved, and Lady Faye disappeared back into the drawing room.

The door shut behind her, not quite cutting off Lady Faye's remonstrations. 'I pay for your services, and you should be good enough to remember that next time you decide to come barging into my house during reading time...'

'Poor man,' Chakrabarti whispered with a wince, before hurrying down the passage towards the kitchen, the tails of his black coat tapping gently against the backs of his legs.

Ellen took the stairs two at a time, hurrying to her bedroom. She could hear Pamela and Adelynn chatting in Lady Faye's chamber next door. If she didn't open the letter soon she just might die from the not knowing, but she couldn't risk opening it in front of anyone. Despite Calum's probing questions about her bruises, nobody else seemed to have noticed not everything was as it should be, and Ellen was desperate to keep it that way. She crept downstairs, seeking peace and quiet to read.

On the first floor, the stairs opened directly into a large room, and she stepped off the landing, hardly bothering to glance around.

With trembling fingers, she broke the seal.

Dearest Ellen,

Do not be panicked by my writing to you. I'm happy to report Gwen and Maggie are both safe. For now, all is well.

Geoffrey is more determined to locate you than we first suspected and is already on our trail. Maggie and I have decided we need to move Gwen to a safer location, somewhere that has no connection to either you or her. I fear it will take me some days to find a new place, but I am unwavering in my commitment to keep them both out of harm's way. As an extra precaution, I will not disclose any more details in writing.

Your friend always,

Verity

Ellen let out a deep breath, tears stinging her eyes. Maggie and Verity had done more for her than she could ever thank them for. There was nothing—nothing!—she could ever do to adequately repay them for their kindness.

'Ye're crying.' Calum's voice was blunt. He stood in the middle of the large room. It was long and narrow, probably half its original size.

Tzar was asleep near the window but otherwise the room was empty.

'Have you been here the entire time?' She hurriedly wiped her eyes with the back of her hand.

'Aye.' He limped closer. His brow was furrowed and there was a darkness in his gaze that reminded of her of clouds right before a storm. He patted his pockets as though searching for a handkerchief but came up short. 'Is someone threatening ye, lass?'

'It's nothing.' She pulled out her own handkerchief from her reticule and discreetly wiped her nose.

The duke's frown deepened. 'Is the letter from the lout who hit ye? The one ye ran away from?' His Scottish accent had returned. It made his voice somehow heavier, as though it held more substance than his English voice.

She narrowed her eyes, suspiciously. Why wasn't he yelling or sulking or being just generally annoying? Was he actually ... concerned for her? She didn't want him to be concerned. She relied on him being infuriatingly miserable. She didn't know how to deal with a concerned Calum, a caring Calum. If he kept this up, she might just find herself confiding all her problems to him and that would be disastrous. In London, nobody knew who Ellen Burney was. Her secrets were safe. Her reputation was intact. She had an opportunity to build a new life—a life of independence as Ellen Smith. A life where her self-worth came from her ability to support Gwen and not from who her brother was.

'Tell me what's wrong.'

She found herself leaning towards him, being drawn in by the worried tone of his voice. She pulled back, wrapping her arms around herself. 'Please, just leave it, Your Grace.' She turned away from him, but he caught her shoulder. His grip was feather-light. She could have easily pulled away, but his touch was more than just a physical bond. It was a touch of comfort, of solace, of solidarity. She looked at his hand. His fingers were mainly undamaged though a couple of smaller scars still crisscrossed his skin.

'Ellie...'

What did he see when he looked in the mirror?

Crazy Calum. How could the newspapers have done that to him? He wasn't crazy. Just sad and lonely and grief-stricken.

Her bruises were slowly healing, but Calum's scars would always be a part of him. He could leave London, but the rumours and the speculation would always follow. Everywhere he went, Calum would always be known.

He turned her around to face him. He had that haunted look in his eyes that she had seen on the faces of parents who'd lost sons to the war or on the faces of son who had returned.

She didn't resist as he tentatively pulled her closer, wrapping his arms around her waist, careful to avoid touching her sore wrists.

He was so tall and broad and muscular. His embrace was a cage around her. But he wasn't locking her away; he was keeping her safe. A moment in his arms couldn't hurt. Just a moment, and then she would stand on her own two feet again.

She rested her cheek on his chest until all she could see and hear and feel and breathe was Calum.

Chapter Eleven

Surely she'd read that wrong! The hero was licking what part of the heroine? Ellen stared down at the boudoir novel lying open on the table before her.

Lady Faye laughed. 'You look like you've suffered a revelation.'

'I didn't realise...' Her breath was trapped in her chest. 'Do people really do that?'

She was reading aloud to the dowager. Unconventionally, they were sitting in the dining room, enjoying the sun before it disappeared behind clouds and smog again. One of the bay windows was open and the faint smell of scented geraniums perfumed the air.

'Only the very best men, gel.' There was a twinkle in Lady Faye's eyes. 'Only the best.'

'Oh, my.' Ellen let out a puff of air. The smooth-talking *on dit* -dropping Frenchman who was the hero of this particular story wasn't really her cup of tea. Perhaps if he were a little gruffer ... Calum kneeling before her. Calum tugging up her skirts. Calum's tongue at the centre of her throbbing heat. She squirmed on her seat, her blood suddenly singing with profound need. 'This is one dangerous book.' And it was giving her too many wonderful ideas.

'Is there any breakfast left?' Calum limped into the dining room, as though her very thoughts had conjured him into existence. 'Your dratted cook just kicked me out of my own kitchen.' He'd left his jacket off again and his shirtsleeves did little to hide the sinewy muscles of his arms. She had to wrench her gaze away before they caught her staring.

'Go away,' ordered Lady Faye. 'You're interrupting our reading, and Ellen's only just getting to the good part.'

'What part is that?'

'You should have come looking for breakfast earlier,' Lady Faye said in lieu of an answer. 'You're hours too late. Now you'll have to wait for afternoon tea.'

'I was busy earlier.' His gaze slide over to Ellen. The heat of it touched her skin. She pretended not to notice, even as the throbbing intensified. She locked her knees together and worked hard to keep her expression neutral. What would Calum think if he could hear her thoughts now?

Lady Faye crossed her arms over her large bosom and stuck out her bottom lip, making it clear she considered Calum's lack of breakfast to be nowhere as important as her boudoir novel. 'This isn't even the dining room anymore. Ellen and I have commandeered it for our own nefarious purposes. Didn't you see the sign on the door?'

'What sign?' He opened the door the rest of the way. *'Ladies of the Scandalous Romance Morning Room.'*

'Precisely.' The dowager tapped Ellen's hand with a finger. 'Remind me to remind Chakrabarti to hang another sign on the door. It shall read 'No men allowed'. Unless...' She turned her gaze back onto Calum. 'Did you want to take over reading?'

His voice reading those words: Ellen would melt from the inside out.

The duke gave the book one quick glance before stalking back out of the room.

Ellen watched his retreating back with a shaking breath. If she were a writer, she'd dedicate pages and pages just to the breadth of his shoulders, to the black depths of his eyes and to the way her heart seemed to backflip whenever he walked unexpectedly into a room. *Oh lordy.* Why had she tied her stays so tight that morning? She could hardly breathe.

She fiddled with a corner of the book, sure that if she tried to keep reading in this state she'd fumble the words. Her face heated. Could everyone tell what she was thinking? Her face grew hotter.

'Lizzy!' Owen's call pulled Ellen back to the present. He strutted inside, waggling his cane before him as would a dandy parading through Hyde Park.

'If you're looking for breakfast, you won't find any in here.' Lady Faye tilted her head to one side so her ward could press a chaste kiss to her cheek.

'Miss Smith.' Owen darted forward, pressing a less-than-chaste kiss to Ellen's cheek before she could pull away. 'I make a point of never leaving my house without breaking my fast. My own man makes the most superb kippers.' He dragged an empty seat from its place further down the table and wiggled it into the small space between Lady Faye and Ellen, where a chair did not belong. His hand brushed Ellen's knee as he sat down.

Mr Tattershall: master of the 'accidental' caress.

She closed the book.

'Ellen's reading me the most delightfully educational novel. It's about—' Lady Faye snapped her mouth shut with a wink.

Owen moved to read the title, but the dowager snatched it off the table and tucked it under her posterior. 'It's much too shocking for your young, innocent ears.'

'My feelings!' Owen pressed a hand to his chest. 'Innocent, indeed!' Today he wore a green waistcoat embroidered all over with dragonflies, a crisp cravat and his beaver hat, which was doing a rather fine job of highlighting the hazel specks in his otherwise blue eyes. A fact he undoubtedly knew and which was probably the sole reason for him wearing the hat inside.

'What I really want to know,' continued Owen, 'is why Wood is prowling up and down the hallway like an angry bear? When I knocked, he actually opened the front door to me. I thought you had a butler now?'

'He's sulking. Calum, not the butler,' Lady Faye clarified. 'Besides, it's the servants' day off.'

Owen rolled his eyes. 'What's got his cravat in a knot today?'

'Apparently news of my visit is spreading around London and people are beginning to breach the front gates to leave their calling cards. The horror of it all!' She gave a fake gasp. 'I daresay he's trying to scare them away.'

'He is?' Ellen hadn't seen Calum by the door when she'd come down that morning. 'For how long?'

'Since the crack of dawn, I believe. He's afraid someone will sneak a calling card onto the tray when Chakrabarti isn't looking.'

'And he told you all of this?' Ellen's heart started thumping against her chest. 'Did he mention anything of letters?'

'Calling cards, letters, the Prince Regent himself.' Lady Faye's smile faltered. 'Are you all right, gel? You've turned ... pasty.'

Ellen nodded, gripping the edge of the table. She'd told Calum to forget about the letter. She'd told him it was none of his business. What did he think he was doing guarding the front door? This wasn't a coincidence. He hadn't bothered guarding the door any other day since Lady Faye's arrival.

He was being nosy or overprotective or ... goodness only knew what thoughts entered that man's head. He was beyond belief!

Remember Rule No. 1, pleaded a desperate voice at the back of her mind. *Behave. Behave! Keep your temper.*

Oh, fie on Rule No. 1. The duke had overstepped the mark and he was going to be getting an earful at her earliest convenience. She crossed her arms. *Behave indeed. It was he who needed to behave.*

Lady Faye and Owen were staring at her in confusion, so Ellen quickly schooled her expression into one of calm. 'If he doesn't want callers, why doesn't he just take the knocker off the door?'

'Men,' ejaculated Lady Faye. 'They never think.' She turned to Owen. 'Was there a reason for this visit, dearest? Not that I'm not pleased to see you, of course.'

'I spoke to Grace this morning.' His expression turned solemn.

'I see.' Lady Faye stared down at her hands. The change was instantaneous. Where a moment ago she'd been jolly, she was now sorrowful. 'It was silly of me to think anything would have changed.'

'Lizzy.' Owen rested a hand on her arm. 'I'm sorry.'

Whatever was happening, it was a private moment. Ellen rose, intending to give them space, but Lady Faye stopped her.

'My daughter hasn't spoken to me for nearly four years. She thinks I took Calum's side when Pierce died in that horrible fire. But there were no sides. Cal was hurting just as much as she was. And we all know he didn't have anything to do with that fire.'

'It was a terrible accident,' Owen agreed.

'Sometimes I think there are two Graces,' said Lady Faye. 'There's the kind and thoughtful Grace who loves her family. That's the Grace I know. But now there's also the angry and sad Grace who won't have anything to do with me or Calum.' Her shoulders slumped like she was sinking in on herself.

'She misses her son,' said Owen.

'We all miss him.' Lady Faye touched a hand to the mourning brooch pinned to her bodice.

'I'm so sorry.' Ellen couldn't begin to imagine the heartbreak of being hated by her own daughter.

Lady Faye stood up abruptly, the legs of her chair scraping against the floorboards. 'I want to visit Grace myself.'

'Are you sure that's wise?'

Ellen and Owen both stood up too, exchanging a worried look.

The dowager was pale, and she suddenly looked ten years older. 'I don't care about wise. I care about my family. Will you take me?'

'Of course.' Owen offered his arm.

'My gel.' Lady Faye turned to Ellen. 'I won't be needing your services this afternoon. Why don't you take some time to yourself?'

'If you're sure.' Ellen curtseyed as the dowager swept from the room, Owen at her beck and call.

***

Cal turned on his heel, limping down the passage. He could still feel Ellie pressed against his chest, taking comfort in the arms of a man nobody had dared take comfort from for many years. Reaching the far end, he turned again, pacing back towards the front door.

To hell with morning callers! Apparently the allure of the dowager marchioness, lately returned to London, was too great for the *ton* to ignore. Even the threat of Crazy Calum wasn't enough to keep them at bay.

Well, I'm not having it. The *ton* had abandoned him when he'd been at his most vulnerable; now he was determined to abandon it.

Patrolling for unwanted visitors had absolutely nothing to do with the crying lass who'd accepted his comfort yesterday.

He dropped into the porter's chair, the cracked leather squeaking with age, and closed his eyes. He could still see her tear-stained cheeks and the quiver of her lips. The need to be doing something, anything, to help her was eating him up. But there was nowhere for him to go, nothing for him to do. He gripped the handrests until his knuckles turned white. He didn't even know who the letter was from.

'What are you doing?'

He started. *Ellie.*

'You're guarding the door.' She pressed her hands to her hips in that way he was quickly coming to associate with an oncoming lecture. A thrill of anticipation raced through him.

'Aye ... nay ... If ye already knew the answer, why ask the question?'

'But *why* are you guarding the door?' She ran a hand over her hair. It was tied back in a soft bun, and the wisps that framed her face had been lightly curled. Or maybe they were natural curls.

Chocolate! That was the word he'd been trying to think of the other day to describe the colour of her hair. Too dark to be brown but too light to be black; it was the colour of thick drinking chocolate, rich and delicious—the perfect companion to her strawberry lips.

She clicked her tongue expectantly.

'I'm watching for ... birds.' He took his jacket from the coatrack and slipped it on just to give his hands something to do. To stop himself pulling her chocolate hair free of its pins, until the silky strands caressed her neck and shoulders.

'Bird watching?' Her tone boded nothing good. 'Since when have you been able to see through solid wooden doors?'

'Well, I'm opening it without warning. That way I catch the birds unawares.' He demonstrated, gesturing out the open door. A large crow sitting in the low branches of the old yew tree cawed mournfully. 'See, surprisingly effective.'

'So your prowling has absolutely nothing to do with the correspondence I received yesterday?'

'What correspondence?' He pulled his lips into an innocent smile that felt entirely unnatural.

She glared at him, and he felt suddenly two feet tall.

'Oh, that correspondence. Nay. This has absolutely nothing to do with *that* correspondence. Nothing to do with ye at all.'

'Your grandmother has been in residence for close on two weeks now, and in all that time you never once guarded the door from visitors. Not until I received a letter.'

Her eyes narrowed even further. Was she challenging him to another staring contest? The last one had left him half naked in front of both his grandmother and his cousin. He'd be dammed if he was going to let that happen again. 'For gods' sake, ye were crying!' He blinked once, twice, three times.

'Which was clearly a mistake.' Her voice rose too.

'Do ye routinely cry by mistake?'

'I meant it was a mistake to let you see.'

'Ye meant it was mistake to let me hold ye, to offer comfort.' He could read between the lines. Ice burned its way through his veins. 'Dammit, Ellie. We didn't do anything wrong. We didn't break one of those precious rules you outlined so thoroughly the other day in the garden.'

He should have kissed her that day instead of letting her rant and rave. He should have tossed to her to the damp earth and kissed her breathless. Kissed and kissed her until she no longer cared about propriety. 'Ellie.' He reached towards her, but she was having none of it.

'Don't call me that. Nobody calls me that.' She stepped back.

He followed without even thinking. 'Is that wrong too?'

'It's...' She pursed her lips. 'I really don't understand you, Calum. You push everyone away. Nobody's allowed to talk about your brother or your scars. But you're constantly pushing your way into my life. That letter has nothing to do with you.'

He opened his mouth to respond, but she pressed her advantage. 'You mope around this house, yelling at me and Owen, arguing with Lady Faye and scaring the servants half to death.'

'It was ye who came barging into my house. I was happy'—wrong word—'content'—still not right—'minding my own business until ye pushed yer problems onto me.'

'I did nothing of the sort. I've specifically tried to keep my distance. It's you who's been asking about my bruises and my letter. It's you who chose to guard the front door.' She tossed her arms into the air as though despairing of him. 'There's no point. I'm not expecting another letter. You can give up.'

'Yer problems became my problems the instant ye climbed through my front window.' He pointed an accusatory finger at her. This was all her fault—all the questions swirling around his head, all this confusion and all these unwanted feelings. Every inch of his body yearned to press against Ellie, to surrender to her touch, to drown in her scent until his whole world was Ellie.

'My problems are nobody's but my own, Your Grace.'

"Tis 'Your Grace' again. What happened to Calum?'

But she just shook her head. 'What are you doing with your life?'

He froze. 'I went to war. That's what I did with my life.'

If he thought that response was going to slow her down he was very much mistaken. She crossed her arms and, without missing a beat, said: 'As admirable as that is, it doesn't answer my question. If you've free time enough that you're guarding doors and locking up cake tins, it really begs the question: what are you doing with your life?'

He grit his teeth. This wasn't supposed to be his life. Pierce was supposed to be alive. He was supposed to have his brother by his side.

He wasn't meant to be in this damned house with this infuriating woman demanding he have some grand plan.

Until the age of ten he hadn't even known he was a duke's heir. Hell, he hadn't even known he was half English!

And then his grandparents had died and he'd been taken in by his father. And then his new-found brother had been killed at war because he'd followed Cal into the Navy. And then, to top that all off, his father had died of a bloody broken heart. Shakespeare had penned tragedies with less death than his family had suffered.

A smarter man might have thought fate his enemy. Cal didn't believe in fate. He didn't believe in anything anymore.

Except maybe Ellie. As infuriating as she was, she made his skin burn with need. She made him feel alive again.

'You have money, an inheritance, a loving family. Why are you sitting around wasting it all?' Despite the quiet way she'd spoken, it was as though she'd yelled again, as though she'd shot a cannonball straight at him.

He wanted to shout or to hit something. He wanted to toss her out the front door. He wanted to lock the front door to keep her from leaving. He wanted to keep her safe forever and ever.

He couldn't think straight. He could barely even meet her steady, waiting gaze. So he did the only thing he could do, the only thing that made any sort of sense. He stepped forward, wrapped one arm around the back of her head and the other around her waist.

It was as though she'd read his mind. Or maybe his expression had said it all, for she moved the same instant he did. Her fingers gripped his collar, pulling his head down so she could reach his lips. He was almost caught off balance, but she'd seemed to have accounted for that as well. Pressing her back to the wall, she remained steady—a rock to which he clung.

The feel of her overshadowed everything else. It was just Ellie and himself and this desperate shared needed between them.

She tasted sweet, like the sugary tea she favoured. With a lurch of his heart he realised it was becoming a familiar taste—a wonderful, heady taste. He was never going to take his tea unsweetened again.

He pulled her closer, as close as they could get with their clothes still on, trying to drink in the taste and feel of her.

Why were they still dressed? And why were they still standing in the passage? He stepped to the side, slowly sliding Ellie along the wall. They just had to navigate two flights of stairs...

He was dimly aware of the front door opening, of someone standing before them, of Tzar barking. And then someone shouted in his ear, harsh and angry.

'What the hell are you doing to my sister?'

Chapter Twelve

Ellen's heart leaped and she clutched at Calum's shirt. 'Geoffrey?'

Her brother's mouth twisted into a self-righteous scowl. He stood on the top step, laying claim to the threshold.

'What are you doing here?' Her lungs tightened, her breath trapped in her throat. *Gwen! Had he found Gwen?*

'Just as I suspected.' His gaze lingered on her kiss-swollen lips.

Old shame filled her stomach like heavy rocks and she barely resisted the urge to wipe her still-tingling mouth on the back of her hand.

Beside her, Calum stiffened. She was acutely aware of his presence, of the strength of his shoulders, of the warmth of his chest. And of the horror he must be feeling standing face to face with her brother.

It was clear Geoffrey hadn't cleaned his teeth, hadn't shaved, hadn't washed his hair. Seeing them face to face, it was hard not to draw a comparison between the two men, so very different were they. Where Calum's very presence seemed to draw the eye, Geoffrey was just ... less.

She straightened her shoulders. They'd done nothing shameful, and the day she'd left Geoffrey's house was the day she'd given up letting his snide comments dictate her emotions. She took a steadying breath, focusing on much more important matters.

Gwen. For a second all she could see was the little girl's face, as though she stood in Geoffrey's place—large, bright owl eyes peeking out from behind a curtain of dark hair as naturally curly as her grandmother's had been.

But Ellen didn't ask what she most wanted to know. Years of experience had taught her drawing attention to Gwen only made matters worse when it came to dealing with her brother. 'How did you find me?'

'Couldn't have been easier,' Geoffrey preened, puffing out his chest. 'You always did take me for a fool.'

'Fool enough to be standing on my doorstep without even a card of introduction,' Calum snapped, finally breaking his silence.

Only then did Geoffrey bother turning his attention to the large Scotsman before him. His eyes narrowed on Calum's face, his scowl turning feral. His thoughts were written on his face as clear as a newspaper headline.

A lurch of panic started her heart to racing. 'Geoffrey, please,' she implored, 'at least let me take you around the back. This is my employer's house.' She reached out to take his hand, desperate to separate the two men, but Geoffrey grabbed her wrist in his vice-like grip, sending pain shooting up her arm.

'A cripple!' He goaded her, his shrill voice magnified with his growing excitement. 'You came all the way to London for a cripple!' A squawk of laughter. 'I bet he was the only one who'd take you in.'

'Who the hell are you?' demanded Calum, his voice dangerously low.

'None other than Geoffrey Burney, Baron of Blackford, and I demand you address me as such, sir.' He gave Calum sanctimonious sneer. 'The runt before you is my sister, and I'm here to return her home to where she belongs.' He turned his attention back to Ellen, pressing his free hand to his chest. 'No man bears the burden of such a sister as I do.'

'Burney?' Calum looked him up and down for a full ten seconds, no doubt comprehending the extent of her lies. Then his gaze locked on Geoffrey's hold of her arm. 'Let her go,' he ground out between clenched teeth.

'It's fine.' Ellen stepped in front of Calum, trying to crowd her brother and force him into taking a step backwards. 'Please, Geoffrey. Let's not do this here.'

The distinct smell of horse clung to his crumpled shirt, testimony to his recent arrival in London. Despite the dust, he was clearly wearing new clothes. His jacket was finely cut; tailor made. She frowned. When had Geoffrey been able to afford such clothes?

Despite it all, he was still wearing those same old boots of his—the ones with the tin toes and the heels that had been replaced so many times she'd lost count. He'd once thrown those shoes at her head.

Some things never changed.

'She isn't going anywhere with you. She's clearly reached her majority which means you have no legal rights to force her to do anything she doesn't wish to do. And if you don't let her go in the next five seconds, I swear—'

Geoffrey let out a derisive laugh, cutting Calum short. 'And who, pray, are you to be telling me the law?'

'I'm a bloody duke, and you're trespassing on my property.'

'Is that what you told Ellen to get her into your bed?' Another laugh.

'Did you want to see my entitlement deeds?' Calum asked with a leaden stare. 'I keep them handy for just such occasions.'

Ellen winced.

Her brother's eyes narrowed ever so slightly, and his gaze finally moved from Calum's face down his superfine jacket with its twin tails to his black calf-clingers and his well-worn buck-skin boots. For a man who spent so little effort or time on his appearance, he certainly looked the part.

'If you are a duke,' drawled her brother, 'then what happened to your face?'

'It's none of your goddamn business. Now, you're either going to leave or I'll be demanding satisfaction.'

Geoffrey's grip on her wrist loosened, and Ellen pulled free. Calum instantly whipped her behind him, bringing himself face to face with her brother.

'Calum, please.' She tugged at the back of his jacket. He was like a bull at the farm gate, waiting for one wrong move, one tiny excuse. But she couldn't let them fight. Calum's size gave him a clear advantage but she wasn't sure how long his wounded leg would hold up.

And Geoffrey never picked a fight unless he was sure he could win—especially a physical fight. He was either taking Calum's scars for weakness or he had another plan.

Gwen.

'You're not helping, either of you,' she snapped, suddenly desperate to put a stop their confrontation. 'Whatever will the neighbours think?'

Neither paid her any attention.

'What is she to you, anyway?' demanded Geoffrey.

'Lord Woodhal is my employer's grandson.' Ellen answered before Calum could. She pushed her way between them again, pressing a hand to Geoffrey's chest. If Calum could just give her moment alone with her brother, maybe she could persuade Geoffrey to leave. She could promise to send home her wages or something—if she still had any wages at the end of this. 'I'm the lady's companion of Lady Faye.'

'That old bat. *My employer, the marchioness,*' mimicked Geoffrey, in a high-pitched voice. '*My lover, the duke. Woe be me.*' His eyes flicked back to Ellen's face, and she knew what he was going to say before he'd even opened his mouth. 'I'll tell them. I'll tell them all. You'll be shunned by every respectable man and woman until the day you die.'

And there it was. The reason why he knew he could win any fight with Calum without even raising a fist. Her secret. The reason she'd stayed with him for the two years after their father's death. The reason it had taken him hitting Gwen before she'd had the courage to finally leave.

Keeping Gwen safe was so much more important than her own reputation. But without her reputation she'd never find respectable employment again and would never be able to support herself or Gwen. It was her own Gordian knot. She couldn't have one without the other.

She felt ill.

'You should have thought of that before you ran away.' There wasn't a flicker of concern for her in his steel grey eyes.

***

'What's happening here?'

Cal glanced over Geoffrey's head to see his grandmother marching up the garden path. The gate was open behind her and a borrowed barouche was pulling away from the side of the road, Owen waving goodbye from the open-air box.

'It's nothing, my lady. Just a simple misunderstanding.' Ellie pushed on her brother's chest, trying to make him move so Lady F could pass. 'I'm sorry. He shouldn't never have come here.'

Geoffrey held his ground. He was a small man. While small suited Ellie, it most certainly didn't suit her brother. His head was too big for his body; it seemed to sit haphazardly on a neck too thin to support its weight. And what he lacked in height, he obviously thought to make up for in temper and fists.

There was no question in Cal's mind that this was the man who'd bruised Ellie, that this was the man she'd run away from. His fists itched to sink themselves into Geoffrey's stomach.

'Ellen and Gwen are coming home with me,' the blackguard said, wrinkling his nose as his surveyed Lady F. 'I remember you from that time you visited Evendale, years ago.'

Wait. Cal frowned. 'Who's Gwen?'

'She's six. And she isn't here.' Ellie let out a shaky breath. For all that she looked distressed, a little tension had slipped from her shoulders. Whoever this Gwen was, Ellie was clearly relieved her brother hadn't found her too.

'I don't believe you,' Geoffrey growled.

'I can assure you that we are not hiding any children in the house.' Icy undertones froze Ellen's usually warm voice. She glared at her brother with such force it was a mystery how he didn't melt into a puddle of dirty wash water at her feet. In fact, it was mystery how Geoffrey had ever thought he could tell her what to do.

All of a sudden Cal wasn't only worried about what he might just do to Geoffrey; the look in Ellen's eyes was practically murderous.

He quickly wrapped an arm back around her shoulders, pulling to her close to his body—not leashing her, just trying to remind her he was there and that she wasn't alone in all this mess. Because he knew without a doubt if she did something to hurt her brother in anger or fear now she'd hate herself for it later.

'And I'm just supposed to believe you? You're clearly pitching the gammon.'

'What a vulgar expression.' Lady F tapped her foot disapprovingly on the overgrown garden path. 'Search the house if you must. You won't find any children inside.' And just like that his big-mouthed grandmother waved the brute inside.

'No you don't.' Cal moved to stop them, but with Ellie by his side he couldn't move fast enough and Geoffrey managed to push his way in.

He threw open the drawing room door. Seeing nothing to interest him, their unwanted guest moved to the next room, tossing open the door to the library with such force a year's collection of the *Weekly Dispatch* tumbled from a shelf to sprawl over the rug.

Stepping over the footrest, he marched to the far wall, tugging open a small door Cal had long since forgotten about. It led to a disused housekeeper's sitting room.

'This is ridiculous.' Ellen hurried after her brother as he rushed down the narrow corridor, past the modified room with the stairs, towards the kitchen. 'You cannot barge inside like this. This isn't your house.'

Ignoring them all, Geoffrey burst into the kitchen, waking the dog. He wrenched on the door leading from the kitchen into Grace's half of the house and it opened with a protesting groan of hinges long unused, and a cloud of shimmering dust rose into the air. A darkened hallway, a rush of cold air—

Cal's lungs constricted. This man actually thought the world should lay down at his feet. Worse, the bastard thought Ellie was his property to do with as he pleased. 'That's enough!' Cal slammed the door shut. 'Let me make this very clear. There's no child in my house. And there's no way in hell you're taking Ellie.'

'Or what?' Geoffrey sneered. 'You'll set your dog on me?'

Tzar growled, pulling back his thin, black lips to display a row of old, worn teeth.

'We've been over this already,' Geoffrey continued. 'I have leverage. I know things.' And for the second time that day he grabbed at Ellie's arm.

Something inside Cal snapped. Anger like which he hadn't felt in years pumped through him. He jabbed a finger against Geoffrey's chest, forcing him back a step. 'Unhand my wife.'

Chapter Thirteen

His what now? Ellen swallowed the wrong way and started choking. *His wife?*

Calum clapped her on the back and glared daggers at Geoffrey. 'Get out and don't come back.'

Her brother's mouth had dropped open. He looked like a stunned fish. He looked how Ellen felt. Out of water, out of depth. He blinked, glanced once more around the room, then turned on his heel and hurried from the house.

'What just happened?' Lady Faye pressed a hand to her throat.

My idiot brother happened, Ellen wanted to answer but it was like her voice was suppressed under the weight of all the panic and anger and guilt. Her legs were like bricks. She was tethered to the spot. Her very own statue.

Calum gripped the table edge with both hands, his knuckles turning white, his head bowed.

What should she do? What *could* she do? Comfort Lady Faye? Explain herself to Calum? Beg for their help? Cry for Gwen? Scream over Geoffrey?

Weeks of hard work trying to be the perfect lady's companion snatched away in just a few moments. No number of rules could ever have been enough to keep her old life at bay. 'Calum...' His name was heavy on her tongue.

His wife!

What could she possibly say to him? How could she possibly start to apologise?'

Lady Faye blinked, coming back to life like a clock whose mechanisms had been wound back up. She dived at Ellen, grabbed both her hands and pressed them to her ample bosom. 'You poor, poor gel. How could you possibly be related to such a horrible man? He's absolutely despicable.'

'Despicable,' Calum muttered under his breath, still unmoving. He could have been carved from marble. 'That's one word to describe what just happened here.'

'Geoffrey shouldn't have pushed his way into your home like that. I'll begin packing immediately and be out the door within the hour.'

'Pack?' Lady Faye pulled her closer, forcing Ellen to stoop a little. 'Surely you're safest with us.'

'I don't know.' Ellen's heart lurched. Why wasn't Lady Faye demanding she leave? It could only be a matter of time before she did. 'I don't know how he found me so fast.' Verity would never have revealed her location, and it was clear

Geoffrey was yet to find Gwen and Maggie. Maybe the coachman...?

'Who's Gwen? That child he was searching for?'

Ellen jumped at the sound of Calum's voice. It was a low rumble in his chest as though he still didn't quite trust himself to speak without shouting. And he still wasn't meeting her gaze. Was he ashamed of her? It was impossible to tell what he was thinking.

And her heart was breaking.

'Is she your sister?' Lady F was gentle but persistent.

'She's only six,' confirmed Ellen. 'Practically still a baby. I've hidden her away in the country.'

'Why did you never mention her to me before now?' Calum sounded calmer than she'd ever thought he could be. Where was his temper? Oh, what she wouldn't give to see his temper right now.

'None of that matters right this moment, Cal.' The smile lines around the old woman's mouth were all turned down. 'We need to be thinking of a plan. We need to prepare for when he returns.'

'Calum's right.' Ellen pulled her hands free of the dowager's grip. She let out a swoosh of air, straightening her shoulders. 'I shouldn't have lied. But I did what I thought was the right thing for Gwen. I couldn't leave her under Geoffrey's roof for a moment longer. He's ... not a nice person. Not anymore.'

She looked between them—her employer who'd become her friend and the duke who sent her heart pounding and her toes curling. 'I'm sorry,' she finally said. It was all she could say, but it would never be enough. She'd brought Geoffrey to their doorstep and he'd come crashing into their lives like a team of carriage horses. She, more than most, knew how important solitude and anonymity was to Calum. She moved towards the kitchen door. A hard ball settled in the pit of her stomach. But she ignored it. She ignored everything but her determination.

Her determination to keep Gwen safe.

Her determination to retain her freedom from Geoffrey.

And her determination to bring no more shame or hurt or anger into Calum's house. Because he deserved none of it.

'But what happens when Geoffrey realises we lied about the two of you being wed?' Lady Faye clutched Calum's arm.

'I don't know. If I leave now, maybe nothing.' Ellen sighed. 'My brother is a gambler, but he's smart and resourceful, and now it looks like he has some money, so the sooner I leave, the better.' And the sooner she left before Lady Faye realised her continued employ was untenable, the better.

The need to reach out to Calum was a physical pain. With what felt like a Herculean effort, she clamped her hands behind her back and took a step away.

'Calum McKenna Callaghan, I demand you do something. Stop her! Marry her!' The dowager actually stamped her foot. 'It isn't fair. Ellen cannot leave us. We cannot let her brother bully us around.' Her voice sputtered into silence as she stared up at her grandson. Tears clung to her invisible lashes. For an instant, she looked like a child.

An oppressive silence filled the kitchen.

'Miss Burney.' Calum nodded towards the hallway just beyond the kitchen door. 'A private word.'

Miss Burney. It was like that, was it?

'Yes!' Lady Faye ushered them both into the passage. 'Talk. Sort this out between yourselves. And don't you dare come back into the kitchen until Ellen has dispensed with this ridiculous idea of leaving us. It will not do.' With another stamp of her foot, she slammed the door in their faces.

They were plunged into gloomy darkness.

Ellen narrowed her eyes, trying to make out the finer features of Calum's face, but he was just a looming shadow against a backdrop of more shadows. There were no windows in this part of the house; with a solid wall down one side and the kitchen door closed behind them, it was almost impossible to see with any clarity.

He pulled in a shuddering breath, the gentle rustle of his superfine jacket against his waistcoat the only sound in the otherwise silent passage. It was a heavy silence, like a weight on her shoulders, grinding her into the floor.

'Why didn't you tell me about your siblings?' His voice was low, as though he suspected Lady Faye of having her ear pressed to the door. Which she probably did.

'Family problems aren't something one usually discusses in polite society.'

'Like hell. Answer me straight. Why didn't you tell me about your brother?'

She let out a deep breath, bracing herself. 'Because I wasn't sure you'd care.'

'Of course I care.' His voice was harsh. 'Why did you really come to my house?'

'I didn't lie about that. My friend Verity knew your grandmother was looking for a lady's companion and she wrote to Lady Faye on my behalf.'

'You said you have no other family.'

'No. My mother died when Gwen was born, and my father passed away two years ago. He made a provision for my dowry, which Geoffrey paid little attention to.'

'Gwen—'

'Is my responsibility. Geoffrey knows nothing of children. He...' she faltered. 'The day he hit her was the day I knew we couldn't stay under his roof any longer.' Her eyes were beginning to adjust to the darkened passageway. There were small spots of light leaking out from the bottom of the closed kitchen door. And then a shadow and the slight creaking of floorboards, probably the dowager moving around just on the other side of the door.

'And that's when your friend, this Mrs Nott, started making employment inquiries?'

'Yes ... no.' She frowned. 'I went to Verity to ask for her advice, and she showed me Lady Faye's acceptance letter. Verity was a childhood friend of my mother and was happy to help.'

Leaving Calum's house was the last thing she wanted to do, but it would be better for them all if she wasn't here if Geoffrey returned—when he returned. Better to get the goodbyes over with before she lost her nerve. 'I really do appreciate everything you and your grandmother—and Owen—have done for me, but that doesn't mean I expect you to risk the reputation of your family any more than need be just because of my idiot brother. He's my problem, not yours.'

'That's far from the truth. You're under my roof and therefore under my protection.'

'I don't expect—'

'I won't let Blackford near you or your sister.' He cut her off, his words abrupt. 'Tell me exactly where she's hiding and I'll bring her to London.'

'Back here? To London?' Her mouth opened. Why wasn't he demanding she leave? It made no sense.

'Aye. Where is Gwen hiding?'

'Tell him!' demanded Lady Faye through the closed door.

'Um ... near Evendale. With another of my mother's friends and her sister-in-law.'

'Good. It shouldn't take me more than three days at most, there and back.' He started down the corridor, but she caught at his arm. In the half-dark, her sense of touch was heightened. She could feel his corded muscles practically quivering with tension even beneath the layers of his clothing.

'Think about this for a moment. Geoffrey knows I'm here. If we bring Gwen to London, we'll practically be handing her over to him. And if I'm going to find new employ, I can't have a child with me. No position—'

'Who said anything about new employment? This is your home. I'll keep you both safe here.'

'But—'

'No buts.'

'It isn't that simple.' He was infuriating! 'You lied to Geoffrey about us being married.' If the newspapers found out, her reputation would be ruined. She'd never find new work. She'd never make a living of her own. Never have her independence. Never be able to provide Gwen with safety and security.

'I've been a sailor and a soldier. For a while, some people even thought me a traitor and a murderer. But I've never lied. Not to you, and certainly not to your idiot of a brother, not entirely at any rate.'

'What do you mean?'

He reached out as if he meant to brush a strand of hair from her face but stopped, letting his hand drop back to his side. 'I mean, by week's end both you and Gwen will be safe forever. By week's end, you and I will be wed.'

***

Cal clenched his hands by his sides, keeping as still as humanly possible, not trusting himself to move or speak any more than necessary. His Ellie had a Jack o'Dandy for a brother and she hadn't told him because she didn't think he'd care enough to do anything to help.

His insides twisted into a knot.

She stood just inches away but there might as well have been a chasm between them. The urge to take her by the shoulders and shake some sense into her small frame was almost too strong to resist. Of course he bloody well cared.

The narrow passage seemed to be shrinking, pushing them closer and closer together.

He pressed his eyes closed, barely trusted himself to breath. He wanted ... so many things he could barely think straight. He wanted to kiss her. He wanted to hold her. He wanted to beat Geoffrey senseless. He wanted privacy in his own house, away from his spying servants and his meddling grandmother. He wanted the newspapers to burn in hell.

But most of all he wanted Ellie to trust him.

What of that secret Geoffrey was threatening to tell everyone?

That was just another thing she'd kept from him. Another thing she hadn't thought he'd care about.

Blast it all. Cal had seen the bruises on her arms that first night. He should have demanded she tell him everything there and then.

Even as he berated himself, he knew pressuring her wouldn't have worked. She'd had enough of that from her brother.

Nay. If he was going to get Ellie to finally trust him, he was going to have to give her good reason to do so. If he wanted her trust, he'd have to keep his word. They would be married, and he would keep both her and her sister safe from Geoffrey.

A husband had legal rights over a wife where a brother did not. Geoffrey would not be able to get a look in once they were wed. He'd be forced to return to Evendale with his tail between his legs.

Cal gave a self-satisfied nod. It was the perfect plan.

And the niggling voice at the back of his mind asking why Ellie's trust was so important to him—He was much too busy to contemplate that now.

***

By week's end, you and I will be wed.

Seconds of pregnant silence ticked by. In the drawing room, the pendulum clock stuck the hour, and the other clocks answered in kind.

Calum stood stock still, a mountain of a man: immovable and so frustratingly stubborn.

'I'm not going to marry you.' Ellen wanted to punch him. Instead, she let out a frustrated sigh. 'Come here.' She led him into the library, away from Lady Faye's listening ears.

The heavy brocade curtains were open, letting in the last of the afternoon sun. Expression was beginning to return to Calum's face. It appeared he couldn't keep his emotions under such strict guard for long. The corners of his mouth were turned down.

She turned her back on him, afraid she wouldn't be able to keep her distance if he kept looking at her like that. They should have stayed in the dark passageway where she couldn't see his face.

For such a small room, the library housed an impressive number of books. They were packed into the bookcases, double stacked in some places, and newspapers had pushed into all remaining available space. Old papers littered the floor. Adelynn hadn't dared tidy a room so obviously the duke's private space. Ellen's eyes lingered on the books stacked knee high beside the outdated cerulean armchair.

'I daresay you don't understand.' He spoke slowly as though her level of comprehension had dropped considerably in the last half hour. Or perhaps it was just his estimation of her that had dropped now he knew what type of family she came from. He walked around her so they were face to face again. 'As my wife you'd be free of your brother. I would give you a monthly allowance, and Gwen would live with us in London. Or in the country if you prefer. I have several estates—'

'I understand perfectly well. I'm not a goosecap.' And she wasn't a charity case either. She ran a hand over her hair, and the pins in her chignon prodded painfully into her scalp. If they married, she'd be behoven to Calum for the rest of her life, unable to even earn a simple wage. Independence had been so hard won. She wasn't going to give it up so easily just to scare away Geoffrey.

'I'm not suggesting—' He made a noise of exasperation, and his mouth snapped shut in a way that made it perfectly clear he was too frustrated with her to finish his sentence.

The dark shadow that always clung to his face was darker than usual. He rubbed at the thigh of his wounded leg as though trying to rub away the pain. As though he were readying himself for another fight.

Lady Faye had described him as a happy child, but Ellen had rarely seen him smile all the time she'd known him. The war had left more damage than half a body of scars. Now she'd brought the threat of violence into his own house, the very house he'd hidden himself in to get away from the gossips and the noise and the brutality of life.

The shadow was there because of her.

'When was the last time you ate a proper meal?' she demanded.

'I'm asking you to marry me and you want to talk of food?'

'If I might be so forward as to point out that you didn't ask me to marry you. You demanded, and I refused. Thank you all the same.'

'Can't ye see I'm trying to help?' he practically yelled, slipped back into his Scottish accent.

'Shouting isn't going to change my mind. You need not concern yourself with my welfare. I'm perfectly capable of looking after myself and Gwen. My brother ruffled your feathers, and you spoke in haste. I won't hold you to your word. I have my own plan. I can—'

'Concern myself? What exactly do ye mean by that?'

'I mean marriage to me wouldn't suit,' she said simply, truthfully. 'You can barely tolerate servants living under the same roof as you, let alone your own grandmother. What do you want with a wife?'

A pause. A flash of thought crossed his face. And then he slow-blinked, his heavy-lidded eyes softening. 'But Ellie dearest, there are so many answers to that question which would have ye blushing.' His voice was almost a purr. A complete turnaround from a second ago.

She missed a breath. Getting angry hadn't worked, and now he was ... seducing her? 'That isn't going to work either.'

He raised a single eyebrow. 'Isn't it?' Another purr.

Tingles prickled her skin. Starting at the top of her head, they rolled down her body beneath her sensible grey gown and tightly laced stays like waves against the water's edge until a light sheen of sweat broke out on her forehead. 'Um...' Her mouth was dry. 'I ... It will not do for us to marry,' she said finally. The safest course of action was to ignore his attempt at flirtation. She was suddenly aware of just how much space he took up in the small library.

'Marriage is the simplest solution,' Calum replied, taking a step closer.

'A married woman cannot work. I wouldn't be able to support myself. I have a plan.' She tried to focus on her reasons for refusing his suit, but it was like trying to trap water in her hands. Thoughts were melting out of her head. He was so close she could see his Adam's apple bob as he swallowed. 'A good p-plan. I'll find new employment...' She licked her suddenly dry lips. 'And make money ... and save Gwen...'

'But I could support ye. I have more than enough money for the both of us. More than enough money for the three of us.' He slipped an arm about her waist, sending a wave of heat through from body from where his arm held her. And he wasn't even touching her bare skin.

'But not nearly enough patience,' was all she could manage in answer. It took an enormous effort of will not to lean into his embrace. His lips brushed against hers in light, temping kisses, causing the tingling to settle between her legs.

He ran his tongue along the seam of her lips, inviting Ellen to open her mouth to him. Even as the rational part of her mind begged her to turn away, to reject him, her arms wrapped around his neck, lacing her fingers in his soft hair, giving him full access. She kissed him as he kissed her, tasting his mouth, breathing his breaths.

'Marry me?' he whispered against her lips.

Head bowed, he rained kisses along the line of her jaw and down her throat. His fingers unhooked a catch at the back of her dress with a single flick, tugging the sleeve down over one shoulder and exposing her skin.

'I can't.' She released the words on a sigh as he pressed kisses to the sensitive area where her neck met her collarbone. The air was chilly on her skin, his lips hot and so soft.

'What if I do this?' He dropped a hand to her leg, running his fingers along her thigh as he slowly gathered up the hem of her old muslin dress.

Oh, she was in so much trouble.

'I can't marry you because...' Her tongue was heavy in her mouth, her mind turning to thick, sticky honey. *Something about independence. Something about...*

Cool air tickled her thigh just above her garter. His hand skimmed higher.

'No drawers.' A sly smile of approval curled his lips. 'I've never been a fan of these new undergarments that some women insist on wearing.'

Who was this Calum? The man petting his way up her leg was far from the man who'd threatened to toss her from the front window the first time they'd met.

She wanted the old Calum back. She knew where she stood with the old Calum.

I want ... I want ... To ravish him.

'Ye gods, Ellie. If ye keep saying things like that this isn't going to last nearly as long as I had planned.'

She'd spoken aloud? Ellen froze, surprised at her own daring. But then she realised exactly what he'd said, and a thrill of excitement had her grinning. 'You have a plan?'

'Oh, aye. A most devilish plan that has consumed my thoughts these days and nights.'

The glint in his eyes had Ellen tugging up her skirts the rest of the way, and then his fingers were miraculously, wondrously gliding through her sex, parting her, exploring her. Her hips bucked towards him in a single violent, uncontrolled movement as she clung to his shoulders.

'An admirable plan,' she managed to gasp.

Calum gave her a wolfish smile and then leaned forward to nibble at her earlobe. His fingertip continued moving in tight circles, around and around that sweet spot that was making her arms tremble and her body vibrate. She gripped his shoulders. Otherwise she'd turn into a puddle on the floor at his feet.

It was never like this when she touched herself. That was always a half-rushed job, in the middle of the night, hidden away in the dark and under her counterpane.

This was slow and sensual; Calum was taking his damn time about it. It was the middle of the afternoon, and they stood before a window. If anyone came around the side of the house, there'd surely be a scandal.

'Ye feel like satin and cream.' His voice was a husky purr.

The last of the starch slipped from her body, followed by all rational thought. It was just Calum and his magic fingers. She half sighed, half moaned against his neck.

He chuckled under his breath. 'Music to my ears. Was that a once-off performance or can it be made on demand?'

The pressure building between her legs was almost unbearably glorious. She never wanted it to end, yet it was like she was dangling at the edge of a cliff, desperate to jump into the deep waters below. And then his thumb rolled over her nub. Her hips started to move again, seeking his touch. She grabbed his hand, dictating the pressure and direction of his fingers. *Harder.* 'Please!'

Calum was all too happy to comply. She raised one knee against the firm mass of his good leg to allow him better access.

Another sighing moan. Another chuckle.

Her eyes rolled, and she caught sight of their reflection in the glass panes of the long window. It was oh-so-beautiful. Calum's bottom lip was trapped between his teeth, his eyes were locked on her face and his back was pressed up against the closed door. Her own head was flung back, a dark stain of colour high on her cheeks. Her chest rising and falling with panting breaths, her breasts straining against the confines of her stays.

Fleetingly, she wondered if this was how Calum had been before the war, before the fire and the heartbreak. But then all thought escaped her as she fell, cascading down the waterfall on a cry of pleasure.

Catching her around the waist, he straightened and tucked her against his chest. His breathing was as erratic as hers. Two racing curricles headed down parallel roads.

'Marry me?'

Her head dropped to his shoulder. She was still trembling with the aftershock. 'Calum—' She struggled to contain her breaths. She was languid, sated even.

His gaze still burned hot.

She wanted more. She wanted him.

'Nay,' He growled a warning. 'Marry me.'

She hid her face in the lapel of his jacket, breathing in his scent: Clean like soap. A little tangy like orange marmalade. Heath, the undertones of whisky. If she could bottle it, she'd make a fortune. The women of the *ton* would probably crown her as their leader.

'I can't think straight with you so close.' She pressed a hand to his chest, intending to push him away. His heart beat against her palm, hard and fast.

He pressed his face to the top of her head so that every inch of her was touching some part of him. She could feel the hardness of his own arousal pushing aggressively against her stomach. Yet they still weren't close enough. Not while there was fabric between them.

'I could protect ye from the world. I could look after ye, give you a home. Ye'd want for nothing.'

She stumbled back a step, her feet as heavy and cumbersome as bricks. Cal's grip fell from her waist only as she moved beyond his reach. His arm hung in the air between them, his fingers twitching as though to pull her back against him.

'I know.' But being cared for wasn't enough. Being somebody's burden wasn't enough. She wanted more out of life. Maybe if he was offering his heart ... But that wasn't what he was doing. He didn't love her; he thought of her as someone to be saved. As he had been unable to save his brother.

His arms dropped to his side like a stone. 'I can hear the silent 'but' at the end of that sentence.'

She chose her next words with care. 'I want to be in control of my own life and not somebody's dependant. Surely you can understand that?'

Dependant: there was that word again. She hated it. Probably every woman in existence hated it.

'I didn't realise a life with me was so distasteful an idea. Ye'd rather risk the welfare of yerself and yer sister than marriage to me.'

'That's not what I meant and you know it.' She didn't take the bait, clenching her fists to keep herself from reaching out to him.

It had taken merely a fortnight for Geoffrey to track her down in London. How long would it be before he finally found Gwen, regardless of the efforts of Verity and Maggie? They couldn't keep moving Gwen from hiding place to hiding place. What kind of life was that for a child?

Better than being under Geoffrey's control.

Which was precisely why she couldn't marry Calum, despite her growing hunger for him.

As an independent woman, she could do all that was in her power to keep Gwen safe. As a married woman—married to a duke no less!—she'd be restricted both by Society and the law. No, earning a wage and paving her own way was the best thing she could give Gwen right now. Even if that meant Gwen had to live in hiding for a while longer.

She was still wet between the thighs. Perhaps she was supposed to feel ashamed, but she didn't. It felt more like a gift Calum had given her. It was just one she couldn't reciprocate.

She closed her eyes and clenched her legs together, seeking any sort of friction, any sort of release from this second wave of need.

She heard the rustle of his jacket tails as he stepped closer and she opened her eyes. He stood less than a foot away but made no move to pull her back into his arms.

She could see each of the small twisted scars of his burn. They cascaded down his forehead, narrowly missed his left eye and then moved down his cheek, twisting the left side of his mouth ever-so-slightly out of proportion. Running down his neck, the scars finally disappeared beneath his messily tied cravat.

She'd seen him without his shirt, seen the scars on his chest and back. He was touched by fire. There was fire in his veins, fire in his voice and fire in the heat of his kisses.

'Why is everything a hundred times harder when ye're around?' he demanded.

'I don't mean for it to be. I never meant for you to get caught up in my mess of a life.' Her gaze dropped to the hand he'd touched her with. Were his fingers still wet too? Did he smell like her? And now she'd refused his marriage offer, again, did he regret pleasuring her as he had?

Following her gaze, he shoved his hands into his pockets. 'If ye're not going to marry me, then what are we going to do?'

Chapter Fourteen

Tension crackled.

Cal didn't want to hear for the hundredth time of her idiotic intention to find employment elsewhere. 'In case ye've forgotten,' he said before she could start, 'Lady F is just down that hallway, and if ye think she's going to let you walk out of this house without a fight...' He shrugged, giving her a surely-you-know-better look. He couldn't help himself. Ellen might have made it abundantly clear she didn't want his help, but there was no way she could so easily brush aside his forthright grandmother. For all that she was short, Lady F had the temper of a lion and the voice of an elephant. And when it came to getting what she wanted, she could throw a tantrum better than any two-year-old.

'You're angry with me.'

'Nay.' He tried to school his expression into one of haughty disinterest.

Her frown deepened. 'Don't take it personally—'

How else am I supposed to fucking take it?

'Nay?' His voice dripped with sarcasm.

'For goodness sake, Calum, don't try to make me feel ashamed of what just happened here.' Colour burned her cheeks.

His fingers were still slick with her need and the air around her smelled of sugar and sex and hunger, drawing him in. Holding his ground, he clenched his hand still hidden in his pocket, holding onto a small essence of the beautiful, intelligent woman who wouldn't have him. 'I would never—' be began, but she wasn't finished with him.

'Yes, you're a duke. Yes, you're wealthy. Yes, you had a terrible war, family tragedies and horrible social injustices. But, Lord Woodhal, the world most certainly doesn't revolve around you.' She stalked towards him to poke a finger against his chest. 'My only concern is keeping Gwen safe from Geoffrey. And as far as I can tell, marrying you would only provide a short-term fix. I need to consider the wider consequences.'

The world doesn't revolve around you. He'd had a similar thought about Geoffrey.

'What do ye mean by a short-term fix?'

'Well, it would certainly free Gwen and me of Geoffrey, but then you'd be stuck with us forever.'

'And ye want yer independence.' Did she really think he'd lock her away like her brother had? Did she really think he'd keep her chained to his bed?

Nay. He'd give her an allowance and freedom to do as she wished.

But is an allowance freedom? No matter how much space he gave her, no matter how much money he gifted her, if they were married, she'd always be tied to him. She'd never be free to marry a man of her own choosing. A man without half his face torn up with scars. A man who wasn't haunted by thoughts of his dead brother.

He looked down at his chest where she was still touching him. It was just her fingertip but it felt like a tether. Through the touch of that single finger he could feel the rise and fall of her chest with each breath. He could feel the beat of her heart.

As though reading his mind, she snatched her hand back, stumbling away. Her calves hit the velvet footrest behind her, and she toppled backwards.

Cal caught her around the waist without hesitation. *Mine,* barked his inner voice, temporarily expelling all other thoughts from his mind.

She bristled at this helping hand, even as she struggled to find her footing. Upright, she pushed away from him and brushed her hands down her skirts, attempting to brush away the wrinkles. It was a fight even the enterprising Miss Ellen Burney couldn't win. They'd inadvertently crushed the faded cotton when they'd hiked her skirts up. Short of starching them, they were beyond saving. Any discerning person of an even slightly quizzical nature would surely guess what the two of them had been up in the library alone together.

Suddenly his need was as hard as it had ever been; his need to hold her, kiss her, love her was almost unbearable. *Hell and damnation.* He was so far out to sea, he couldn't see the shore.

He ground his teeth to keep from saying something stupid as lust and want and need began to fog his mind. If he tried to lay claim to her, she'd only back further away. Of that he was certain. Everything else was a bit hazy, like his plan to get her to trust him. That clearly wasn't progressing as smoothly as he'd have liked.

Marriage was still the most obvious and the easiest path to take. But it was also the path Ellie had upfront rejected. Short of forcing her—which he wouldn't ever consider doing—he'd just have to think of another way to keep both her and Gwen safe from Geoffrey. And, in doing so, show Ellie that he could be trusted.

He moved slowly away from the library door, providing her with an escape route, and planted himself firmly by the window. Normally he'd have sat at his desk. Sitting was kinder on his wounded knee than standing, but he didn't think being behind the desk would work in his favour right now.

Sunlight warmed the back of his neck, and he turned slightly so the light was on his face. He didn't have anything to hide, not from Ellie. 'What do ye think we should do?' he asked again.

She continued to bristle, reminding him of a loaded canon—her tinder line was burning down and she was lining up her shot, about to fire.

'I'm sincerely trying to help,' he hurriedly added, raising his hands before his chest in a gesture of surrender.

'I'm not sure you've been sincere about anything in your life, Calum Callaghan,' she scolded in that prim and proper voice she used when admonishing him. 'But, since you asked so nicely, maybe Lady Faye will return the character reference Verity wrote for me. The letter will be of some assistance when looking for new employment. After that, I'll keep a low profile so Geoffrey won't be able to find me again, and I'll continue to save my wage for Gwen.'

'And when Lady F tries to lock ye away in one of the upstairs bedrooms for yer own safety?'

She started pacing circles around the library, running a hand along the dusty bookshelves.

'Or, saying ye do find respectable employment, what will happen when Geoffrey tracks ye down again? Because he will. Ye can't remain hidden forever. And I didn't think any other employer will be quite as understanding as Lady F.'

'He won't...' She faltered.

'Maybe he doesn't stay in London. Maybe he returns to the country. Ye said Gwen is near Evendale, so what happens when he eventually finds her? It took him hardly any time to find ye.'

'Fine!' She smacked down on the bookcase. 'What do you suggest I do?'

'I'm not trying to discourage ye from action,' he said honestly. 'I'm just not sure ye've thought everything through with clarity. I personally think we were on the right track earlier. I should bring Gwen to London. She'll be safer under this roof where we can all keep an eye on her. After that...' He ran a hand through his hair. An absurd idea was beginning to form. But it might actually work. 'What if we pretended we're engaged? I could have an announcement printed in newspaper.'

'Whyever for?' She wrinkled her nose in confusion.

He tried not to take it personally.

'It's not going to take Geoffrey long to realise we're not actually married. But if he sees the engagement notice in the papers, he'll realise there's nothing he can do to make ye return to Evendale with him, and he'll eventually get bored and leave.' His plan had absolutely nothing at all to do with not wanting to let Ellie out of his sight ever again. Absolutely nothing. This was all for her benefit.

'I see...'

She didn't look convinced. Or perhaps she couldn't even stand the idea of a fake engagement with him of all people. He flexed his hands. 'Ye needn't worry about being tainted by my reputation,' he assured her, trying but failing to keep the peevish edge from his voice. 'Owen tells me I've been quite forgotten these last few years.' He looked towards his desk. His collection of newspaper clippings on the ship fire had been haphazardly pushed to the far corner and his estate papers, which usually graced the dining room table, had been rearranged over the free space, courtesy of his meddling family.

'I wasn't suggesting that would be the case.'

'As soon as Geoffrey leaves London, we can break the engagement and ye can spend the rest of the Season gainfully employed as Lady F's companion, and yer sister will be safe here with us.'

'Are you sure you want another person living under your roof?'

'Aye. I've been alone for four long years. I think I can survive a couple of months with house guests.'

She still didn't look convinced.

He wanted to throw his arms in the air and start swearing black and blue. Instead, he held his temper in check. 'What are ye worried about now, lass?' Sure, it wasn't the best plan. Sure, life would be better if she didn't have a malodorous brother trying to manipulate her every move. But as she'd said herself, he was offering her a temporary solution to all her troubles.

'I just don't see why you're doing this for me. What do you get out of it?'

You! that traitorous voice in his head yelled. *All of you.* 'Do ye really think I'd get a second of peace from Lady F if I did nothing to help?'

***

Calum left London within the hour. Ellen only wished she could have gone with him, but travelling always made her feel so ill she'd only have slowed him down. And right now, speed was of the essence. There was no knowing what Geoffrey would do next.

As soon as he was out of sight, Owen locked the front door with a large brass key. 'The whole house is under martial law,' he declared. 'Nobody's to leave without informing me first.'

'Piddle paddle!' scoffed Lady Faye.

'It's called a safety precaution.'

'It's called power hungry.'

Owen just shook his head. 'I'm going to make sure all the windows are latched closed.'

'Whyever for?' the dowager frowned at his retreating back. 'It's not like Geoffrey's going to climb in through a window. What's gotten into him?'

'He loves you, and he's worried,' replied Ellen, desperately trying to ignore the guilt swirling around her stomach. They wouldn't have to be doing all of this if it weren't for her.

'Idiot boy.' But Lady Faye's gaze softened. 'Cal told me of your engagement.'

'Fake engagement,' Ellen hurried to correct.

'Details, details. I'm absolutely delighted. I was beginning to doubt he'd ever leave this house again. And now he's out and about, rescuing a lassie and marrying—'

'*Pretending to be engaged* to the sister of a bankrupt baron.'

Lady Faye's levelled her gaze on Ellen. 'I have a new house rule for you, gel. Stop defining yourself by the actions of your brother.'

'I'm just—'

'And no apologising for his indiscretions either. Understand me?'

'Yes, but—'

'And promise you'll let me help plan your wedding.'

'We're not really getting married!'

'Perfect.' The dowager smiled. 'Now kiss my cheek, for you're to be my first granddaughter.' She titled her head to the side, presenting Ellen with one papery cheek and no way to argue.

Her skin was cool to the touch and she smelled of lavender soap.

'Ah, I've just remembered,' said Ellen. 'I should have asked you earlier, but how did your visit to Grace go?'

Lady Faye's face clouded over.

Ellen winced. 'I see. I'm sorry.' No wonder she'd returned home so soon—returned home to find Geoffrey ranting and raving.

A bell rang, the sound echoing from the kitchen down the narrow passage.

'What was that?' Owen dashed towards them. There were spider webs in his hair, like he'd been crawling around the attic or maybe through Grace's half of the house. His poor waistcoat.

'Evidently someone wants to come inside,' answered Lady Faye turning to the front door. 'Who's there?'

'It could be Geoffrey returned,' hissed Owen.

'Or it could be one of the servants. You locked the back door too, remember.' The dowager pressed her eye to the keyhole. 'I can see you. Announce yourself.'

A shuffling. A cough. An awkward silence. 'Umm ... I have a delivery for Lady Faye from Miss Bond.'

'Fantastic!' Lady Faye straightened. 'Well,' she demanded of Owen. 'You heard the boy. Open the door immediately.'

'I'm not so sure.' Owen teetered on the spot. 'He could easily be lying.'

'Open. The. Door. Tattershall.' Her voice held a warning note, and Owen relented. Snatching the box from the frazzled carrier, he thrust a generous tip at him before slamming the door closed and locking it again with a swift click.

Lady Faye took the box, indicating Ellen should follow her back into the drawing room. 'I ordered this as a surprise for you, back when we had that dress fitting. Mademoiselle Bond promised to send it along as soon as it was ready.' She snapped the door closed, leaving Owen high and dry in the passage without an apology. 'She finished it sooner than I was expecting. Lucky this one didn't need a return fitting.'

'My lady...' Ellen gestured towards the door.

'Serves him right for thinking he can refuse my delivery.' She handed the box to Ellen, crowding in close to get a good look. 'Open it.'

'You shouldn't have.' More guilt lumped in her stomach like a waxy ball of tallow.

'Open it.' She nudged Ellen with her elbow.

Nestled in a cloud of white tissue paper sat a small card with the words 'Mademoiselle Bond of House of Bond, Bond Street' printed on one side, and on the other side there was a handwritten note.

Something to make you glow.

With shaking hands, Ellen lifted out the most exquisite nightdress she'd ever seen. Made of the lightest cream muslin with delicate lace edgings and tiny mother of pearl buttons, the nightdress had an empire waistline and short puffed sleeves. The matching wrapper was a little simpler with a single tie that fastened under the bust.

Her mouth dropped open.

'I know you didn't want me to buy you anything else,' Lady Faye said with a self-satisfied smile. 'But, if the state of your morning dresses are anything to go on, your nightrail isn't fit to be seen either.'

'It's...' Beautiful didn't seem adequate. *Pure decadence.*

'Rather French, eh?' Lady Faye wiggled her eyebrows.

'Now you mention it.' It did look rather like the nightdress described in the boudoir novel.

'A happy coincidence,' Lady Faye assured her with a chuckle. 'Put this on and Cal won't be able to take his eyes off you, my gel.'

'That's your grandson you're talking about! And you do realise we're not actually getting married?'

'Phiff! Details, details.'

Chapter Fifteen

Miss Guinevere didn't like him one bit. She clung to the skirts of a woman he could only assume was Miss Miller and glared at him through the curtain of her dark curls with such ferocity her displeasure was almost palpable. He paused on his way towards the front door, keeping his distance.

'Who are you?' An aggressive flush sat high on Maggie Miller's cheeks. She had her hands tucked behind her back and her shoulders set straight as a ship's main mast. With her mottled brown and grey hair she resembled a tall tabby cat guarding her precious kitten.

There was another woman who watched him warily through the kitchen window. Probably the sister-in-law who's cottage this was.

'I'm not going to hurt you,' he repeated.

'Then what exactly are you doing here?'

'I'm a friend of Ellie's ahh ... Miss Burney.'

Gwen started at that the sound of her sister's name, but she didn't make a sound. Even half hidden, there was no doubt she was related to his Ellie. They shared the same dark eyebrows, the same small chin.

He knew nothing of children, so he forced a smile. 'Hello there ... little one.'

Gwen's glare instantly magnified.

He turned hastily to Maggie. 'I have a note of introduction from Miss Burney explaining why I've come and what's to be done next.' There'd be no point trying to explain anything else until Maggie had read the letter. Judging by his less than warm welcome, they wouldn't believe him even if he tried. He held up the sealed letter to show her.

Maggie's stern manner didn't relent. In this scenario, he was like an unknown dog. To them, he surely looked a lot like Tzar—with his scarred muzzle and the chunk missing from his ear.

Cal turned his head, presenting them with his good side. 'I'll give you time to think in peace. When you're ready to talk, I'll be waiting in the lane.' He placed the letter on the garden path, donning his hat and retreating back down the lane to his waiting horse.

**

Sophy Calder appeared overnight.

Ellen rested a hand on the cool glass of the half-window of the ballroom. It couldn't be a coincidence that the woman she'd bumped into at the fireworks was now surveying the house from across the street.

Her dress was almost identical to the one she'd been wearing the other night, with its faded linsey apron. In the sunlight, her hair shone an even brighter red, the old straw bonnet doing little to disguise her locks.

The neighbour's second footman, dressed in ostentatious livery of blue and gold, approached. They conversed for a few minutes, but Sophy shook her head and eventually he retreated. A few moments later the second footman returned accompanied by the first footman and the butler. They kept gesturing for her to leave, but she would not be told.

The servants disappeared inside again, and a family of five girls and their mother stepped out. They marched from the house, resolutely ignoring Sophy as they passed, and clambered into a crowed closed-roof town coach. The driver set the greys in motion and they disappeared around the corner in the direction of the Pantheon Arcade at a fast trot.

Their papa's pocketbook was going to be considerably lighter by day's end.

The old townhouse creaked in the silence. Everything seemed so much quieter without Calum around. Ellen shuffled from foot to foot. He'd only been gone a day and a half and wasn't supposed to return for another day and a half.

To make matters worse, her menses had arrived the other night. Her breasts and abdomen ached and she felt generally out of sorts, like she was on the verge of crying.

She watched as Sophy's gaze roamed over the large yew tree and its resident crow to the two matching front doors and the disused ballroom balcony. Looking straight at the ballroom window, she raised a hand and waved.

Ellen spun on her heels, retreating to the kitchen.

'Miss.' Cook bobbed head and knees. 'I'm just about to take up a tray for her ladyship. Can I get you anything?'

'No. Thank you.' Ellen's stomach churned at the thought of food. She bent to pat Tzar's head. He was sitting by the range, keeping an eye on the tray of food Cook was carrying. As she left the kitchen, Tzar sighed, clambered to his feet and trotted after her, his waging tail in a wave goodbye.

The stockpot full of Calum's marmalade was still on the sideboard. Cook had tried to decant it into smaller jars, but it was particularly thick and nothing short of sheer determination was enough to move more than a teaspoon at a time. And at the centre of the long table was the square cake tin wrapped in a thick chain and secured with the padlock. Chakrabarti had tried to pick the lock to no avail.

Ellen walked a lap of the kitchen, letting the warmth from the hearth seep into her hands and feet. This room even smelled a little of Calum. There was a bottle of half-drunk whisky on the sideboard and one of his old cloaks hanging on a hook by the door. He was probably the only duke to ever make himself comfortable in his own kitchen. She smiled. He was probably the only duke who even knew how to find his own kitchen.

'I have a missive for you, Miss...' Chakrabarti stood on the threshold, one foot in the kitchen and one foot out. 'It was pushed under the front door. I didn't mean to read it, but it's not sealed.' He held it out to her, refusing to make eye contact.

'Not sealed' was an understatement. It was just an old calling card with battered corners. The name and address had been crossed out and on the back someone had scrawled a single sentence.

I'm coming for you, whore.

It hadn't even been signed. Not that it mattered. There was no mistaking Geoffrey's handwriting. 'Did you see who delivered it?'

'No, Miss ahh ... Burney.'

She winced. Burney, not Smith. The servants knew about her brother. Did they all hate her now they knew she was a liar?

'Are you all right?'

He nodded, staring down at his shoes—a reliable pair of black buckled boots.

'My brother—' She stopped, unsure about where to take that sentence. Then another thought occurred to her. 'I like to think we were friends when I was her ladyship's companion. And we're friends still, if that's alright with you.'

'Now you're His Grace's fiancée?'

Fake fiancée. But she couldn't tell him that. The fewer people who knew, the safer it was for Gwen. *You're good a keeping secrets,* scoffed a voice in her head. *Will you ever not be living a lie?* 'Still friends,' she repeated allowed.

He smiled, visibly relaxing. 'We'll keep you safe. Your brother won't find his way back into this house.'

'Thank you.' She forced a return smile then looked back down at the card in her hand. Geoffrey was like a snake in the grass. He'd always preferred to do his bullying from the shadows. Verity called it a muzzle move, like in boxing. Ellen just called it cowardly.

A ring sounded and they both glanced towards the bell board. Someone was at the front door.

'I didn't realise we were expecting visitors.'

'We aren't.' Chakrabarti hurriedly tugged at the lapel of his jacket and headed down the passage to answer it. He reappeared a few moments later and passed Ellen another calling card. This one was clean and crisp, with elegant handwriting announcing their guest.

'She asked for her ladyship,' he said, as Ellen stared down at the name.

'Then you'd better send Pamela up to wake her at once. Lady Faye isn't going to want to miss seeing her daughter.'

***

Cal gave a well-practiced bow, acknowledging Maggie as she strode towards him down the lane. The overgrown gooseberry hedges either side provided the perfect cover for a private conversation. Howbeit, they prevented Cal from seeing very far in either direction, so if anyone came across them there wouldn't be much warning.

Ellie's friend dipped into a curtsey. 'It seems you were telling the truth after all, Your Grace. I would know Ellen's handwriting anywhere.' Her eyes flickered to the scars on his face. She was uncomfortable being so close to him but doing a very good job at hiding it—a better job than the half the *ton*.

Judging by her worn dress, her deportment and her manner of speaking, she was probably the daughter of the local parson or a respectable farmer. Her hand was free of a wedding ring though she was closer to forty than he was.

'I'm to take Miss Guinevere to London, to Miss Burney.'

Maggie nodded. 'I'm a little relieved. We've been convinced Geoffrey will appear up the lane at any moment, but Verity—that is, Mrs Nott is having trouble finding us new accommodation.'

'If you pack Gwen's belongings into a small bag, we'll leave as soon as possible.'

'Where's the carriage?' Miss Miller leaned around him to frown at his single horse.

As he'd ridden almost non-stop for a day and a half, resting only for a few hours at a posting-house, he'd long since swapped the black gelding he'd borrowed from Owen for a hire horse. His current ride was a chestnut mare who'd been slow to get going but who'd kept up a steady pace with a little bribery.

'We don't need a carriage. Miss Guinevere will be quite safe riding in front of me.' The mare would barely even notice the added weight of the child.

'You're not leaving me behind.' Maggie's eyes flashed something fierce. 'Your Grace,' she added quickly.

'We don't have time for this.' Calum barely resisted tossing his hands in the air in suddenly exasperation. 'Gwen will come with me. You're not in any personal danger from Blackford, are you?'

'He doesn't care a tuppence about me. It's the girls he wants, but that doesn't mean I'm letting you take Gwen away from me. She'd terrified of men. You'll give her palpitations.'

'It cannot be all that bad.'

'Just because you say something doesn't make it true. Geoffrey hit her, for goodness sakes.' She stared him down. She was nearly as tall as he was, nearly eye to eye with him. If Ellen and Lady F had taught him anything about women it was that this fight was over long before it had even begun.

'Fine,' he growled. 'I'll hire a carriage from the village. Be ready to leave in two hours.'

***

Evendale proper liked Cal about as much as the wee Miss Guinevere did.

Passersby glared at him as he rode down Main Street. Their eyes bored into his back and their snide whispers stung his ears. They mightn't know he was a duke, but half his face looked like it had been to hell and back, and that was more than enough fodder to feed their imaginations.

Which was exactly why he hated leaving his house.

Yes, he was used to people staring. They'd stared at him most of his life. After all, he was the half-Scottish son of a duke and he looked nothing like his father. But since the age of ten, he'd had Pierce by his side, and the two of them had held their heads high. It had made him feel dangerous and desired. Between Pierce's blond hair and blue eyes, and Calum's darker looks, they'd been the centre of everyone's attention. The ladies of the *ton* had found the pair irresistible, and, if he was being completely honest, he'd rather enjoyed the attention.

But now the staring was nothing more than judgemental. And he no longer had Pierce by his side.

Not that he'd left his townhouse much these last four years; he hadn't travelled further than the House of Lords and only when they were to vote on a particularly important piece of reform legislation. He was a Whig and an abolitionist loud and proud. Ten years fighting at sea could do that to man.

Cal tugged on the upturned collar of his greatcoat, refusing to meet anyone's eyes. He was here for one reason and one reason only.

Ellie. He had better things to worry about than a handful of ill-mannered country knaves.

A row of cottages lined Main Street, a medieval church dominating one end. Its graveyard likely housed more headstones than people currently living in Evendale, including Ellen's parents.

With those bruises, Ellie was lucky not to be buried in that graveyard. *Lucky?* He ground his teeth. There was nothing lucky about being dragged about by your own brother until your wrists turned black and blue.

The air might be clearer out this way and the fields greener, but this was where Blackford lived and that made it rotten.

He dismounted outside the one and only posting-house, aptly named *The Sinking Ship*, and left his horse with the waiting ostler, a boy of no more than eleven or twelve. If he was going to find a carriage in this middle-of-nowhere village, the posting-house would be the place to ask.

A loud bang reverberated around the village.

Cal's heart leaped into his mouth. 'What the hell was that?' He sought signs of an attack. His wounded knee started to give way and he to press a hand to his horse to keep himself upright.

The ostler squinted up at him, his hand shielding his eyes from the glare of the sun. 'It's just a farmer popping a couple of rabbits.'

'Right.' Cal forced his knee to straighten and take his weight again. Just a farmer. Shooting rabbits. Of course. This was the country after all. *Goddamn country!*

'You good, sir?'

'Aye, of course.' He wiped a hand over his mouth, where sweat had gathered on his top lip, then tossed the ostler another coin.

Inside, a hush fell over the diners as Cal shrugged off his greatcoat and stamped his feet to rid his boots of excess mud, then he shoved his shaking hands into his pockets.

Mismatched tables littered the taproom. The grimy windows let in very little natural light and the candles had dripped tallow over all the tables. Everything smelled of burned fat.

He ordered food and found an empty table.

'You're not from around here.' A gentleman stopped by his table. He smiled down at Cal, his thumbs tucked into the pockets of his catskin waistcoat.

'Nay.' Cal focused on his meal, waiting for him to leave. He wasn't in a very charitable mood. He was still a little clammy, and his gaze seemed determined to jump continuously towards the door as though Boney and his army were going to come sailing into the taproom at any moment. Maybe he should have requested a table in the private parlour.

'A Scot?' The catskin pulled up a chair.

Calum preserved a weary silence, choosing not to grace that question with an answer.

'Never mind my forwardness, sir. It's my unofficial job to keep an eye on any strangers we have passing through. Although'—his eyes roamed over the cut of Cal's mud-splattered jacket and looked impressed—'you're not exactly the normal type of visitor we get.'

'You the local magistrate?' He very carefully kept his voice clean of his childhood accent. He was tired, otherwise he wouldn't have made such a slip already.

'Ha! Nothing so sinister. Dr Audley. Pleased to make your acquaintance.' The catskin stuck out his hand, confident his unorthodox introduction couldn't be unwelcome, an idea that likely originated from the same place as his ridiculously flamboyant lace shirt cuffs. He was by far the most exuberantly dressed man in the establishment. His clothes would have given poor Owen nightmares for weeks.

Then again, his eyes were rather glassy and his speech slurred. This catskin wasn't so skilled at holding his drink.

He pulled his chair even closer, completely unfazed. 'Look, I didn't want to say anything but you've kind of got everyone on edge.'

Cal met his gaze, refusing to break the tension. The other man had started this conversation; he could damn well finish it.

'Those are really quite impressive burn scars? Get them in the war?'

Still Cal held motionless.

'I served too.' He pulled back a little of his cravat to reveal a small, shallow scar about half the length of Cal's smallest finger. He had to squint to see it.

Still, service was service. 'Navy,' Cal acknowledged grudgingly.

'Army for me. Spain. So, what's brought you to our small corner of the world?'

'I'm looking for someone.' There was no way Cal was going to tell this busybody—even if he had been a fellow man-in-arms—about Gwen. 'Baron Blackford. You know of him?'

'Blackford, sure. He's in here most days.' He jerked his head towards the back of the taproom. At a glance, there appeared to be a gambling table, with cards and dice and coin and men with that look of desperation they always seemed to wear when they'd lost their wages to vice. 'Although I can't say I've seen him in here for a while. Apparently his sister went missing, the minx.'

'Er?' Cal raised a single eyebrow, preserving a calm composure.

'Blackford's gone crazy looking for her. He's even offered up a reward. Whoever uncovers her whereabouts gets twenty pounds.'

'A considerable sum.'

'I know. The sop actually won at cards.' The catskin shook his head with a laugh. 'After all these years, he finally found some Irish luck.'

'And he's willing to spend all his winnings on finding his sister?' What did Geoffrey want with Ellie? The man was obsessed.

'Not just Ellen. He wants that dumb girl too. Guinevere. Blackford's face almost turned purple when he found out they'd gotten away. He was in here ranting and raving.' He pulled a flask from his pocket, opened it with long-practiced ease and gulped down a mouthful, with a furtive glance towards the barman.

If he wasn't drunk from dawn to dusk, Cal would be very surprised. God help his patients. 'Why do you think he even cares about finding them so much? Wouldn't he be glad to be rid of them if he was having money problems?' Geoffrey hadn't exactly struck Cal as a family man.

The catskin's eyes narrowed and he pulled away from Cal. 'Why exactly are you looking for him?'

'No reason concerning yourself.'

He gave Cal a blurry-eyed once-over. 'Ho! You know where is she.' He threw back his head and laughed. 'I'm thinking you're not interested in twenty pounds.'

'Not particularly.' Cal returned to his dinner.

'She's not worth your effort, friend. She's gotten herself into trouble before. A disgrace to her parents.' He was grinning like a fool, relishing the power a little information gave him. 'Of course, I can't tell you what she did. I've been sworn to secrecy.' And he patted his breast pocket, jiggling a couple of coins.

'Tell me.'

'Not likely. Unless...' He patted his pocket again. 'I reckon you've got more money than anyone round here. How about helping out a former soldier?' He laughed again. The snide jackass.

Cal ran a hand over his scratchy chin. He hadn't had time to shave since leaving London. And he certainly didn't have time for games. He stood, the legs of his chair scrapping along the sticky floor. Pressing his hands to the tabletop, he leaned over the doctor. 'You want to know who I really am? I'm the goddamn Duke of Woodhal. Now tell me what I want to know.'

'A what now?' His month opened and closed. He couldn't have looked more stunned if he'd been kicked by a fish. Suddenly his eyes widened in shock. 'Captain Callaghan? *The* Captain Callaghan? I didn't recognise you.'

'Not Captain anymore. I sold out.' But not before his ship had caught fire, his brother had died and his reputation had been destroyed. 'And you've been disrespected my future duchess.'

'Crazy Calum.' The doctor licked his lips, glancing around the taproom. 'I ... That is ... Blackford blames Ellen—ah, Miss Burney for everything.' He spoke quickly and quietly. 'His gambling and money problems. He says everything changed seven years ago, when...'

'When what?'

'I'm not supposed to say. The family made me swear.'

'When what, Dr Audley?'

'When Ellen went and got herself pregnant.'

Chapter Sixteen

'Lady Grace Callaghan isn't one to be kept waiting,' said Owen, ushering Ellen out the door before him. She'd found him in the dining room reading the boudoir novel with an open mouth, but he'd put the book aside as soon as she'd announced their unexpected visitor.

'Surely she doesn't want to see me?' Ellen looked at him over her shoulder. Beads of sweat dotted his brow.

'She couldn't have come at a worse time.' Completely ignoring her query, he corralled her into the front room. 'Grace,' he said with a formal bow. Then he gestured towards Ellen. 'This is Miss Burney, your mother's companion.'

'So the rumours are true.' Seated in the very centre of the settee, the duchess surveyed the room as though atop a throne. Her shoulders were so straight even Maggie would have been impressed, and she swept her gaze around the room with a disapproving frown, clearly having decided Ellen deserved no more of her attention. It was quite remarkable the furniture didn't sink through the floor in shame. 'I see some things never change.'

Ellen pressed her mouth closed. As a companion, it was not her place to speak unless spoken to. Grace's own lady's companion was seated at the desk, the only other seat available. Her hands were tucked neatly in her lap and she was resolutely staring at the Persian rug.

'Lizzy is resting at the moment,' continued Owen. 'But we've sent her maid up to wake her, so she should be down in a—'

'I'm not here to see my mother. I'm here to discuss something with my stepson.' One of Grace's eyes twitched at her mention of Calum. Tzar nudged her knee with his nose, his tail wagging feverishly.

'Wood isn't home at the moment.'

'Not home? Whyever not? Did he die or something?'

'Of course not,' snapped Ellen without thinking. 'Your Grace,' she added quickly. *What a ridiculous thing to say.* Calum was perfectly safe and sound. As were Gwen and Maggie and Verity. She resisted the urge to cross her arms and glare at the duchess.

But Grace didn't even favour Ellen with a glance. 'His whereabouts matter little to me,' she said to Owen, her self-composure returning as quickly as it had slipped. 'What I really want to know is why this house is closed to visitors?'

'Wood never has any visitors.'

'But my mother does. And while Society is being turned away at the door, gossip is spreading faster and further around London. It's the latest *on dit,* and it reflects badly upon me.' She flicked an invisible fleck of dust from her skirt. Four years after her son's death and she was still wearing half mourning.

Where Lady Faye was short and plump, Grace was tall and curvaceous. The weight sat well on her figure and her gown hugged her body in all the right places. She was a woman who knew the power of her curves and she used her size to command the attention of the room.

In that way, she looked more like Calum than Calum's own blood relatives, with her dark hair and her dark eyes and her widow's weeds.

'Lizzy would never do anything intentionally to hurt you,' said Owen. 'It's just that she didn't come to London to entertain. She came to see her family.'

Grace's eyes narrowed. 'What's going on here, Tattershall? What aren't you telling me?'

'Absolutely nothing.' Owen spread his arms out before him in the least convincing lie of all time.

'What's. Going. On?' Grace punctuated each word with deep, angry exhales.

A knot of annoyance tightened in Ellen's chest, and Owen tugged at his cravat. Only Tzar appeared unfazed. He pressed himself as close to Grace as possible, sitting on her slippered feet—ridiculously fashionable shoes of crimson wool that would probably die of fright at the first sight of a muddy puddle.

Ellen's own half-boots were decidedly more practical, but beside the duchess's rich wardrobe, she must look a fright. *You look like a down-on-your-lucky lady's companion,* she reminded herself. Which was precisely what she was.

'Tattershall,' Grace warned.

'There's nothing ... Wood's not home ... wedding...'. Owen mumbled, staring at the shiny buttons of his own waistcoat.

'I'm afraid we can't offer you tea,' Ellen said, hurriedly. 'Our cake is rather tied up at moment. And as Owen said, Lady Faye isn't receiving visitors at the moment. Although I'm sure she'd be delighted to see you.'

But Grace had frozen. 'Wedding? What wedding?' Finally, painstakingly slowly, she turned her full attention onto Ellen. 'You! He might be a duke, but you do realise that he's half Scottish and a murderer? What, Miss Lady's Companion, could possibly have you desperate enough to marry Calum of all men?'

Geoffrey! Ellen plastered a smile onto her face even as her heart started racing. She wanted to wipe that knowing expression off Grace's face. Calum might be a little grumpy—a little, ha!—but he was also kind and thoughtful, and he absolutely positively wasn't responsible for Lieutenant Callaghan's death. Whyever couldn't Grace understand that? Lady Faye and Owen could. 'Oh, phiff,' she said dismissively. 'Haven't you heard? It's a love match.'

Grace rose, dislodging Tzar. The difference in height had Ellen almost despairing. 'Is this true?' she demanded of Owen.

'Y-yes.' He nodded. 'Wood can't keep his hands off her.'

Thank you, Mr Tattershall! Ellen rubbed the back of her neck. Was he bluffing, or had he seen them together?

'Calum is making the wedding cake himself,' she added quickly.

'Now that I do believe. He was always messing around in the kitchen when he was a child. May I assume I'm invited to the wedding?'

'Of course,' said Owen. 'Lizzy wouldn't have it any other way. We'll send you an invitation with all the details. It's only going to be a small, family ceremony with breakfast back here at the house.'

Was it? When had Owen decided on the details of her and Calum's fake wedding?

'I suppose that means I'll have to give you a wedding gift.' Grace sighed just as dramatically as her mother was prone to doing. 'I know. I'll gift you my side of the house.' She smiled.

'You're going to need it.' And with that she glided from the room in a swirl of mauve skirts, followed by her lady's companion and one ratty old dog.

The front door shut, and from the hallway came Tzar's whimpering cry.

'What just happened?' Ellen blinked.

Owen wiped his face with his pocket handkerchief. 'Sweetheart, she didn't mean—'

'Yes, she did.' Two wedding gifts in the space of two days. The beautiful nightgown from the dowager and now half a house. She didn't know which one to feel more guilty about. It was a lonely, empty half a house that had already seen one broken marriage and was about to be caught up in the drama of a fake engagement.

'Grace?' Lady Faye hurried into the drawing room. There were lines on her face from the wrinkles in her pillowcase. Her smile faltered as she looked between Ellen and Owen. 'Where's my daughter?'

***

Gwen watched him from across the table through eyes as dark as her mother's.

'Are you not hungry?' Cal nodded to her untouched dinner. 'We won't be stopping again until morning, so you should eat something now.'

She looked questioningly towards Maggie. The older woman wrapped an arm about her shoulders, pulling the child closer to her side.

When he'd first set eyes on Gwen, he'd thought Ellen's likeness strong in her face, and now he knew why.

Ellen only went and got herself pregnant. The doctor's words raced each other through his mind along with many questions, each worse than the last. It was like there was a storm raging inside him, and Cal was hard-pressed to keep it from showing on his face.

Who was Gwen's father? Where was he now? Was he still alive? How much did Geoffrey know? Was Gwen illegitimate? Hell, what if Ellen was actually already married?

A lump the size of a large boulder settled in his stomach, and he pushed his own plate of food away.

Is that why she'd refused his offer? Because she was already married.

Ellen. Pregnant.

After his shock announcement the doctor had glanced over his shoulder as though worried Geoffrey might come striding into the taproom. 'It all happened back when their parents were still alive, Johnathan and Guinevere Burney,' he continued.

'Gwen was named after Ellen's mother then?'

The catskin shrugged, clearly uninterested in names. 'I'm still not entirely sure how it happened but it was put about town that the baroness had fallen pregnant and was ill with it.' He leaned forward conspiratorially, the inside of his collar dampened with sweat. 'Ellen stayed up at the house for months and months supposedly looking after her mother. Only I know it was Ellen who was actually pregnant because I attended the birth. It was complicated.' He blinked, memories clouding his vision for a heartbeat. 'That's why they called me up to the big house. All the servants had been given the night off. Nobody was ever supposed to know the truth but the family—and then me.'

And now Cal.

'You won't tell anyone about this conversation, will you?'

'Scared of Geoffrey?' Cal scoffed. The doctor was at least a head taller than that numbskull and an ex-Army to boot.

'Blackford pays me well to keep my mouth shut.'

'I see.' A doctor who was easily bought off. Cal's estimation of the man sank even further. What other secrets was he being paid to keep? 'I thought Blackford was broke.'

'Doesn't matter how much he loses at the tables, he always makes sure he can pay me on time.'

'And Gwen's father?' The moment the words left his mouth Cal hated himself for asking. He shouldn't be prying. It wasn't any of his business. But then again, how was he supposed to protect Ellie if he didn't know the whole story? She certainly hadn't offered up the information freely. Just another secret she hadn't trusted him with.

The catskin shrugged. 'Don't know. Doubt it's anyone local, otherwise it wouldn't be such a secret. Things like that tend to rise to the surface in a place this small.'

'And Ellen's parents: what did they think?'

He shook his head. 'Her mother was dead in the next room.'

'What?' Cal's mouth dropped open. 'You mean...'

'That's right. Turns out she really was ill.' He took another swing from his flask. 'The baroness died the same night Ellen's daughter was born. The timing couldn't have been more perfect, and word spread that she'd died in labour. Nobody ever questioned it.'

Perfect timing? *Jackass!* 'And Blackford—ah, Geoffrey?' he corrected, making the distinction between Ellen's brother and her late father.

He shrugged again. 'Up at Oxford. He came home for his mother's funeral of course. But he wasn't around much those next few years. I always got the impression the old Lord Blackford didn't want his son in the house.' He raised his arms behind his head, once again comfortable with the conversation. He actually thought he'd done Cal a favour warning him off Ellen.

Cal gave his head a little shake, focusing his thoughts back on the present. It was Little Miss Guinevere and Maggie Miller sitting before him now, not the good-for-nothing country doctor. And they were many miles from Evendale.

Still, he should have called out that doctor. He should have challenged him to a good ol' fashioned illegal duel—pistols at twenty paces at the crack of dawn.

To hell with the man. So what if Gwen was Ellen's daughter. Who was Cal to judge? His mother had abandoned his father and run back to Scotland when she was supposedly pregnant with him. She'd sworn with her dying breath that he was Hammond's true son, but they'd never looked anything alike. Everyone in London had thought it.

An illegitimate duke?

Cal pushed his chair back with such force it toppled over. Gwen jumped. 'I'll give you two some space to finish eating. But don't take too long. We're running late as it is.'

In just two days he'd gained a fake fiancée, a fake soon-to-be stepdaughter and a ... Maggie. God help him. Lady F was going to be simply thrilled. The more the merrier in her opinion.

Verity

Duke of Woodhal ... To London ... Saved at last...

Verity read Maggie's missive three times in quick succession.

She'd come to tell Maggie that she's finally secured a new hiding place for them. She'd called in favours she'd been saving since before her husband's death and had found an elderly woman in Bath who was happy to take in a respectable 'governess' and her young charge for the spring months—for a fee, of course.

The fee had been more difficult to find. The annual interest on the dowry her husband had been presented with on their marriage was barely substantial enough to cover the rent of her small cottage. So in the end she'd had to sell the last of her mother's pearls.

All of that and she'd missed Maggie and Gwen by just a couple of hours.

The coins sat heavy in her pocket. It felt like dirty money. Like she'd somehow betrayed her mother's memory. But it had been worth it, to keep Ellen and Gwen safe from Geoffrey. To keep Maggie safe.

But what could Verity do for them that a duke couldn't do tenfold? A hundredfold?

She looked around. She'd subconsciously started walking away from the cottage and down the lane towards ... This wasn't the way home. This was the way to London.

She looked down at the letter again. However had Maggie expressed it?

The duke will personally accompany us to London. I think, finally, the girls will be safe. Geoffrey will surely not attempt anything foolish under the watchful eye of a duke.

Verity let out of a huff of air. It was ridiculous thinking she could follow; she'd never catch up to them now.

A minute ago, she'd had a purpose—to protect. Now she was at a loss. She turned around. Perhaps it was time to head home. Although, somehow, the empty cottage no longer felt quite enough.

Chapter Seventeen

'Lo! That's startlingly red hair.'

Ellen jumped then smiled at Owen over her shoulder. 'I didn't realise you were there.'

He stepped up beside her, resting a hand on the windowsill. 'What's she doing?'

'I'm not sure.' Ellen turned her attention back to Sophy Calder. 'She appeared two days ago and has been watching the house ever since.'

Owen's lips formed an O shape. It was obvious what he was thinking, because it was exactly what she was thinking. Did Sophy know Geoffrey?

'It's probably nothing.' She forcibly turned her back to the window. 'How are you this morning?'

'Dapper.' Owen's easy smile returned. He was staying in one of the other guest chambers. His valet had arrived the morning of the second day with three large travel trunks holding more clothes than Ellen had ever owned in her whole life. Today he was wearing a magnificent red waistcoat with gold buttons that brought to mind the militia.

Did the man have a waistcoat for every occasion? And probably more besides.

Noting the direction of her gaze, he peacocked his chest to best display the fine cut of his clothes. But there were dark shadows hanging under his eyes.

'You didn't sleep well either?'

'No.' He sighed. 'I couldn't stop thinking about Lizzy and Grace.'

'Is she still crying?'

'Thank goodness, no. Now she's sequestered herself in Wood's library and is reorganising all his papers.' He gave her a look that clearly demonstrated what he thought Calum's reaction to his grandmother's interference would be.

'Quite.' Ellen grimaced. Knowing the dowager, it was highly likely Calum would return home to find all his newspaper clipping of the ship fire tossed away. Perhaps she should stage a rescue mission.

'Speaking of Grace, this just came for you.' Owen handed over a letter, sealed with a wax stamp into which had been pressed the monogram GC.

She tore it open.

To the Hon. Miss B—

On the happy occasion of your forthcoming nuptials, I gift you my half of the Callaghan London townhouse.

Yours in earnest,
Grace

True to her word, Grace had included the deed for the other half of the house.

'It's not a genuine deed.' Owen squeezed her hand reassuringly. 'She can't actually give you half a house when Wood is the actually owner. It's just a gesture.'

A rather smug, self-satisfied gesture that made it perfectly clear the duchess hadn't been fooled by Ellen's proclamations that their wedding was a love match. 'I know.'

She didn't want to think about Grace right now. Or Sophy or Geoffrey or anyone but Calum and Gwen. Her heart backflipped in her chest. They were a day late.

'There was another note left for you.' Owen dragged his heels.

Her stomach sunk. 'Another one from my delightful brother?'

He nodded, reluctantly handing it over.

It was another old calling card with the name and address of someone she'd never heard of crossed out and a short message scrawled on the back.

I'm coming for you.

'Did anyone actually see Geoffrey push it under the door?' She suddenly felt very vulnerable standing with her back to the window for anyone to see.

'No.' He glanced over her shoulder and she was sure he was checking on Sophy. 'Wood will be back soon. He's probably just around the corner.'

'It's been longer than three days. He said three days.' She tried to keep the panic from her voice.

'I know, but travel is like that sometimes.' He pulled a small key out of his waistcoat pocket. 'The old man wanted me to give this to you. He said you'd spend too much time worrying, and that you're to eat cake and stay calm.' He backed away. 'Why don't you try to get some rest? As soon as I see him approaching the house, I'll give you a shout.'

Owen's love for Lady Faye was unmistakable. And now he was taking such good care of her too. 'Thank you.' She tried to put as much sincerity as she could into those two words.

He waved his hand dismissively—'Get some rest'—and slipped out of the ballroom.

She jammed both notes into her reticule. If only the old saying 'out of sight, out of mind' were actually true.

She fingered the key. It was warm to the touch. Maybe cake was exactly what she needed right now. Cake and a lovely cup of hot, sweet tea. Calum was absolutely right.

***

The iron gates of No. 7 Roseworthy Street towered over even Cal. When compared to Gwen's wee stature, they appeared visually insurmountable. The house itself was shrouded in the gloom of gritty London smog, and a heavy weight settled on Cal's chest. It had always been an ugly house. Ugly and claustrophobic despite its grand size.

He pushed open the whingeing gate, stepping aside for the other two to enter first. Gwen looked up at him and he nodded his encouragement. She still clutched the paper bag of honeycomb he'd bought her at one of their few stops.

From somewhere out of sight, a crow gave a mournful cry. Otherwise, the street was surprisingly quiet. Eerily so. The neighbours probably all had their noses pressed to their front windows, wondering who had finally lured Crazy Calum from his seclusion.

'Ellen will be waiting for us inside,' he said in an attempt to break the unnatural silence. *Waiting inside for her daughter. Not for me. She doesn't want me.*

He unlocked the front door. The sooner this fake engagement was over the better it would be for everyone. Having Ellie so near was leading to too many thoughts of self-worth. He had no future; he deserved no future.

As he led the others inside, he recited the list of reasons why marrying Ellie was such a bad idea.

1. Pierce was dead.

2. He was too damaged.

3. She didn't want to marry him and was possibly already married to someone else.

Well, hell, that last one really soared to the top.

Yet she cared for him; he'd tasted it upon her lips each time he'd kissed her. *Or so you were foolish enough to believe. She lusts after you, that's all.*

'You're back. Finally!' Owen sprinted down the narrow passage to greet them. 'We were starting to get worried. You're a day late.' He shook Maggie's hand with over-familiarity and clapped Cal on the shoulder with a smile of welcome he didn't reciprocate.

Why did Owen have to be so damned happy all the time?

'You must be Miss Guinevere, Ellen's sister.' He kneeled before the child, but she ducked behind Maggie, using the woman's skirts as a shield. Maggie clicked her tongue in warning.

'I'm sorry.' Owen straightened, startled. 'I guess it's been a hectic few days. You'll probably—'

'I'm going to wash,' Cal interrupted. His guests were now somebody else's concern, and he desperately needed a shave. At least, half his face did. 'You'd better tell Miss Burney her family's here.' *Miss Burney. Not Ellie. Never again Ellie.* He started forward, but Owen grabbed his elbow, halting his progress.

'What are you doing? Don't you want to see Ellen's face when she sees they're safe?'

'No.' To hell with Ellie and love and happiness. To hell with family. He was bachelor and a hermit.

He wrenched his arm free but Owen had already thrown back his head. 'Ellen. Ellen! Lizzy. They're here.'

Hurried footsteps sounded on the stairs and down the hall from the kitchen, and suddenly Cal was trapped between Owen, Maggie and Gwen, and an approaching fake fiancée and loud-mouthed grandmother. Ignoring Owen's protests, he limped into the drawing room and kicked the door shut in their faces.

To hell with the lot of them. He'd had enough for one day.

Ellie—*Miss Burney!*—so very happy to see her family. But that wasn't him. Never would be. He unstopped a decanter, gulping down a mouthful without even bothering with a glass. Sweet and fruity. *Sherry?* He coughed. Where the hell was his whisky? He'd only been gone four days!

He slumped onto the settee, leaning back as the old springs squeaked. Was he actually jealous of a child and a spinster? Was he so desperate for Ellie's affection that he was angry because she cared more for her own daughter than for him? Apparently he was even more pathetic than he'd realised.

Tzar was sleeping half under the settee, half on the rug. His snores did little to drown out the chatter on the other side of the door. Owen was chattering too, pushing his nose into business that had nothing to do with him. He was always doing that—going where he wasn't wanted, prying where he shouldn't be.

Cal tossed down another gulp of vile sherry, kicked off his shoes and stared up at the ceiling. His jaw was so tight his head ached. He closed his eyes, trying to remember what his life had been like before Ellie had clambered through his window and into his heart.

***

Ellen found Calum lying on the settee, his legs dangling over the armrest. Night had fallen and tentacles of soft firelight tickled his face. There was a discarded—mostly full—decanter of

Lady Faye's sherry on the ground by the sleeping dog.

He groaned, rolling onto his side before sitting up. His head dropped into the cradle of his hands, his elbows on his knees.

It wasn't often she had the advantage of superior height. His clothes were travel worn. He'd kicked off his shoes and shrugged out of his jacket. Dark stubble had grown in on one side of his face, the other was just as rough and tormented with scars as ever.

'Are you all right?'

He jumped, looking up at her blurry-eyed. 'Are ye already married? Is that why ye said no to me?'

Her insides coiled into tight knots and the warning bells in her head starting ringing a full peal. 'W-wherever did you get an idea like that?' She tried to sound nonchalant but it was an exercise just to get her mouth to work.

'I know Gwen's your daughter.'

She froze. *Oh lordy.* 'Calum, I ... You...' She pressed her eyes closed. 'W-who told you?' It came out as a whimper, as a barely-there question.

'Dr Audley.'

Emotions bombarded Ellen like a volley of coach horns. The sound of her blood pumping through her ears was deafening. Was this why

Calum hadn't greeted her? Did he hate her for lying to him? Did he hate for her straying, for being an unwed mother? As Geoffrey hated her. 'W-why did Dr Audley tell you?' Her voice was rising, but it sounded distant, like it was someone else yelling. 'What did you do to him?'

'He was maudlin drunk. How is he even a doctor?'

'Drunk?' Dr Audley? That was news to her. Then again, she'd been rather isolated these last few years.

'Why didn't ye just tell me about Gwen? I'm supposed to be yer goddamn fiancé.' He hit his fist to his thigh.

She flinched. 'My fake fiancé. *Fake*.' On that note at least she could correct him. Or rather reassure him. 'It isn't something one goes around blurting out at every available opportunity. It's a secret.' A pox on Dr Audley. A pox on Calum Callaghan!

Excluding herself and Gwen, only five living people knew Gwen was her daughter. Geoffrey, her mother's two best friends, Dr Audley. And now Calum, her fiancé—*fake fiancé!* Why were they having so much trouble remembering that? *Fake. Fake. Fake!*

'I understand that, but I'm not everyone and their twittering gabster. I'm...' His mouth worked in silence. 'I'm yer friend. And I'm trying to help ye.'

Friend? Is that what they were to each other?

Her friends were few and far between, but she'd certainly never kissed any of them as she'd kissed Calum.

Friend. That word annoyed her. A second ago she could hardly breathe for fear. Now her panic was intermingled with annoyance. None of her friends, God forbid, had ever pleasured her down there as Calum had. Not even Gwen's father, for that matter.

If we're not friends, then what are we? Lovers? They hadn't quite gone that far, but they were well beyond friendship.

Weren't they?

'The fewer people who know the truth the better,' she said eventually. 'It's always been that way.'

'Better for who?' He rose, suddenly towering over her again. They were so close. Almost chest to chest. Well, chin to chest.

What an obnoxious question. A little more of her panic turned to annoyance, like water freezing to ice. 'Better for Gwen. For Gwen.' She didn't give an inch. He could sit up there on his high horse like the rest of the world, like her own brother, but there was no way she was ever apologising for Gwen's existence. Gwen was the best thing in her life—her difficult, confusing, scary life. 'Everything I've ever done has been to keep my daughter safe.'

A pause so heavy with tension it was like lightening crackled in the air between them. And then he deflated. His shoulders sagged and all the fight left his eyes. 'Of course. Ellie, ahh, I'm sorry. I got a shock, that's all.' He sagged back down onto the settee.

She narrowed her eyes, suspicious of his speedy withdrawal, not quite believing what she saw. 'Calum,' she said slowly, 'I hate to be the one to break it to you, but women bear children out of wedlock all the time. It might not be socially acceptable but it happens, and you can't—'

'I know,' he interrupted. 'It's not that. I just got a shock thinking ye might already be married.'

'Oh.' She sat down too. 'Well, I'm not.'

'And Gwen's father?' He sounded so hesitant, so unsure of himself. She'd been preparing for the moment when someone confronted her about Gwen's parentage for the last six years. She had her retorts well in hand—if not her panic—but now...

She took another deep breath. What should she say?

The truth. He deserved that much. 'I don't know. The colonies, mayhap? I haven't seen head or tail of him since well before she was born. He wants nothing to do with us.' She shrugged, attempting a careless attitude. 'Even before my father died and Geoffrey gambled away my dowry.'

'I'm sorry.'

There was a light scattering of grey hair near his temple. She hadn't noticed when she'd cut his hair. Had that really only been less than three weeks ago?

Calum shifted. The settee sunk lower under his greater weight, and she slipped a fraction closer. 'You have more questions,' she surmised. If she were in Calum's shoes, she'd have a million.

'I do.' He actually looked sheepish.

She almost laughed. 'Ask away.' This was what friends did, wasn't it—talk about their lives, discuss their problems, share their secrets? She winced. Maybe they were just friends.

You didn't want to be anything more. She had, after all, been the one to refuse his offer of marriage.

Because he was only offering protection, nothing more. Did she want more? More than just friendship? More than just kisses?

'What I still didn't understand is why ye're running away from Geoffrey. He isn't yer guardian because ye've reached yer majority, and now I know he isn't Gwen's guardian because she's yer daughter. Surely ye could have left his house and found employment long before now.'

And the spell was broken, again. Of course there couldn't be anything more between them. He was one of only eighteen dukes, the highest in the land, aside from the royal family, while she had a daughter to think of and a secret to keep. 'With an illegitimate baby in tow? I think not.' She shook her head, focusing her thoughts on Calum's questions and only Calum's questions. Not thinking about how his scars pulled at the left side of his mouth so that on those rare occasions when he actually smiled it was lopsided. And most definitely not thinking about how he liked to keep his eyes open when they kissed so he could watch her every response.

'It was only possible to accept work with her ladyship because Gwen is a little older now and because Maggie agreed to hide her. Maggie's sister-in-law wasn't too pleased about the whole arrangement, but she'd never turn Maggie away.' The two sisters by marriage, while not all that friendly with each other, shared a bond of love for Maggie's older brother, who'd died many years ago falling from a horse.

'I see.' He ran a hand through his hair, setting it on edge. He was pale and dark circles hung like half-moons under his eyes. Like usual, he hadn't been looking after himself properly. She ran the bell, organising for a tray to be brought in, before resuming her place by his side.

'Ye could have trusted me, ye know. I wouldn't have told anyone.'

'I've been keeping Gwen's identity a secret her entire life. It's more natural for me to not talk of it. And, as I'm sharing the truth with you now...' she hurried on before she could back down, 'I didn't know how you would react. My own brother, my own flesh and blood, can't stand the sight of my beautiful daughter.'

'I'm not—'

'No, you're nothing like Geoffrey.' Truer words she'd never uttered.

'If ye married me, the courts would award me guardianship of Gwen.'

'But...' Her heart stared hammering against her chest again until she could count each beat. Beside her, Calum froze, still as a statue. A log slipped in the fire, causing the embers to flare, and for the briefest moment his dark eyes flashed pure gold. 'I'm Gwen's guardian.'

'I didn't mean—' Calum looked panicked.

'And if you did that, then all and sundry would quickly realise the truth of her parentage. All these years of secrecy would have been for nothing.'

'Aye. But, lass, Blackford is probably going to tell everyone the truth if ye don't go home with him anyway.'

'I know. It's a complete mess.' It was her turn to bury her face in her hands. 'But I couldn't have stayed under Geoffrey's roof a moment longer. He hit Gwen.'

'Ye know I would marry ye in a second if ye thought it would help.'

'I do. But I don't want to live in a world where people have to get married just to escape their dunderheaded brothers.' She looked at Calum though the cage of her fingers. 'As it is, you're risking your reputation even just pretending to be engaged to me. If—or when—Geoffrey tells everyone I'm a fallen woman. I'll be shunned by all of polite society.'

'I'm hardly *du jour* myself. And ye know I don't care what other people think of me.'

'But of course you care.' Could he not see that? She didn't want Calum to keep himself locked away from the world because of her. And she certainly didn't want to lock herself away. She wanted to hold her head high. She wanted to live her own life and provide Gwen with a life worth living. A life free of Geoffrey and every other person who'd try to bring Gwen down because her father and mother hadn't been married when she was born. 'I don't think this house is very good for you, Calum. You don't seem very happy to be back.'

For a moment afterwards everything was perfectly still, as though time had stopped. She'd hit a nerve.

'Where's Gwen now?' he eventually asked.

'Lady Faye tucked both Gwen and Maggie under her arms and marched them upstairs to bed.'

A ghost of a smile touched his lips. 'How did she get them to both fit?'

'Surprisingly, with little difficultly.' Considering the height difference between herself and Maggie. 'I had the impression Maggie took an instant liking to Lady Faye. It was almost as if they're old friends.'

He slipped an arm about Ellen's shoulder, closing the last inch between them so they sat hip to hip. 'Ye know my grandmother wouldn't care one pence about Gwen's parentage if ye told her the truth.'

Ellen exhaled, leaning into his one-armed embrace. 'Your grandmother is hardly a pattern-book marchioness.'

'That's one way to put it, gel.'

Chapter Eighteen

'My lady!' Ellen leaped to her feet, dipping into a curtsy as a sudden rush of heat collected on her neck and cheeks. How much had the dowager overheard?

'Didn't anyone ever teach ye to knock?' Calum growled at his grandmother.

Lady Faye just smiled. 'I put to you both that Calum isn't a pattern-book duke. And you, my gel, are hardly a pattern-book companion.'

'I didn't mean...' Ellen began, not having any idea where she was going with her utterance.

'I'll have you know that I don't care one dusting that Gwen is your daughter. Of course I don't. She's the sweetest, dearest little thing I've ever met. And if the reason you never told me about her was because you thought I would toss you out on your ear, I shall never forgive you. In fact, I might just suffer from my first ever fit of the vapours.' She pressed the back of one hand to her forehead, tottering forward on bended legs.

Ellen rushed to her side, guiding her to the settee, more out of obligation to fulfil her role in this dramatic display than from any actual necessity. Lady Faye had the constitution of a hardened soldier. If anyone was going to suffer a fit of the vapours, it would probably be herself.

Displaying the true gentleman Calum was, it took a light kick to the shins to persuade him to give up his seat. His scowl deepened but eventually he rose laboriously to his feet. 'Listening through the keyhole again, were you?' he asked dryly, taking up his new position by the dampened fire, one hand resting along the length of the mantel.

He looked more relaxed than at any point during their private conversation. And now his surprise had lessened, he'd slipped back into his Oxbridge voice. One day she was going to ask if he did it on purpose—although she suspected not.

'You insult me,' scoffed Lady Faye with an equally formidable scowl. She reclined along the settee, one leg up, one leg down. 'I was delivering you the tea tray myself.' And she gestured to the ground by the door where the deserted tray sat. 'You really should redecorate this room, Cal. It's not fit for entertaining. A couple of armchairs at the very least. A mirror or two—'

'Don't try changing the subject,' he growled, and Ellen could have kicked him herself.

Yes, change the subject.

'You're right. For once.' Lady Faye gestured for Ellen to sit on what little room was left on the settee.

Ellen perched on the very edge, ready to make a hasty withdrawal. Not that there was anywhere she could withdraw to. Her very presence in this house was at the sole discretion of the dowager. The dowager who now knew her greatest secret.

'How much of our conversation did you overhear?' Calum asked, his words as direct as his gaze.

'I didn't overhear anything because I wasn't listening at the keyhole, as you so crassly put it.' Lady Faye stuck out her lower lip, like a wilful child who'd be accused of stealing sweets.

'But then how—'

'I cut my eye-teeth many years ago.' She chuckled. 'That girl is the mirror image of her mama. I knew the instant I set my sights upon her. And then everything else just fell into place. That odious brother of yours kept going on about a secret he was prepared to reveal.' She looked pointedly between her and Calum. 'So, what are you going to do about it?'

'We brought Gwen to London to keep her safe from Blackford.' Close on, there was a tightness to Calum's jaw and a tension to the set of his shoulders.

'Absolutely right. She's safer under this roof than anywhere else. We can be sure of that.'

'Maggie would never have let anything happen to Gwen,' said Ellen, feeling rather rattled. She hadn't just abandoned her child to the wilds of the moors when she'd come to London.

'Of course not.' Lady Faye straightened, patting Ellen's shoulder. 'The two of you were extraordinarily brave leaving Evendale like you did. I take my hat off to you.'

To her shame, tears pricked Ellen's eyes. She was very tired all of a sudden. Gwen was just upstairs, sound asleep, and there was nothing she wanted more than to curl up beside her daughter. She slumped back in the chair, running a hand over her face.

'Here.' Calum poured a cup of tea from the tray by the door, adding a generous spoonful of sugar. 'Drink this.'

'The tea was supposed to be for you,' Ellen reproached.

Cal grunted a non-response and pressed the fine bone china into her hand.

'The both of you look dead on your feet,' said Lady Faye. 'Drink that down Ellen, and Cal can use the cup after you. You're engaged, after all.' And she winked. 'Now, since the two of you clearly don't have any idea of how to solve your current predicament, the burden again falls to me.' She pressed a hand solemnly to her heart.

'What do you mean, again?'

The dowager pressed on, ignoring Calum's interruption with practiced finesse. 'The answer came to me in a flash of brilliance, as many of my great plans do. In fact, I'm thinking of writing a book. *The Complete and Truthful Cyclopaedia of the Marvellous Exploits, Hair-Breath Escapades and Ingenious Plans of a Lady of Quality.* She wrinkled her nose. 'The title's still a work in progress. I'm not sure about the "lady of quality" part ... Does it make me sound too self-righteous?'

'Och, get on with it,' snapped Calum, almost smiling. Almost.

'You take all the fun out of life.' Another pout. 'Very well, very well. I propose to launch Ellen into Society.' She flung open her arms, pausing for effect.

'Sorry?' Ellen asked. Calum just narrowed his eyes.

'Humph. I guess I'll have to explain it word for word for you two scatterbrains. I intend to launch Ellen into Society.' She turned to Ellen. 'With a marchioness as your sponsor and a duke as your affianced, you'll be the instant belle of the ball. Everyone will want to either be with you or be you.'

'Those fools,' Calum dismissed. 'They wouldn't know a good thing if it—' He turned his back on them, obviously tempering his language.

Lady Faye rolled her eyes. Taking both of Ellen's hands in her own, she wiggled closer. 'Can you see? We'll make you the star of everyone's attentions and they won't give Geoffrey a second glance, no matter what he starts saying about you or Gwen.'

'Ahh..' Ellen could see one rather large hole in this plan. 'My lady, London Society is notorious for gossip.'

Calum shifted slightly. London had chewed him up and spat him back out when he'd been at his most vulnerable. Ellen didn't want anything to do with Society. Not a single one of them deserved the time of day. It was no wonder the dowager had disappeared to the Faye estate for four years. And Calum ... well, he'd locked himself away in his old, rundown house.

Lady Faye refilled the cup, handing it to Calum. 'Society will take one look at you, a sweet country gel, newly arrived to Town, an almost-duchess, and then they'll take one look at your brother and see—'

'A notorious gambler and general bell swagger,' supplied Calum.

'Precisely. They'll say Geoffrey's spinning Barnaby tales just to spite you. Sibling rivalry or something of the sort. And from then on, Gwen will forever be your baby sister and Geoffrey nothing more than—'

'A lowly fulham.' Calum turned back to face them.

'Precisely.' Lady Faye beamed.

'But I'm hardly the nonpareil,' he pointed out. 'Won't Ellen being seen with me only ruin her chances of a successful Season?'

'Nonsense. Four years have passed since the *ton* rejected the Duke of Woodhal. Your name has long since been cleared of any wrongdoing. By now I bet everyone is clamouring to see how you've been faring.'

'Maybe...' Calum looked thoughtful, like he was actually considering this crazy scheme. 'Owen suggested something similar.'

'But, my lady, you said yourself that Gwen looks just like me.' If Lady Faye guessed, what was stopping anyone else realising the truth when they saw the two of them together?

'It won't matter. Geoffrey could build an entire castle of evidence against you but nobody will ever believe him. It won't be fashionable to believe him.'

'I see...' Did she? Not fashionable to believe Gwen was her daughter? Had it been fashionable to believe Calum had murdered his brother on the high seas? Apparently so.

'What I mean is that it'll be an open secret—something everyone knows is probably true but doesn't talk about,' clarified the dowager. 'Trust me, it's not often Society works in someone's favour, but, if we play our cards right, you'll be the exception to the rule.'

'So we're actually going to put Gwen's future in the hands of the people who ruined Calum's?'

Lady Faye nodded. 'Precisely.'

Calum tossed back the hot tea. 'It's about bloody time they did something right.'

***

There was a crease between Ellie's brows that spoke volumes about her continued worries, despite Lady F's assurances her plan was 'topping' and 'of the first water'.

'Don't worry,' Cal said, his chest tightening. 'We're just taking precautions to prevent a possible scandal. We don't even know if Blackford will carry through with his threats.' A second later he found himself standing beside the settee, a comforting hand on her shoulder. He could barely remember making the journey across the room.

He snatched back his hand, but not before Lady F had caught sight of it. She could barely suppress her smile of delight. Rising, she hurried from the room. 'That's right, dearest. Kiss some sense into her.' And she snapped the door closed behind her.

'Your grandmother is quite the chaperon.' A light blush crept up Ellie's neck to stain her cheeks.

If he peeled back the layers of her dress would he uncover the origin of her blush? Did it sweep down over her breasts too? His gaze dropped lower before he could help himself. Did he even want to help himself? Ellie's breath hitched. He loved that after all the kisses they'd shared, she was still so responsive.

His cock hardened. The glorious image of Ellie with her head thrown back, her breasts practically bursting from the confines of her stays and his hand up her skirt was one he'd cherish for the rest of his life. She was a fascinatingly sensuous creature, one who'd barely begun exploring all her needs and desires, despite her efforts to hide that side of herself from everyone.

Mine. That possessive and all-consuming need to touch her, to pleasure her, to bury his cock inside her until a little of her goodness seeped inside of him washed over Cal like a storm crashing against the side of a ship.

Tzar woke with a start, jumping in surprise to see Ellie sitting on the settee in place of Cal himself. The old dog clambered to his feet, his tail wagging and his eyes fixed on the tea tray. He might be deaf but he certainly wasn't blind. And he was always hungry. Or so he liked them to believe.

Cal took the opportunity to kneel, ignoring the shooting pain in his knee, using the arm of the chair to steady himself. He ruffled Tzar's fur. He hoped his new position would hide the fact that his cock was tenting his breeches. While he wanted nothing more than to throw caution to the wind, he'd bet against the worst odds that Lady F had her ear pressed to the door. For all her exclamations of innocence, she was planning something, and he didn't trust his grandmother any further than he could throw her.

And there was nothing more cock softening than the thought of his snooping grandmother.

'I'm feeling a little guilty about Geoffrey.' Ellie broke the silence.

'Whyever for?'

'It's just...' She tapped her forehead, obviously trying to voice her wayward thoughts. 'He's still my brother. And I feel like ... like we're setting him up for ridicule.'

'Nonsense. If he keeps his mouth shut, nothing will happen.' He had no time to spare for Geoffrey.

Ellen's hair had been braided and wrapped around her head like a crown, and the golden firelight had turned her usual chocolate colour bronze. Majestic: that was the word that sprung to mind. But the crease between her brow had returned.

'You're over thinking it. If your brother's smart, he'll use the money he won to pay off his debts and return to Evendale. He's a baron. Does he have much land?'

She nodded.

'Then he's better off than most in this world.' And much better off than he deserved to be after everything he'd put Ellie and Gwen through.

'Other brothers would have done worse in my situation.'

'That's no argument.' Were Pierce still alive, Cal would have stuck by his side come hell or high water, just as Pierce would have stuck by him.

Something in his eyes must have betrayed the direction of his thoughts.

'Thinking on it,' she said with sudden bravado, flashing him one of her beautiful smiles, 'this plan will probably work in your favour too. When I break off the engagement, I could contrive a devilish story about you being a rake and breaking my heart. If that doesn't have all the eligible young ladies of the *ton* chasing after you, I don't know what will.'

He frowned.

'Or ineligible ladies, if that's what you prefer,' she quickly added.

His frown deepened.

'Don't try to tell me you weren't a rake before the war? No woman would have been able to resist a face like yours.' She laughed. 'Mark my words, Calum Callaghan. There's nothing so appealing to woman than a rake with sad eyes. Especially an exceptionally wealthy rake with sad eyes and a ducal estate.'

'I don't have sad eyes.' He clambered to his feet, feeling much older than his thirty-three years.

'Not right now you don't,' she conceded, leaning forward the better to see. 'In fact, you're looking more than half peevish.'

'And it's entirely your fault.' Incorrigible woman! It wasn't his life they were supposed to be meddling with. 'I don't want women of any eligibility chasing me, thank you very much.' None but the one seated before him.

Chapter Nineteen

His Grace, the Duke of Woodhal, to wed the Honourable Miss Ellen Burney, eldest daughter of the late Baron of Blackford. The soon-to-be duchess appears to be even more of a recluse than her bridegroom. Rumour has it, she's to make her first public appearance at the Theatre Royal this coming Tuesday. She hasn't even yet been introduced at the drawing room of St James. Let us hope news of the duke's scandalous past reached whichever corner of the English countryside this innocent rose has been hiding in.

—*The Ladies' Gazette*

'Chin up, dearest. An evening at the theatre won't kill you.' Lady F tapped the underside of Cal's chin as she spoke. 'It was your idea, after all.'

'Don't remind me.' He crossed his arms. With four of them in the hired carriage, space was scarce, particularly for his long legs. Ellie was sitting across from him, and it was all he could do to keep their knees from touching.

The last few days had been filled with preparations for their fancy-dress engagement ball. Invitations had been sent out that very morning. His grandmother had devised the guest list, including His Royal Highness, the Prince Regent himself. Then this afternoon had been consumed with preparations for their evening at the theatre. Who'd have thought being social took so much work! They'd all been rushing around the house with last-minute dress fittings and the procurement of shoeroses, hairpins, boot polish and other such 'necessities'. He'd hated every single second.

Now, trapped in the carriage, Cal's eyes once again seemed to have a mind of their own. And they were firmly set upon Ellie. No matter how many times he turned his head, they always drifted back to her. She was looking positively virginal in a new muslin gown of softest pink, almost the same colour as her skin. Instead of washing her out, the gown made her dark hair and eyes shine all the brighter.

For just a little while, the world would wonder how scarred, damaged Calum Callaghan had managed to capture such a stunning lass. Then Geoffrey would leave London, and Ellie would break the engagement, and the world would quickly realise it was his heart that had been caught, not hers.

The carriage jostled to the side, and Owen practically tumbled into Cal's lap. Scowling, he pushed his cousin away.

'Careful!' Owen scolded. 'I'll have you know my waistcoat is new.'

'Don't mind him. You look positively modish, Mr Tattershall,' Ellie assured Owen with a warm smile. 'In fact, I don't think I've ever seen such a waistcoat as yours.'

'Modish' was certainly one word to describe his cousin's appearance. Tonight he was sporting not only a pineapple-coloured waistcoat so bright it actually hurt Cal's eyes whenever he looked directly at it but a black opera hat—a crescent-shaped hat that was designed to be flattened and carried under the arm rather than actually worn on the head. Though apparently common sense alone wasn't enough to dissuade Owen from wearing his opera hat and almost poking everyone in the eye each time he turned his head in the cramped carriage.

'Yes,' Lady F agreed with Ellie. 'You're sure to draw the eye. Which is more than I can say for you.' She gave Cal's new monochrome ensemble a dark look. 'A little colour won't kill you.'

'These clothes are the height of fashion.' He tugged at his starched cravat, procured especially for this evening. Following the illustrated instructions in a fashion pamphlet Owen had lent him, he'd finally managed to tie the ornate Waterfall knot rather than his usual Oriental. And it was devilish uncomfortable.

'Fashionable, yes. Adventurous, no,' muttered Owen, cleaning his immaculate spectacles on a crimson handkerchief.

'At least the audience will be able to tell me apart from the actors,' retorted Cal. He was unfairly taking out his feelings on his cousin, but anything was better than contemplating jumping from the speeding carriage and scuttling back home again.

'Of all the nerve—' Owen spluttered.

Cal allowed his eyes another quick glance in Ellie's direction. Her hair had been pinned into an elaborate bun with curls framing her face and tickling the back of her neck. He wanted nothing more than a few moments alone with her in the carriage. He wanted her to crumple his perfect cravat and rumple his styled hair. He wanted her to kiss him until his lips were deliciously red and swollen.

'I really don't understand why the two of you won't just be married for real,' said Lady F, catching the direction of his gaze. 'He's not such a bad catch, you know, gel. He still has all his teeth, and it's not like you pay much attention to his temper. You could easily—'

'We're here.' Cal threw open the carriage door and jumped down before the footman could lower the steps. As soon as the steps were lowed, he offered his arm, helping the ladies down. Ellie followed his grandmother, but when she started to remove her hand from his, he tugged her closer. Purely for show. Not at all because he wanted her near.

Owen jumped down last, waving their box tickets and leading the way into the theatre. The building itself was new, at least new to him. The old one had burned down or fallen down or something. He couldn't quite remember—or care.

They were relatively early but still a crowd had gathered in the entrance foyer. A hush fell and the crowd eyed his family warily. Cal faltered, but Lady F raised an arm to wave at a friend—if any of these coxcombs could be called friends—and dived into the crowd, apparently at ease. Owen followed suit.

'They're not going to eat us,' Ellie muttered. 'At least I don't think they are.' She tugged on his arm, pulling him forward also.

The crowd parted like the Red Sea. Nobody gave him the cut direct, which was an improvement on the last time he'd been in Society four years ago, but they didn't exactly acknowledge him either. Sideways glances and mutterings behind fans and hands were his only greetings.

To Ellie's credit she neither abandoned him to his fate nor seemed to take any notice of their mutterings. In fact, if it weren't for her arm, his wounded knee probably would have given way under the weight of all the judgemental backstabbing.

Slowly, they made their way to their seats. The hired box provided them with an excellent view of the stage—which was a shame because Cal had never been much of a Shakespeare fan, particularly not miserable *Romeo and Juliet*—and an even better view of the crowd in the pit below. He and Ellie took the front seats; Lady Faye and Owen sat behind them.

Unfortunately, or was that supposed to be fortunately, everyone had a perfect view of them also. Even the dandies in the pit below turned around to stare up at them.

He wiped his sweaty palms down his thighs. Damnable crowds. All the pushing and shoving, the not being able to see what everyone was doing, the threat of unknown danger—it all brought up too many old memories of being back on ship, cramped onto the deck with seven hundred other men, all waiting for the enemy's next attack.

Excitement and expectation hung in the air like a heavy fog.

After all these years of self-imposed isolation, why the hell was he subjecting himself to this torment again?

Ellie. He turned his head to look at her. His love.

His *fake* fiancée.

***

Just looking at the back of Cal's head, Lizzy could tell he wasn't happy. Not even close. His shoulders were tense and he kept running his hands through his hair in a way that made her sure he was trying very hard not to touch his scars.

The players took up their positions on the stage, but Lizzy barely spared them a second glance. She'd seen *Romeo and Juliet* too many times for it to be of particular interest. And judging by the chatter coming from the rest of the audience, they weren't paying the stage much attention either. Tonight, the cloistered Duke of Woodhal and his intended bride were the centre of everyone's focus.

Cal shifted in his seat, his long legs cramped against the front of the box.

He's always been handsome, even as a child. Both he and Pierce. Although it had been impossible to find two half-brothers so completely different in appearance. Still, it was a shame Cal didn't look a little more like his father, if only to stop everyone speculating.

Lizzy hadn't doubted Finella for one heartbeat. She'd known Cal's mother in passing, mainly by reputation, but she'd come from a good family and there was no reason for her to have lied about the identity of Cal's father. Her own family had been almost as wealthy as Hammond.

What if she did lie? asked the rebellious voice at the back of her mind, the one she never heeded. *Well,* she told that voice sternly, *I'd love him all the same.* He was her grandson, regardless of blood—or the lack of blood as it was. Just as Owen was her adopted son even though the law didn't recognise him as such.

Almost as though Cal could sense her watching him, he twisted in his seat to look at her. Lizzy smiled innocently, completely ignoring his suspicious look. She wasn't always up to something, for goodness sake.

And even if she were, Cal would never be able to prove it. She was an excellent secret keeper.

Evidently content with what he saw, he shifted back around to face the front. Lizzy gave herself a mental pat on the back. Nobody could outsmart Elizabeth Debelle! Even if she did say so herself—or think so herself...?

Cal might be a duke now, but she was still the matriarch of this family—of the Callaghan and the Debelles and the adopted Tattershalls alike. Her stomach sank with the thought. Three families combined into one and there were only four of them left in all the world. And Grace wasn't talking to her.

So much death. So much loss.

So much heartbreak.

Ellen leaned fractionally closer to Cal and whispered in his ear even as an over-eager Romeo exclaimed: 'She speaks, O, speak again, bright angel!'

A thrill of excitement ran through Lizzy. Four family members plus the two Burney gels. Six was a nice number. A much nicer number than measly, lonely four. Her family was slowly but surely growing.

Yes, one could argue that technically Cal and Ellen weren't engaged. But that could be easily fixed with the gentle administrations of Grandmother Lizzy.

Why, if the two of them weren't married by Michaelmas, she'd ... She looked around the box for an adequate punishment and caught sight of Owen's cocked hat on the chair by his other side. He'd been loath to part with it when the theatre attendants had collected everyone's outerwear. If Cal and Ellen weren't really, truly married by Michaelmas, she'd eat Owen's beloved hat.

If anyone deserved a happy, loving family it was little Gwen. That poor gel. She'd called out in her sleep last night. Lizzy had heard the yelling through the wall that separated her room from Ellen's, Ellen having insisted Gwen sleep with her.

Lizzy ground her teeth. How many nights had Ellen laid awake, guarding the youngest Burney child from the ill temper of her brother? He was a bully if ever she'd seen one. An insufferable blustering hardhead!

Even now, dear Maggie was back at Roseworthy, minding Gwen, trying to keep the nightmares at bay.

'What are you planning? You're huffing and puffing on the back of my neck.' Cal hissed, again looking at her over his shoulder again.

'Nothing.' Lizzy feigned innocence, quickly moderating her breathing.

Ellen was also watching her suspiciously.

'Why don't I believe you?'

'Because you're a deeply distrustful young man.' And she tapped his cheek lightly with her closed fan so the two of them would turn back to the front.

There'd be no point having come to the theatre if Cal and Ellen spent the whole night staring over their shoulders, their faces turned away from the eyes of their gobsmacked audience. And then Ellen touched a hand to Cal's cheek, looking like a woman in love, and the audience gave one collective sigh.

From her stage balcony, Juliet pressed her hand to her heart: 'If that thy bent of love be honourable, Thy purpose marriage, send me word tomorrow.'

Ha! Owen's cocked hat couldn't have been safer. Wedding bells would be ringing before too long, even if she had to procure the special licence herself!

***

Two minutes earlier

A lifetime would never acclimate Ellen to the heat of the Herculean man seat beside her. It seeped through the delicate crepe of her new evening gown despite the inches of space between their plush seats, a welcome contrast to the cool stares of the audience. She rubbed at the back of her neck and then didn't know what to do with her arms. Resting her hands in her lap seemed too meek an action when so much was at stake.

She trained her gaze on the ardent lovers currently gracing the stage, but the actors could barely be heard over the jostling of the crowd. People were pointing. People were whispering. People were not bothering in the slightest to keep their fascination with the duke a secret.

By now all of London must be alight with the news of Calum's sudden engagement. Surely all of London was in the pit below, pointing up at them. And there was no way of knowing if Geoffrey had started gossiping about Gwen's illegitimacy.

She let out a shaking breath. Gwen was worth every single second of pain she'd suffered these last two years.

Calum shifted uncomfortably in his seat. Although the box itself was generous in size, he always seemed too large for any enclosed space. And it didn't help that Lady Faye was muttering excitedly under her breath behind them. What was she even saying?

She watched Calum from the corner of her eye. The candelabras overhead sent flickering light directly over his face. There was a tightness to his jaw that suggested he was having a hard time keeping control of his rising anger. And then suddenly his gaze snapped down to the crowd as though daring anyone to call out in mockery.

A hush rippled through the theatre. Everyone below was holding their breath, waiting for a glimpse of Crazy Calum.

'Look at me.' She moved to the edge of her chair, desperate to close the gap between them. He was putting himself through this torture for her and Gwen.

'Calum,' she hissed, tugging on his arm. 'Love, look at me.'

Finally, with what seemed to be a monumental effort, he wrenched his gaze from the crowd, turning his dark, stormy eyes to her face.

'They don't know you. Not like your family does. Not like I do.' And she raised a hand to his scarred cheek, claiming the wickedly handsome man sitting before her as her own for all to see.

A flash of surprise crossed his face, as though he'd forgotten she was seated beside him. It was quickly replaced by something much darker and more possessive. He turned in his seat, his whole body facing her, her hand still on his cheek. 'I think the crowd's had its fill. Let's get out of here, bonnie lass.'

Chapter Twenty

Calum's gaze burned its way down her body. His legs were stretched out before him and even in the dim light it was clear he was enjoying the freedom of a partially empty carriage.

A knowing smirk played over his mouth, and wariness stole over Ellen. She'd seen that look before—back in the library when he'd seduced her, when he'd persuaded her to throw caution to the wind if only for a couple of minutes. Back then, he'd had a hand up her skirt and that same glint in his eyes.

'You're staring.' She kept her voice steady even as her heart started dancing an enthusiastic quadrille in anticipation.

'After everything, I declare tonight a raging success.'

'Oh, you do?' She grinned despite herself. 'And did you enjoy yourself, Your Grace?'

'Immensely so.'

'Ha!' A very unladylike laugh escaped her mouth. He couldn't have been more obviously lying if he'd been standing on his head and telling her he had his feet on the ground.

His mouth slipped into something more serious but equally dangerous. 'I thought I asked ye not to call me that.'

'Oh?' she pretended innocence. 'I'm not sure I remember...'

He slipped off his seat and moved onto hers. One of his large legs pressed along the length of her leg and his arm bumped gently against her shoulder with each small jilt of the well-sprung carriage.

The look he bestowed upon her this time was something hotter, something filled with promise. Vibrant, happy Calum had come out to play once more. *Oh lordy.* She should not have teased him. She should not have tempted fate.

'You're just delighted we left the theatre early.'

'And that Owen has to stay until the end.'

She laughed. 'Well, someone has to keep your grandmother company since we ran out without her. It will probably cause a scandal you know, and after all our hard work.' Guilt twinged.

'I don't know. There's no act more chivalrous than a besotted fiancé escorting his soon-to-be bride home when she was suddenly struck down with a headache.' He chuckled, a sound she'd never thought to hear him make, and relaxed back into the padded seat. 'I imagine all the gentlemen are wildly envious of me right now.'

She hurriedly turned her head to stare out the window, but night had well and truly fallen and there wasn't much to see other than darkness and spots of candlelight from other carriage lamps and house windows.

Even with her face turned away, it was impossible to ignore the scent of him. He smelled of big open space in a crowded room, of heat in the middle of a frosty winter, of firelight in the middle of a stormy night. Of whisky and sex. A smell she wanted nothing more than to wrap herself in. To bathe in. To drink in.

'Ye touched my cheek before half of London proper.' His voice was low, his accent thick. It was like a secret he only shared with her. 'Ye were claiming me for yer own.'

'No, I wasn't.' She turned back to him. 'I didn't...' But she had. It had been a touch of ownership, of belonging. A sign of solidarity before all the wolves and vipers of the *ton*, just as Calum claiming to be her fiancé to save her from Geoffrey had been a mark of intimacy, of belonging, of partnership.

The driver took the corner sharply and Ellen was tossed against Calum. He pressed his advantage, wrapping an arm around her waist and pulling her onto his lap. 'I've been keeping my own list of all the reasons why we shouldn't marry, lass.' His mouth was so close his words tickled her cheek. 'But it's quickly getting shorter and shorter as the days go on.'

Something hard nudging against the side of her leg. He did nothing to disguise it.

A rush of heat flooded her veins. Was that all it took? A glint in Calum's eye and a hint of pleasure to come? Apparently so. Apparently so! She hadn't been able to resist him since the first moment they'd first met.

'Wait, you have a list?' Her eyes widened, the meaning of his words only just penetrating her befuddled mind. Was he actually trying to seduce her into marriage again? He really was one of a kind.

'Of course. Every self-respecting bachelor has a list. Though I suspect mine's a little more dramatic than most others.'

'Is that right?' Calum? Dramatic? She'd never have guessed. She laughed. 'So what's on your list?'

He flexed his hips ever so slightly, seeking friction against her leg. She looked down before she could help herself. His form fitting breeches framed rather than hid his growing enthusiasm. In all its magnificent glory.

'Number one.' He pressed a light kiss to her temple. 'I knew ye were hiding from someone. At first I considered the possibility that ye'd run away from an abusive husband. I now know the truth of that.'

'Not married. Just the mother of an illegitimate daughter.'

'A moot point in my book,' he said, dismissively. 'Number two.' He pressed a kiss to her cheek. 'Ye, Miss Burney, are much too good for the likes of me.'

'A baron's daughter without even a dowry too good for a duke?' She focused on his words, resolutely ignoring his hand on her thigh. Her breath caught in her throat. Where had all the air suddenly gone? She licked her dry lips.

'What I mean is that beautiful, intriguing, feisty Ellen Burney is too good for a half-Scottish, damaged and decidedly grumpy Calum.'

'You're not—'

'Please, Ellie. I'm trying to tell ye that I love ye. And that while I'm far from perfect, I've come to realise over these last few weeks that ye're not too good for love. Hell, ye deserve love more than anyone I've ever met.'

Something inside her chest tightened, and she pressed a hand to Calum's arm, straightening. *Love? But ... That...*

'Calum—' She felt frozen.

Her expression must have given him cause for concern for he pressed more kisses down the side of her face, lingering at the corner of her mouth. She turned to kiss him, but with another sly smile he straightened a little.

'And number three?' she prompted, rather breathlessly, barely resisting the urge to straddle him. It wouldn't take them long to reach Yew Tree House, and she didn't particularly like the idea of being discovered by the driver.

'Number three has been the hardest one to come to terms with.' A little darkness settled back into his eyes.

'Lieutenant Callaghan.'

'Aye. Pierce saved me. He pulled me back from the fire, risking his own life. And he died because of it. My wee brother, who followed me to war because we'd always done everything together from the moment we first met.' He rubbed a hand over the burn scars on his cheek. 'I've always thought that because he will never have the chance to fall in love and live a full life, I shouldn't be allowed to either.'

'Lady Faye and Owen don't blame you for his death. And neither do I. The fire was an accident—'

'It doesn't matter what they think. It doesn't matter what Grace thinks or what the rest of the world thinks, not any more. It doesn't even matter what ye think in that regard.' He gave her a tight-lipped smile as a silent apology. 'It matters what I think, and I know that a small part of me is never going to stop blaming myself. Even though I logically know that, at the end of the day, they were all Pierce's own choices. He could be ridiculously stubborn when he wanted to be.'

'Just like another man I know.' She cupped his face in both of her hands, twisting awkwardly in his lap to face him, and brushed her lips against his in a kiss so light it could have been a touch of air.

He growled low in his throat, leaning forward, and she rewarded him by deepening the kiss. She used her hands on his face to guide him, directing the angle of his mouth so she could slip her tongue between his lips.

With her sitting on his knee like this, they were nearly of equal height. The thrill of taking control only seemed to add fuel to the fire burning at that deliciously sensitive spot between her legs. She rocked her hips again, and Calum's grip tightened in warning.

So close.

But she didn't want her first time with Calum to be a rushed and fumbled job. Her first, and only, time with Gwen's father had been that way. Afterwards she'd felt dirty and used.

She slowed the kiss, taking her time to explore his face with her fingers and lips. There was such a delicious contrast between the softness of his lips and the roughness of his scars. Contrast too between the gentle way he held her to his chest, mindful of the fading bruises on her wrists, and the strength of his corded muscles.

Her lips travelled down his jawline to his neck, and he raised his chin, giving her full access—at least as much as his cravat would allow. She ran her tongue along the ridges of his burns, where the skin was pulled tight. He was a magnificent man, in all his unabashed glory. She had to grip his shoulders to stop her hands from pulling open his waistcoat and shirt and exposing his chest. She'd seen it once before—but once would never be enough.

Following her lead, his hands began an exploration of their own. From hip to waist to breast and finally to tangle in her hair.

Eventually, they broke apart, breathless and flushed.

'Was that a pity kiss?' he asked with a raised eyebrow.

'Maybe...' She almost winced, worried for a second he'd take offence.

But Calum just shrugged, then tugged uncomfortably at his breeches. 'If I knew pity came as kisses, maybe I wouldn't have locked myself away for four years.' The carriage jerked to a halt and a second later they could hear the footman climbing down from his seat beside the driver.

Ellen scrambled off Calum's lap, tugging at her skirts and running a hand over her ruined hairstyle. Next time they were likely to be caught in a compromising position, she was going to have to ensure Calum was the one who looked thoroughly ravished and not her. Just as a little pay back.

That would mean ... She cast a sideways glance at the bulge in his breeches even as the carriage door opened and the footman offered his arm to help her down the steps. She sat frozen for a second imaging the possibilities. Calum half naked beneath her fully clothed body...

A handful of moments later, Calum had bade the driver return to the theatre for Lady F and Owen, and they'd moved through the front gate of Yew Tree House. Ellen started up the garden path, and Calum slipped in behind her, walking so close she could feel the heat of his chest seeping through the back of her borrowed pelisse and something hard pressed against her spine. Was that his ... his ... She frowned. What exactly was she supposed to call a man's ... display of amorous physical interest? The illicit romance had used words like a 'shaft of delight' and 'pleasure-pivot', but none of those flowery phrases were a good fit with Calum's rather forthright nature.

'What are you doing?' She tried to move to the side but he followed. 'The servants will start talking. We're supposed to be avoiding a scandal, not starting a new one.'

'Would ye rather I take a step to the right so Chakrabarti can see just how enamoured I am of ye at this very moment?'

***

Enamoured? More like as aroused as a rutting bull.

He followed Ellie up the stairs to the second-storey bedrooms, a hand on the railing for support. To hell with these god-awful skin-tight breeches. To hell with all clothes. If he didn't have Ellie undressed and under him in the next five seconds he might just burn up.

He caught her around the waist, but she slipped from his grip with a sly smile. 'Gwen's probably asleep in my bed this very minute,' she whispered.

'Then we'll use my bed.'

She sank against him for another low, long kiss. His cock jumped, straining at the confines of his breeches as though it thought to break itself free. He ground against her, unable to keep still, and she moaned low in her throat. It was the same delicious sound as she'd made back in the library when he'd pleasured her with his fingers. God, he'd loved how she'd taken control, directing the pressure and direction of his strokes. She most certainly knew what she wanted.

He'd never had time for insipid innocents.

'She'll hear us,' Ellie whispered against his lips.

'Then we'll be very, very quiet.' He kissed her again, more urgent this time. Their tongues clashing and their breaths coming in short, sharp pants.

Ellie fisted her hands in his lapels and, without breaking the kiss, started pulling him further down the corridor. When his back hit the door, he reached behind to open it and they practically fell into his room.

Desperately, he tugged at his cravat and ripped at his shirt buttons, until he was stripped to the waist. She watched with eyes dark with desire, her gaze roaming his scarred chest. He'd never felt more desirable.

God, he wanted to kneel at her feet, to touch and taste and worship. But his wounded knee wouldn't support his weight for long, and what an arse he'd look struggling to stand back up. He tugged her towards the bed instead, and Ellie eagerly lay down, fully clothed.

He watched her bounce a little on the mattress, following her with hungry eyes, devouring her curves.

Tzar was startled from his slumber. The old dog tossed them his most affronted look and clambered out of Ellie's way. Cal banished him to the corridor without a second thought. He could sleep on someone else's bed tonight.

'Beautiful.' Her hair had fallen from the confines of its pins in soft tangles around her shoulders.

After quickly toeing off his boots, he stripped off the last of his clothes. His erection stood proud.

Her eyes widened and she sat up, unashamedly wrapping her hand around his length before he could move any closer. *Ye gods,* it felt good. He winced in an effort to stop himself pushing further into her fist. Four years of abstinence was a fierce demon to contain.

'What do you call this?'

'That, lass, is my cock,' he ground out between clenched teeth.

She smiled. 'Much better.'

Better than what? But before he could ask, she ran her fist up and down, and he almost came undone then and there.

'Nay, ye don't.' Reluctantly he pulled her hand away. 'It's too soon.' He'd been fantasising about this moment for too long to let it end like this. He wanted to take it slowly. He wanted to commit every moment to memory so that when he lay in his empty bed at night after all of this was over he could close his eyes and pretend Ellie hadn't left.

He made short work of her gown, fervently kissing the newly exposed skin at her collarbone, but his fingers fumbled on the closure of her stays. Impatiently, she brushed his hands away, taking over.

'I'm a little rusty.' Had stays always been so bloody fiddly? To hell with the person who'd invented them. Surely there was a better, more accessible way of holding breasts. Like his hands.

As her stays fell away, Ellie lay back down on the bed and Cal followed, kneeling over her. He took her breasts, one in each hand. A perfect fit. He massaged them, pulling gently at her nipples, just visible through the thin fabric of her chemise. Peaked and pink and aching to be touched.

Sharp pain speared his knee, and he grunted involuntarily.

'Here.' She pulled him down onto the mattress and straddled his waist, reversing their positions.

He might have initiated sex, but he loved how she took control. Especially as his shaft was now rubbing against her hot, wet centre, the only barrier between them her cotton chemise. Her breasts bounced enticingly. His heart pounded out of control but with the merest sliver of self-restraint left, he managed not to thrust up. It was the hardest thing he'd even done in his whole miserable life.

He reached towards her, intending to pull her down for another kiss, but she hesitated.

'What's wrong?' His breath hitched. Had she changed her mind? There was no way he was going to force her into anything she didn't want. Even if it damn near killed him to let her go. Every moment with Ellie was a gift.

'I...' She gestured between them, looking suddenly apprehensive. 'I'm not ready for another child.'

'My love, neither am I. When was yer last menses?'

'It finished just yesterday.'

'Perfect timing.' With a sigh, he pulled one eager nipple into his mouth until her chemise was wet, turning practically sheer. He admired his work with smug satisfaction. 'But just to be safe, there are many ways to enjoy ourselves without the risk of pregnancy.'

'You mean...' Her brows knitted together, her gaze on her peaked nipple. 'I read about how some men like to ... to use their mouths.'

He laughed, his voice husky with desire. 'Some men. I most certainly do.' And he grasped her around the waist, sliding her up his body until she was kneeling over his face, her chemise tenting his head.

***

The boudoir novel hadn't done justice to this particular kind of kissing. With the first lash of his tongue at the apex of legs, Ellen gasped and instantly spread her thighs wider, offering more. Calum pressed forward with his rampage: tasting, teasing, nibbling until she had to close her eyes from the sheer force of it all.

Large hands on her hips held her still as she strained to move. Her back arched as surges of pleasure pulsed through her. She wanted it to never end, but Calum's mouth was a master and he ruthlessly pushed her over the edge before she could do anything more than clasp a hand over her mouth, muffling her cries of exhilaration.

When she finally came back to her senses, she was lying beside Calum, a hand flung across her face and her breaths short and sharp.

'That was...' But apparently she couldn't find the words any more than the author of the boudoir novel had. She pulled her petticoat over her head and dropped it over the edge of the bed. Naked, she stretched against him, enjoying the sensation of skin against skin.

'Deliciously wicked,' suppled Calum, wrapping an arm around her and gently massaged one bare breast. He looked much as she felt: content. His hair was ruffled and he was smiling smugly.

'Deliciously wicked,' Ellen agreed. She let her gaze drift down his glorious body. His cock pointed unapologetically towards his stomach. Not so content after all.

'Although it's not fair that I've had all the fun,' she amended.

'I'm entirely at yer mercy, love. I think we've both realised that, when it comes to the bedroom, ye're the one wearing the trousers, as they say.' His gaze turned thoughtful. 'That gives me another idea: yer arse in tight breeches.'

'I do believe that view is my prerogative. Although I most assuredly prefer this view.' She gestured towards his straining cock.

He chuckled, and a flush of contentment rushed through her.

'What do ye intend to do about my predicament?'

'Hmm. Take you in hand, I think.' She smiled at her own boldness. This was more than deliciously wicked. She felt happy, pure and simple. Happy and loved and safe to be herself.

What a wonderful gift Calum had given her this evening.

Now it was her turn to bestow a gift on him, and she could hardly wait. She felt free in the knowledge she could touch him as she liked—he'd given his consent, as she'd given hers.

He was watching her as a dying man would watch a plate of food—like he could gobble her up in an instant. He was evidently enjoying the anticipation of what was to come; it was feeding his desire.

She ran her fingers down his chest, exploring the shape of him. He was all muscle, for all that he could use a couple of extra pounds. Maybe after the Season finished, Cook would stay on, ensuring Calum ate three full meals a day. He needed someone to look after him.

Her fingers skimmed the base of his cock, and he made a sound of undiluted pleasure. The sound resonated through her body and she quickly straddled him, desperate to close the distance between them. She rubbed her wet heat against the head of his cock.

'Are ye sure?' Calum ground the question out through clenched teeth. All laugher had dissipated from his face, leaving a look of extreme concentration. He was holding himself back, just.

'Yes. We'll be careful.' She sank down, watching where their bodies joined, watching as him disappeared inside her. Why had the great artists never painted such a scene—a de Vinci or a Rembrandt. But then she moved her hips and all thoughts fled.

'Faster, please.' He was begging her. And just the thought of Calum begging for anything had her moving faster and harder.

Oh, she loved being in control. She loved the freedom and the daring of it. Her hands reached for something to grasp, her fingers frantic, and she leaned forward to fist her hands in the dark, luxurious bedsheets. Her nipples rubbed against Calum's chest, and his cock hit a spot inside her that had her gasping.

Pleasure speared through her body, and Calum wrapped a hand around the back of her neck, pulling her down for another kiss. He swallowed her cries as her internal muscles convulsed around him.

A second later, Calum grasped her by the hips and lifted her off him. As he tensed, his own release washed over him, and it was Ellie's kisses muffling his cries and her hand holding his convulsing cock.

Chapter Twenty-One

Ellen jerked awake. She was spread-eagled over Calum's bare chest, his shoulder her pillow. Something had woken her. A noise?

'What was that?' Calum sat up, an arm about her waist, bringing her up with him. His hair was decidedly rumpled, and she instantly wanted to run her fingers through his short locks.

She blinked sleep from her eyes. 'It sounded like one of the downstairs windows.'

'Ye stay here. I'll go.' He kissed her cheek, barely pausing long enough to grab his dressing gown.

Ellen groped down by the side of his bed for her dress. She'd hardly pulled it over her head before she was hurrying to follow. She paused for a second by her own chamber, checking on Gwen, but her daughter was fast asleep in Ellen's own bed, Maggie devotedly sleeping on a trundle beside her. Neither of them had been woken by the crash.

Maybe what they'd heard had just been Lady Faye returning home with Owen. But when she poked her head into the dowager's room, the first thing she noticed were the soft snores of Lady Faye and Tzar. And, of course, Owen was no longer staying here now Calum was back.

Satisfied her family was safe, she slipped down the stairs, searching for Calum.

It was later than she'd first realised, well after midnight. All the servants had retired for the night, leaving the house almost impossibly quiet. She found Calum in the drawing room, silhouetted against the dying fire. One of the windows was open, letting in a cold wind that stirred the curtains and pulled at the folds of Calum's dressing gown.

He held out his arm, waylaying her progress further into the room. 'Careful. There's broken glass.' And he gestured at the remains of the armorial window. Sharp pieces of stained glass littered the floor, heraldic blues and yellows shining dully in the light of the embers.

In their haste, neither of them had grabbed shoes.

'Was it the wind?' she asked even as cold started creeping its way into her veins.

'Nay.' He bent down to pick up something from the worn rug. It was a large rock wrapped in an old sheet of newsprint. 'Very original,' he grumbled.

Moving carefully to the fire, he smoothed the page open. The newspaper was dated several days ago. Someone had circled their engagement notice, and scrawled a handwritten note underneath. They pressed their heads together to read Geoffrey's message.

Did you really think it would be so easy?

***

Last night the Honourable Miss Ellen Burney, future Duchess of Woodhal, was seen at the theatre accompanied by the Dowager Marchioness of Faye, Mr Owen Tattershall and the elusive duke himself. She wore a simple pale gown trimmed with pink silk. But it was her long sleeves that caught the eye of many a keen observer. Word is, they shall be all the fashion by the morrow.

—The Daily Tatler

Is this is beginning of the end of the duke's self-imposed exile? Perhaps a wife is just what he needs to set him on the straight and narrow.

—The Ladies Gazette

The axe sank into the wall with a satisfyingly loud thwack. Pieces of plaster littered the floor around Cal's feet and a cloud of white dust bloomed into the air, catching the sunlight.

So, Geoffrey wasn't easily deterred. It hardly signified. After their exclusive engagement ball, Ellie would be nestled within the deep folds of

Society's skirts and no respectable person would be caught listening to any rumour Geoffrey tried to spread about her for fear of incurring the cut direct from his peers. In the face of that, not even the most steadfast of men could possibly continue this fiddle-faddle attempt to punish Ellie for whatever crimes their deluded minds had conjured up.

He let out a shuddering breath. Ellie's essence was rooted so deep beneath his skin every inch of his body remembered the feel of her against him. And last night he'd told her as much. With actual words. Like some goddamn normal functioning person.

Aye, she hadn't responded in kind. But he hadn't really expected her to. It was Ellie, after all. She needed space. She needed time. She needed to know she was in control of the situation.

Last night it had just been important that he be honest with himself and with her. And it was even more important that she realise how loved she was.

He chuckled. Who knew he'd ever be the romantic one in the relationship? Hell, when had he become the settling-down type?

The moment I met Ellie, of course.

He pulled back for a second swing, hoisting the axe over his shoulder and really throwing his weight behind it. Another bang, another hole, more flying plaster.

'What are you doing?'

Cal jumped. Ellie stood in the doorway to the ballroom, hands on hips. She wore another of her old, faded gowns. Her hair was a tangle of curls around her shoulders. She'd obviously recently woken.

What a stunning sight. If only she'd woken in his bed, instead of returning to her own after the mess of the broken window.

'It's barely six in the morning,' she scolded lightly. 'You'll wake the whole house.'

'Sorry.' He couldn't help but grin, and she smiled in return, flashing pearl-white teeth at him. Her lips were still red and a little swollen. The only evidence of last night. Hell, he wanted to shout it from the roof for all the world to hear.

I love Ellen Burney.

He leaned the axe against the half-destroyed wall and strode forward, fully intending to pull her in for another kiss, but then he noticed large eyes watching him from somewhere down near Ellie's waist. 'Uh-oh. I didn't mean to wake you too, wee one.'

Gwen didn't smile, but she didn't turn her face away from him either. And she was still holding the paper bag from yesterday, which was now looking a rather worse for wear. He brushed a finger lightly down one of her baby-smooth cheeks, tucking a dark curl behind her ear. 'Did ye finish your honeycomb last night?'

She nodded, slipping her thumb into her mouth.

'And now there are sticky crumbs in our bed.' Ellie nodded to the wall behind him, the one that cut the ballroom in half. 'You know the builders will be arriving this morning. You don't have to do that.'

'I know.' He ran a hand through his hair. 'It just felt right that I be the one to take it down—at least part of it.' After all, the whole reason Grace had commissioned the dividing walls in the first place was him. It was only years later that Cal had stumbled across his father's old receipts—evidence of the bribes he'd paid to ensure the builders kept their silence. He couldn't imagine what Hammond must have paid the servants over the years to keep the secret. To this day, all the wider world knew of the changes was that the house now had two front doors.

That was all about to change in just three days' time, when the house would be awash with London's brightest and wealthiest to celebrate his and Ellie's fake engagement.

'I see.' She stepped forward and pressed a light kiss to his scarred cheek. 'Good morning.' A whisper. Another shared smile.

'Good morning.' Excellent morning. The best of all mornings. 'Did ye want to help me?'

Her eyes widened. 'Is it dangerous?'

'It's just laths and plaster. The wall isn't even strong enough to hold up a painting. Ye just—'

Even before he'd finished his sentence, Ellie rushed the wall, kicking it. With a loud crack, her petite boot smashed a hole.

'Woo!' She hopped backwards until her foot came free, her eyes flashing with excitement. 'I've never broken anything on purpose before.' And she set to work with that same dedication she applied to all her tasks.

He shrugged off his jacket, using his hands to tear at the broken plaster. Out of the corner of his eye, he saw Gwen, still tangled in her mother's skirts, kicking her own small hole with the toe of her tiny boot until the entire room was filled with the glorious sounds of destruction.

Chapter Twenty-Two

One week later

Once again Cal's house had descended into chaos. He sped up, limping towards the sanctuary of his bedchamber. The servants were like spinning tops, rushing around all over the place, putting together the last-minute touches for tonight's engagement ball.

They'd had to hire most of the ballroom furniture, including chaperone chairs and long tables for the buffet. The larger pieces were this minute being taken apart and reassembled upstairs thanks to the too-narrow passageways. For that task, Lady F had hired a whole battalion of labourers, who were traipsing up and down the stairs in shoes that might well have been made from steel for all the noise they were making.

Cal quickly shut the door behind him, resting his forehead on the cool wood. But even in here he could hear the shrill voice of his grandmother, who was barking out orders like Nelson himself, and Tzar, who was just barking. Cal's head was beginning to ache. He needed to stuff his ears with cotton. Hell, he needed a drink.

He limped towards his bed, stopping short. Someone had laid out his costume for tonight, and he instantly wished he'd hidden behind the rosebush in the back garden instead. There was no way he was wearing that.

A pox on Geoffrey!

And a pox on that daft barking dog. Why wouldn't he shut up? It was wholly unlike Tzar to make such a racket. He was usually so mellow, even more now he was deaf.

Grinding his teeth, Cal headed back downstairs. Tzar probably enjoyed having strangers in the house as much as Cal did and needed recusing.

Also much like I do.

'Vouchers to Almack's already.' Lady F practically purred with delight when he stuck his head into the ballroom. 'And to think you and Ellen didn't even to stay until the end of Act II.' She waved him closer.

'You've had an open invitation for Almack's since the day it opened,' Cal reminded her, crossing the room and narrowly side-stepping a pair of labourers hurrying back towards the stairs.

'Calum! Haven't you been taught never to make reference to a lady's age?' She gave his arm a scolding tap. 'Lady Jersey was practically begging me to bring Ellen along. She even asked after you.'

'Did she?' He didn't even attempt to keep the dry sarcasm from his voice. He couldn't care less who or what Lady Jersey asked after.

'Don't you see? They simply love Ellen. She's their queen bee after one appearance.'

'That might be a bit of an exaggeration. But, yes, everything is going to plan,' he conceded, sounding rather ungracious even to his own ears.

'My plan.' She puffed out her chest. 'Didn't I tell you this would work?'

'Yes. Do you know what Ellen intends to do after all this is over?'

Lady F shrugged. 'I'm not a crystal ball. She and Gwen are very welcome to stay with me for as long as they wish.'

'But you'll return to Faye Park at the end of the Season. Has she said anything—'

'Pish posh. Why all the questions? Ellen is a grown woman and perfectly capable of deciding her future all on her own.'

'I know but—'

'But nothing. You're just nervous,' she said dismissively. 'Nerves always make you grumpy.'

He most certainly wasn't nervous. He was ... What was the word for a combination of defensive, contemptuous and bitter? Bedevilled perhaps? On that note: 'There's nothing you can do that will convince me to wear the costume you've picked out.'

But he'd already lost her attention. Lady F had returned to scribbling notes in the margin of a book entitled *A Companion to the Ballroom* with a small graphite pencil. That certainly wasn't a book from his father's library.

On the other side of the room, the formidable Miss Miller was examining a list of her own. It was so long he could have used it to climb out the first-storey window, like Rapunzel's hair.

'Stop being ridiculous,' his grandmother said, not sparing him another glance. 'Your costume is in theme with the decorations.' Lady F waved the pencil vaguely around the room.

Begrudgingly, he silently had to admit the ballroom did look rather magnificent. The builders had removed all remaining evidence of the dividing wall. They'd also refreshed the wallpaper, repainted the moulded ceiling and replaced the chandeliers with ones that were neither dusty nor cracked. They'd also taken down the boarding and opened the double doors leading out onto the balcony, letting crisp, fresh air carry away the last of the plaster dust.

Entire bolts of white crepe had been draped in swathes over the walls, and what looked like an entire flower shop had been arranged into large urns, creating small and seductively private alcoves of each of the four corners. Alcoves that he would undoubtably not have the privilege of visiting tonight, not when he and Ellie were to be under so many watchful eyes.

Turning a full circle, he frowned at a wooden placard that had pride of place by the main entrance.

'From chaos into light,' he read. 'What's that supposed to mean?'

'What?' Lady F looked around, distractedly. 'Oh-oh, that. It was the only excuse I could think of to explain the rest of the house.'

'What about my house?' He pulled back an inch.

'Don't sound so offended. You know what it means—the garden looks like hedgerows and the house is crumbling down around your boots.'

'It's not.'

With a sigh, she finally looked at him again. 'Dear boy, the wallpaper is peeling something dreadful, and the furniture is about a decade out of date. But most importantly, the dining room is where the lady's parlour should be, the stairs used to be the billiards room, and I surely don't need to remind you that there's a wall running straight down the central hallway. I dread to think how some of the ladies are going to squeeze down there in their costumes. The builders simply didn't have time—'

'I get your point.' He cut across her. 'Maybe we should just cancel this whole damned thing.'

'Cancel?' Her near-invisible eyebrows rose. 'We've only just whetted their appetites. If we cancel now, they'll never forgive us for denying them the chance to meet the mysterious Miss Burney in person. Did I tell you that every single invitation we sent has been accepted? Every single one.'

Except for the one sent to Grace, who hadn't responded either way. And just because the Prince Regent has said he'd attend didn't actually mean he'd show. Cal wasn't exactly George's favourite duke, not since Cal had voted so obviously in favour of curbing rising taxes. But he didn't remind Lady F of that.

'Yes,' he said instead. 'You might have mentioned it once or twice or a million times.'

'Not there!' She waved at a short man carrying a chaperone chair. He wore a hat pulled so low it cast shadows over his face. 'Have you even bothered to look at the floor plan I made for you? The chairs go along the other wall.'

'Why are you doing all of this? You haven't known Ellen all that long and ... well, you're going to a lot of trouble.'

'I'm not the one posing as her fiancé.' She swallowed, looking away.

'What is it?' He narrowed his eyes, watching her carefully. 'What aren't you telling me?'

'Nothing.' She shrugged. 'It's just ... Well, Ellen's mother was a friend of Owen's mother, before they both died.'

'You knew Ellen's mother?' His mouth opened. Sure, he'd always known Owen's family was originally from Evendale, but that was so many years ago. Owen's parents had died when he'd still been in leading strings. 'Does that mean you also you knew about Gwen and Geoffrey all along?'

She nibbled her bottom lip.

'You did!'

'I haven't been back to Evendale since just after Ellen was born. I kept in touch with her mother though, and, when Guinevere died, I started writing to Maggie. It was Maggie who told me about all the trouble Ellen and little Gwen were having with Geoffrey.'

'So you didn't advertise for a lady's companion after all?' He'd thought that had been out of character. His grandmother had never been one to sit around expecting others to keep her entertained.

'Not exactly...'

'Does Ellen know?'

'Of course not. Maggie said Ellen would never accept charity. She wants to be an independent woman, not a single mother accepting handouts. Besides, if Ellen had known about me, then there was a chance Geoffrey would have found out too. It's safer this way. At least, it was supposed to be.'

It was all starting to make sense now—why Lady F had taken such a liking to Ellie when they'd first met and how Geoffrey had found her so quickly. He must has remembered Lady F despite all the years.

A light sheen of perspiration gathered on the Lady F's upper lip and she clutched the book close to her chest. An uncomfortable swell of guilt churned in Cal's stomach. Without her interference, whatever her motivations, whatever secrets she'd kept, he'd never have met Ellie.

'You look lovely.' He nodded to the costume she was already wearing. More swathes of white fabric engulfed her large frame. The hem was stitched with peacock feathers and she'd changed her normal white wig for one of tight brunette pin curls. To top it all off, she'd placed a small beauty patch on one cheek like a dimple formed by a smile—a throwback to the last century.

'I'm Hera, Queen of the Greek gods.' The bright smile she turned on him just made him feel even worse. Had it really been that long since he'd paid her a compliment? Hell, what had he been doing with his life these last few years?

'All your shouting has scared the dog,' he grumbled, desperate to change the conversation before he was completely overwhelmed by unwanted emotions. 'I can't find him anywhere, and he won't stop barking.'

'Well, he's stopped barking now.'

'He's—Wait, who's that?' There was a woman sitting in one of the chaperone chairs. She wore a tattered dress, and there was a straw bonnet with a faded blue ribbon resting in her lap. She wasn't a servant or a guest.

Following his gaze, his grandmother gave a small start. 'Who's she?'

He refrained from rolling his eyes. 'I just asked you that.' The stranger had the most shockingly red hair he'd ever seen and spectacles that made her eyes appear much too large for her face.

'Chakrabarti!' Lady Faye waved at the passing butler, who was shepherding around an armful of crystal glasses. There was a long piece of paper sticking out of his pocket—probably another to-do list compiled by Lady F. Poor chap. By the time this was all over, he'd deserve a pay rise.

'Who's that?'

'Sorry, my lady. I don't know. Miss Burney brought her inside a couple of hours ago, sat her in that seat and told her to stay quiet. I heard her say something about, if that woman was going to spy on them from across the road, she might as well be warm and comfortable because it's going to be a long night.' With a bow, he continued on with his task.

'Intriguing.' Lady Faye approached the stranger. 'Good afternoon, lovely. A friend of Miss Burney, I hear?'

The woman jumped to her feet, curtsying low. 'My lady—'

'Who are you?' Cal interrupted what he foresaw as a tirade of sentimental salutations about how wonderful the dowager was.

'Miss Sophy Calder, my lady, Your Grace. I'm sorry, but who is Miss Burney?' She frowned.

'The woman who brought you inside,' Lady F asked, elbowing Cal painfully in his side for his rudeness.

'Ah, you mean Miss Smith. We've only met the once before today.'

'Did Geoffrey send you?' Cal completely ignored the warning looks Lady F was giving him. Ellie hadn't mentioned a Miss Calder to him before.

'For goodness sake, Cal. You're scaring her. You've got everyone on edge.' His grandmother grabbed his arm, tugging him back a few steps. 'Excuse us a moment.'

'Everyone—' he started indigently.

'Most certainly everyone. Now, do you or do you not want to marry Ellen?'

Hell's bells! 'Where on earth did that come from?'

Over his grandmother's shoulder he caught sight of Miss Calder squinting at him shortsightedly through her spectacles, all the better to see his startled expression. He pulled his arm free of Lady F's clutches.

'You've been sulking around this house ever since she refused to marry you.'

'I've been sulking around this house for much longer than that,' he hissed, keeping his voice low.

'Precisely my point.' She didn't bother keeping her own voice low.

'What?' That made no sense.

Lady F pressed her hands to her hips and stuck her chin in the air. 'Well? Do you or do you not want to marry Ellen?'

'I...' She had that look in her eye that told him if he tried to run away she'd follow. She'd probably follow him to the Continent and back. *To hell with it.* 'Of course I do!'

She beamed. 'Cal, dearest, of course you do.' Standing on tip toes, she pressed a hand to his cheek in a moment of unexpected affection, before giving him a light slap. 'So go and put on the costume I laid out for you.'

'I've already told Ellie how I feel, and she still won't have me.'

This time she slapped his arse with her book. 'Perhaps if you weren't so miserable and grumpy all the time she might actually start taking you seriously.'

Chapter Twenty-Three

Downstairs, the ball had begun. Ellen watched as carriages jostled for advantage before the great iron gates. Most of their guests lived within walking distance, Mayfair being the fashionable part of Town, but come by coach and four they did, until the dark street below was awash with the flickering lights of dozens of carriage lamps.

She let the curtain fall back into place and pressed a kiss to her daughter's temple. Gwen was fast asleep, her hands pillowing one cheek.

'Cook said there'd be dinner waiting in the kitchen for you,' she told Maggie in a low voice. Her friend was knitting by the fire. Her hands were never idle. 'Are you sure you don't want to come to the ball?'

'Don't worry about me. I'm much happier keeping an eye on little Guinevere.' The shadows dancing over her face exaggerated the hollows under her eyes. 'Although some dinner would be much appreciated.'

They left Gwen sleeping. The candles in the wall sconces lining the passageway flicked with the closing of the door. Maggie continued on down to the kitchen, but Ellen stayed in the passage, waiting for the music to start.

Sounds from below flowed up the stairs. Chakrabarti was still manning the front door and directing guests upstairs, while Lady Faye was greeting them as they entered the ballroom, Owen by her side.

Ellen took a shuddering breath. This wasn't going to be like the other night at the theatre. Not only would everyone be staring at her; they'd want to talk to her as well. She was seven years out of practice with her small talk.

She ran shaking hands down the front of her costume. Mademoiselle Bond had worked magic. Tonight she wore a simple white dress that hung from her shoulders and gathered at her waist. It was very similar to Lady Faye's costume, although Ellen's hem was embroidered with blue cornflowers rather than peacock feathers and it was her own hair that had been curled to within an inch of its life and pinned into a sweeping chignon, not a wig like the dowager wore.

'Demeter, goddess of the harvest, I do believe.' Calum leaned against the open doorway of his chamber, arms crossed. He looked her up and down, eyes lingering. 'The gardening goddess. How very apt.'

'I thought so...' Her voice died as she took in the sight of him. He was wearing ... She swallowed. He was wearing what could only be described as a white kilt with white stockings and bare knees. His shirt was open at the collar, the top couple of buttons having been cut away.

He followed her gaze down to his knees and scowled. 'Trust me, this wasn't my first choice.'

Her stomach did a backflip, a whole series of them. He was dressed as a Greek god, just as she'd imagined him to be the first night they'd met. Apparently some wishes really did come true.

Who knew Calum Callaghan was sex in a skirt?

Her mouth went dry and her thoughts fuzzy. She searched for words, trying to persuade her mouth to say something half intelligent. 'Ahh...'

She quickly averted her gaze, praying her brain would start working again if she wasn't looking directly at him, and spotted a large four-poster bed with dark sheets over his shoulder. The counterpane had been thrown back haphazardly as though the bed had just been vacated—or was inviting her in.

He chuckled. 'If I'd known ye'd look at me like that I wouldn't have complained half so much about this ridiculous costume.'

'Not ridiculous.' She swallowed to remove the lump from her throat. 'But you cannot go downstairs like that. Your knees...' He had beautiful knees. Even his left one, which was marked by a large scar. 'You'll have all the chaperones fainting and all the debutantes waving their dance cards at you. I won't get a word in.'

'Jealous?' He raised that single glorious eyebrow. 'Ellie, love, haven't I made myself clear? Ye're the only one for me.' His gaze dropped to her mouth, the hungry look in his eyes scolding her skin until she had to lock her hands behind her back for fear of jumping him. 'Perhaps I need to be more persuasive.' He guided her into his empty room. She slid from his hold, but he stalked towards her like a cat hunting its prey, and suddenly she wanted nothing more than to let him catch her, if only for a few heartbeats.

He rested both hands on the wall either side of her head, leaning down for a kiss, a smirk tugging at his lips. His smile seemed to say 'resist me if you can'.

Her traitorous nipples hardened, clearly visible through the thin fabric of her costume.

At the last second, he slipped the straps from her shoulders. The bodice, not supported by boning or buttons or lacing, slithered down her body to hang from her hips. Cal's sharp intake of breath spoke volumes. Anticipation skittered over her skin, and he dipped his head, taking one peaked nipple into his mouth.

Thank all that was good laced stays weren't part of her costume.

'Someone will see,' she breathed even as she arched her back, pressing closer.

'They're all busy downstairs.' He moved his attention to her other breast, and the cool air on the damp flesh of her abandoned breast only stoked her desire for his touch.

She moaned, unable to hold back. He looked up at her, his hooded eyes near black with desire, and his smile turned smug. Somewhere in the passage beyond the open door, the wall sconces flickered as though someone was in the corridor. But there was no sound of footsteps, so she relaxed.

'I'm not sure why you're under the impression you have the upper hand.' Not when his skirt was considerably shorter than her own. She slipped her hand under the pleats, running her finger up his thick thigh. He grunted in surprise.

What was it she'd promised herself back in the carriage after they'd left the theatre? *Oh, yes. It's my turn to crumple his clothes.*

She moved her hand higher and his hips involuntarily thrust towards her. His head dropped to rest on her shoulder. 'I very much approve of your costume,' she purred into his ear.

'I know I'm also supposed to be Greek,' he managed to say through clenched teeth. 'I'm just not sure which one.'

'Atlas,' she replied without hesitation. 'The man who holds the whole world upon his shoulders.'

He stilled, pulling back a little to study her face. 'Remind me again why ye won't marry me, lass?'

She withdrew her hand and pulled her sleeves back up, covering herself. 'Because...' The thought of leaving him felt like someone had pulled all the air from her lungs. She'd miss the way he looked straight at her, as though he could instantly understand each expression that crossed her face, as though he were the only one in the world who could completely perceive her.

She'd miss the way his knee pained him when he was anxious or readying himself for a fight. And it was always her he was fighting for these days, even though he wanted nothing more than peace and quiet after all the horrors of the war. She should feel guilty about that, and she did. But she also felt incredibly blessed.

He was as kind to her as he was angry with the rest of the world.

She'd even miss his grumpy sulks. He was so infuriating when in high dudgeon. The way he crossed his arms and stood his ground, as though he thought neither heaven nor hell could move him.

And that Scottish voice of his did the most delightful things to her imagination. Just the thought of it had her toes curling in anticipation.

She'd never thought to be loved in such a way, and it was simply sublime.

'Marry me.' He pressed his advantage, rightly taking her silence for consideration.

She winced. 'I can't. Not now. I'm sorry. I want the right to choose what I do with my life—and Gwen's. I don't want to be pushed into anything because my witless brother is threatening to make a mess.'

'Ellie—'

'My lord duke.' Sophy turned her back on them, her hands leaping to her mouth. 'I'm sorry. I didn't realise anyone was still up here.'

'What are you doing?' Ellen moved forward, but Calum stopped her.

'I asked for Miss Calder's help. She's looking for Tzar.'

'What?' Her brother's spy was helping Calum?

'She wasn't doing anything and Tzar's missing, so she volunteered to search for him.'

'So ... she's not working for Geoffrey?' She gestured at Sophy's back.

'Nay.' He frowned. 'Weren't you the one to invite her inside? Didn't you want her to speak with me?'

'Yes ... no.' She wrinkled her brow. They were at sixes and sevens. 'Miss Calder didn't actually tell me what she wanted. She was watching the house and I thought...' Ugh, it sounded silly now. Of course the poor woman wasn't a spy.

His frown deepened. 'She wants my help finding her brother. Isn't that right, Miss Calder?'

Sophy turned back to face them. 'Yes, Your Grace. I haven't heard anything of him since well before the end of the war.' She turned to Ellen. 'He was in the Navy, you see. I thought Lord Woodhal might have heard something.'

Near on two years of silence. Sophy must be desperate if she was petitioning a duke—a duke who'd left the Navy more than four years ago and on less than ideal terms. 'You mentioned your brother to me that first night we met at Vauxhall.' And apparently she'd been telling the truth all along.

Ellen's gaze landed on Sophy's feet, clad in a pair of leather half-boots, with black ribbon laces. They were the shoes a governess would wear or maybe a housekeeper—perfectly practical and perfectly respectable in every way. Butterflies named Guilt and Shame fluttered uneasily in her stomach.

'Any luck finding my dog?' Calum asked.

'No, Your Grace.' Sophy bobbed another curtsey. 'About my brother—'

Cal's jaw tightened, the only perceivable change to indicate his growing concern.

'He can't have gotten far.' Ellen fiddled with her skirt in a bid to stop herself reaching out to comfort him before watching eyes. She knew how much Tzar meant to him.

'I've searched the downstairs rooms twice over,' confirmed Sophy rather reluctantly. 'I'm just about to check the other bedchambers.'

'He's not in my room, and Gwen is sleeping.'

'Of course,' said Calum. 'Have you searched the other side of the house, Miss Calder?'

'I assumed someone else lived there.' Sophy glanced between them, seeking confirmation.

'It's empty.' Calum quickly described the door in the kitchen that led into Grace's—now Ellen's—half of the house. 'I doubt he's there,' he admitted. 'But maybe someone opened the door by accident when they were moving furniture upstairs.'

'I'll check straight away.' She hurried away.

'I feel like a sop.' Ellen wrinkled her nose. 'I thought she was watching the house at Geoffrey's request. I should have just asked instead of worrying about it for so many days.' Poor Sophy and her poor brother. 'It was very kind of you to agree to help. Do you know her brother?'

'Nay. I don't think we ever met. But I can easily write Miss Calder letters of introduction for the Navy Office and such so that they can't ignore her requests for information any longer. It's the very least I can do. I suspect the poor lad's dead, but she deserves to know either way.' He forced a smile, a shadow in his eyes at the very mention of the Navy. 'After tonight, hopefully ye won't have to worry about Blackford again. This engagement ball is going to be an even greater success than I first anticipated. Thanks to Lady F.'

Ellen nodded. The dowager had worked tirelessly for days. She'd even hired two artists to chalk the ballroom floor with Mount Olympus, complete with its temple—the finishing touches to a room decorated to dazzle.

All that was left now was the actual ball. Just one long night of smiling and dancing and small talk to survive. The butterflies in her stomach morphed into leapfrogs named Panic and Terror.

Below, the music started playing. Ellen crossed her arms, tucking her shaking hands under her elbows. At least her costume was sleeveless, else she'd probably stain the delicate muslin with perspiration. Her bruises had almost entirely faded.

Calum gave her a reassuring smile. 'You know, the more I think about it the more I'm sure that Demeter married Atlas in the end.'

'No, she did not.' Ellen laughed, but even she could hear the shake in her voice. 'She had a daughter with Zeus. And when her daughter was stolen away, she searched and searched until they were reunited. But she most definitely didn't marry Atlas.'

'Shame. That would have been a much better ending to the tale. And I'm quite sure they would have rubbed along famously together.' He offered his arm. 'That's our cue, though ye need only say the word and we'll run away to Gretna Green.'

She placed her hand on his forearm. For all his laughing words, he was tense.

'Perhaps next time.' He was doing this all for her, and, if it weren't for Gwen, she'd never have agreed to this plan. But there wasn't anything she wouldn't do to protect her child, nothing she wouldn't ask of the people around her. If only there were some way she could wrap both Gwen and Calum in cottonwool and tuck them into her pocket, safe and protected from the world.

But this was real life and real life was never so simple.

'Try to stop worrying, love.' He bent his head and pressed a lingering kiss to the corner of her mouth. 'And consider yerself warned. I intend to spend the rest of the evening persuading ye to marry me.'

***

Bang!

The house reverberated, setting the candelabras chiming.

Ellie clutched his arm. 'What was that?'

'Gunshot.' Cal stiffened. He tried sucking in a breath but his lungs seemed to have forgotten how to work. Only his heart kept beating, thumping so hard in his chest it surely sounded like a military tattoo.

'In Roseworthy?' Ellie's eyebrows rose in question, but before he could answer she started towards the stairs, her white dress fanning out behind her. He forced his legs into motion, using the handrail to leverage his bad knee down the stairs. He reached the ground floor, coming to an abrupt halt behind Ellie. She was staring at a man standing a few feet inside the house, pistol in hand. He wore the clothes of a labourer and had a hat pulled low over his head. It was the same man Lady F had remonstrated with earlier that afternoon for leaving chairs in the wrong place. There was white plaster on his shoulders and scattered around his feet. He'd fired a hole through the ceiling above his head.

'Geoffrey!' Ellie's hand jumped to her mouth. 'What are you doing?'

He laughed. *Laughed!*

Cal's gaze was drawn to the gun. He couldn't blink. He couldn't look away. Ellie was so vulnerable standing in front of Geoffrey as she was. He could practically see how the bullet would tear through her flesh like she was nothing more than meat. Cal tried to push her behind him, but she was having none of it.

'Geoffrey.' She reached towards her brother as though to take the gun from his hand.

Geoffrey jumped back and out of her reach. *Bang!*

Plaster explored above their heads. Instinctively Cal raised his arms to cover Ellie from the worst of it. White specks fell into his eyes and for a second he couldn't see.

'There are people upstairs!' Ellie yelled. She was angry, much angrier than scared, and she was glaring at Geoffrey with renewed ferocity. 'You'll kill someone.'

Footsteps sound on the stairs behind them. But he didn't spare the spectators a glance. He had his family to protect.

'Ye're out of shots.' Cal nodded to the gun. It was a double-barrelled flintlock pistol, very similar to the type British troops had used during the war. 'What are ye going to do now?'

'What's all of this?' A middle-aged woman, of all things, appeared in the doorway behind Geoffrey. She was dressed in a long travelling cloak, and there was mud on her boots. She started at Geoffrey's back with horrified recognition.

Geoffrey laughed again, a maniacal laugh that carried with it notes of triumph and madness.

'What am I going to do now?' he repeated Cal's question as though it were the funniest thing he'd ever heard—the punch line of a hilarious tale. 'I've already done it.' He sprung around, apparently completely unaware of the woman behind him.

'Verity, look out!' Ellie dived forward, but Verity drew back her fist and punched Geoffrey square in the face.

There was a sickening crack, and Ellie's brother went down, his hands grasping at his bleeding nose. Before anyone could move to apprehend him, someone else screamed.

It was Maggie, and she was pushing her way through the crowd towards them.

'Gwen. She's gone!'

Chapter Twenty-Four

Ellen launched herself at Geoffrey, but Calum was faster.

He grabbed her brother by the scruff of his collar and hauled Geoffrey to his feet. Drops of blood splattered his old shoes. 'What have you done with Gwen?'

'Check my pockets. I haven't got her.' Geoffrey's voice was muffled by the sleeve he held to his nose, and he was breathing heavily out his mouth. For all that, he still managed a sneer.

'If ye've hurt that wee bairn in any way—' Calum broke off. The unspoken threat hung in the air, and for the first time that evening a flicker of fear crossed Geoffrey's face. He eyed the sheer size of Calum, and where he hadn't seen a threat before, he certainly saw one now. Calum's muscles held tension, clearly visible though the thin linen of his white shirt. And the candlelight from the small chandelier overhead highlighted the peaks and valleys of his scars.

Geoffrey glanced down at his gun. They all knew he was out of bullets, and he never pushed for a fight when he didn't have the upper hand.

Only he did have the upper hand, gun or no, because he had Gwen.

Renewed desperation clawed at Ellen's throat like someone trying to strangle the life from her. She grabbed at Geoffrey's sleeve demanding his attention, demanding he tell her where Gwen was. Her brother turned his gaze towards her. And his eyes, so like her father's in shape and colour, where filled with hatred. Pure, undiluted hatred.

'But you're my brother.' She stumbled back a step, the sheer force of his look a knife to her heart.

'You ruined my whole life!'

'What rot,' scoffed Calum aggressively. He released Geoffrey to wrap an arm around her shoulders, holding her up when her knees would have given way. 'Ye ruined yer own life. Ye had the world handed down to ye on a silver platter, Blackford, and ye threw it all away at the gambling tables. Ye're a cowardly coxcomb!'

'Of course you've taken Ellen's side. Everyone always does.' Geoffrey laughed for the third time. A bitter laugh. A sad laugh. The laugh of a condemned man.

Suddenly someone was screaming, but Ellen couldn't hear what they were saying. There was a rushing in her ears and spots blurring her vision.

Gwen!

'Hold up there, lass.' Calum pulled her against his hard chest, trapping her hands. 'Ye're all right. We'll find her.'

She realised it was her who was screaming. They were her cries echoing through the rundown house. She buried her face in Calum's shoulder, biting down on her bottom lip until there was pain. Her whole body shook from the force of her sobs and there was nothing she could do to stop.

'Dearest.' Lady Faye was there, rubbing circled on her back. And Owen too. They huddled close, offering comfort with their touch.

My family. The thought came unbidden, offering strength enough that she was able to finally check her tears. She was not alone in this, and crying wasn't going to help find her daughter. She pulled away from Calum's chest, searching for brother. She'd demand Geoffrey tell her where Gwen was if it was the last thing she did.

'He got away, lass. When ye started screaming,' said Calum, and she felt the rumble of his voice in his chest. 'Your Maggie and Verity ran after him.'

'What are we going to do?' Her voice was hoarse. She licked her lips and wiped clean her face with the Calum's offered handkerchief.

'One of the servants is already on their way to fetch the Runners. Until then, we have to trust Maggie and Verity will find Geoffrey. Miss Calder,' he suddenly called over the top of her head. 'Did ye see a bairn when ye searched the house for Tzar?'

Ellen looked over her shoulder in the direction Calum had spoken. There was a crowd of people pressed into the tiny space behind her. She'd completely forgotten about the engagement ball.

Sophy pushed her way through costumed guests towards them. There was a large busted Cleopatra, a sheep-less shepherdess, two knights of the round table and three King Arthurs all squeezed into what was probably the narrowest passageway in all of London. The rest of the guests must still be upstairs in the ballroom. The music had stopped. They probably all had their ears pressed to the floor. She looked up, and there was an eye staring at her through the hole in the ceiling. It blinked, then pulled back.

Ellen's scandalous past was well and truly out to air. Not that it mattered now. Nothing matter more than Gwen's safety.

'No, Your Grace,' panted Sophy. 'I heard the shots. I've just come from the other half of the house, and it's completely empty. I didn't find your dog—or the missing girl.'

Renewed doubt choked up Ellen's throat. Sophy was a part of this. Sophy had taken her child. And Ellen had been the one to invite her into their home.

She broke free of Calum's embrace, rushing Sophy. 'She's only six,' she screamed.

'I know.' Even when Ellen grabbed at Sophy, the other woman didn't flinch away. She looked straight at Ellen, and some of Ellen's own pain was reflected back at her. This woman's beloved brother was missing; and there was a strange sort of kinship in that.

Ellen's shoulders sagged and she felt the fight leave her body again. 'I'm sorry. I'm sorry.'

Only when Calum tried to pry her fingers off Sophy's arm did she realised she'd grabbed her hard enough to bruise. She let go, disgusted at herself.

'She's a very quiet bairn,' Calum said. 'Ye might not have heard her if ye weren't searching carefully.'

'No. I swear I never saw a child.' Sophy looked between them, still steadily meeting their gazes. 'I searched every room save your own chamber, Your Grace, and your's, miss.' She nodded towards Ellen. And with her nod, another piece of Ellen's heart broke.

If Geoffrey hadn't left with Gwen, if Sophy wasn't a part of this, if Gwen wasn't anywhere to be found in the house, then where was she?

'Keep searching,' Calum demanded, desperation creeping into his voice. 'If ye find the lass I swear to God I'll help find your brother.'

Chapter Twenty-Five

Ellie looked just about ready to expire from heartbreak. Cal gently led her to the porter's chair, and she sank down onto the seat, her head dropping into her hands.

'Ye're shaking.' He forced his wounded knee to bend, and kneeled before her, rubbing her shaking legs. If only he could somehow rub a little of her fear away.

If Ellie's heart broke, surely his would too.

He needed to fix this. He needed to find Gwen. Right this very minute. 'Lizzy, stay with Ellen. Owen, guard the door. Call for me immediately if Blackford dares to show his face here again, and don't let any of the guests leave unless ye're sure they're not hiding Gwen on their person. I'll direct the search.' He straightened, ideas about search numbers and reporting stations and plans of attack swirling around his head. It was the same voice he'd listened to when captaining a ship of seven hundred men. The voice he'd stopped listening to after the fire. Now, he didn't have that luxury.

'Right you are!' Owen snatched a sword from a bewildered-looking knight and turned his gaze to the front door as though daring Geoffrey to reappear. He'd come to the ball as Icarus, the man who'd flown too close to the sun, and was wearing white feather wings and a short white tunic. Now, he was an avenging angel.

'Where's Chakrabarti?' Lady F pushed a shot of whisky into Ellie's hand, looking up and down the passage as though the butler would appear on command. 'He was supposed to be manning the door, and he's never not where he's supposed to be.'

'Ye're right.' He frowned. Had Geoffrey stolen away their butler too? Surely not.

'Why has he done this?' Ellie's voice was barely more than a whisper. Calum didn't need to hear a name to know she was talking about her brother again.

'Think about it for a moment, love,' he said, trying to offer words of comfort. Though what he could stay to make any of this better was beyond him. 'What would Geoffrey want with a six-year-old? Nothing whatsoever. She'll be hiding somewhere in the house.'

'Then why did he say he'd got what he'd come for?' Lady F nudged the untouched glass in Ellie's hand, directing her to down the whisky.

'He'd just fired a gun and created a scene that's not likely to be forgotten anytime soon,' Cal reasoned. 'I think that's what he was referring too. Gwen probably heard the shots and hid somewhere.'

'You're right.' Ellie straightened, discarding the glass on the chair arm. 'She's very good a hiding. She's used to hide in the—' Her face froze.

'Ellie?'

She pushed to her feet, her gaze distant. 'What of the old housekeeper's sitting room at the back of your library. That door's half in shadow. Sophy might not have seen it.'

They hurried down the hallway, pushing their way past guests who had their mouths open and were watching everything that was happening like it was some sort of stage drama. In the library, the fireplace was empty and the curtains drawn, leaving the room so dark Ellie nearly tripped over the footrest again. Cal slipped his hand into hers. 'This way.' Reaching towards the door, his hand touched the back of a chair. 'This shouldn't be here.' He pulled it out of the way. It had been blocking the door shut. He opened it, blinking in the sudden light.

A three-arm candelabra was on one of the dusty tables. Chakrabarti sat on the floor, his back against the wall. His eyes were closed and there was a bloody gash on the side of his head. Tzar lay at his feet, gently snorting.

A flash a white fabric was all Cal saw of Gwen as she scrambled to her feet and launched herself at Ellie.

'Mama!' A heartbeat later, the child had buried her face in Ellie's skirts. Ellie dropped to her knees, crying loudly. She pressed wet kisses to Gwen's cheeks, chin and hair.

Chakrabarti groaned, his eyes flickering open. 'Your Grace.' He tried to struggle to his feet, but Cal shook his head and nudged Tzar out of his way so he could bend over the butler and better assess his head wound. Thankfully it looked fairly shallow, despite the blood which had dripped down the side of his face and begun to dry on his cravat. Head wounds could be serious though, and Chakrabarti would need a doctor to check him over. 'Someone hit me.' The young man's words were slightly slurred. Concussed no doubt.

'It was my brother.' Ellie stood up, her daughter in her arms. She bounced lightly on her toes, one arm wrapped around Gwen's back and the other cradling Gwen's head to her shoulder. The girl's arms were wrapped tightly around Ellen's neck. It looked like they were never going to let each other go. He could hardly blame them. It was all he could do not to pull them both into his arms. Hell, he felt like crying too, his relief was so palpable.

'I don't understand.' Chakrabarti ran a shaking hand over his face. 'There was a labourer. He came out of the drawing room after the guests had gone upstairs. That's when he hit me.' He looked at the blood staining his hands as though he couldn't work out where it had come from. Even shallow head wounds tended to bleed a lot.

Cal stuck his head out the library door, directing Owen to call a doctor. then returned to Chakrabarti. Although the young man was slurring his words, his gaze was clear. 'After Blackford hit ye, he dragged ye in here?'

'I suppose.' Chakrabarti shrugged then winced. 'I woke up and found myself locked in here with Miss Guinevere. I think she'd come downstairs looking for Miss Miller.'

'Maggie was in the kitchen getting her dinner,' Ellie clarified.

'Blackford must have locked Tzar up because he wouldn't stop barking at him.' Calum scratch Tzar behind the ear, remembering how much he'd barked at Geoffrey the first time Ellie's brother had come calling. 'Ye've certainly got good taste, old man.'

Tzar wagged his tail in agreement.

***

'I can't tell which way he went.' Verity squinted up and down the street. They'd barely passed through the gate before a sinking feeling had filled her stomach. It was so dark, they'd never find Geoffrey now. 'I should have tried harder to stop him.'

'Self-pity later.' Maggie turned right onto Curzon Street. 'There's only two ways he could have gone. We might as well try this way.'

Verity felt lost, like her thoughts were trapped in golden syrup. All she could do was follow Maggie. In no time at all they'd reached the end of the street, bringing them face to face with another hard choice.

'This way.' Barely pausing, Maggie turned onto Clargest Street, guessing again. Her footsteps tapped out a brisk rhythm that seemed to echo the beating of Verity's heart. 'If that vile man has hurt Gwen...' Her voice dropped away with worry, even as she sped up.

Verity couldn't think of a single comforting word. What could she say? Meaningless platitudes about how it would all work out in the end. How could it? They both knew what Geoffrey was capable of.

They reached the end of the second street and were faced with another impossible choice: left or right along Piccadilly? Unless, of course, Geoffrey had crossed into Green Park. Verity eyed the shadowy wall surrounding the park wearily. Surely not even Geoffrey would risk crossing it after sundown?

'This is hopeless.' Maggie turned a circle.

'We can't give up so quickly.' Maggie's panic seemed to launch Verity's thoughts into action. 'We'll keep searching.' It was all that they could do.

She took Maggie's hand in hers, and they turned back, taking a different direction this time. Practically running now, they made their way along each of the streets in Mayfair, circling around Roseworthy.

'Wait.' Maggie held out an arm, stopping Verity. 'Down here.' Partial darkness hid the bottom of the area steps of the nearest townhouse, but Maggie didn't hesitate.

Verity followed, almost slipping on something dark and wet on the stairs. There was a door, which presumably led to the basement kitchen, and at the foot of the steps lay Geoffrey. His arms were flung wide like he'd tried to stop his fall. He stared up at them, unseeing.

Kneeling, Verity ran her hands over Geoffrey, searching for any signs he still lived, but there was no breath and no pulse. Her fingers brushed something sticky on the back of his head. More blood. 'He'd dead.' He'd died as he'd lived—alone and disgraced. 'It's over.' She sat back on her heels, sucking in deep, shaky breaths.

'I can't believe it.' Maggie's usually stern mouth quivered. 'We knew him his whole life. And now he's ... This is how it ended?'

'He was a rotten egg.' Verity rose, dusting off her skirts.

'That doesn't mean we stopped loving him.' Maggie's voice broke.

Verity handed over her handkerchief. Geoffrey and Ellen were the closest Maggie had come to having her own children. She wanted to wrap her arms about the other woman's shoulders, but that last seed of fear held her back.

'What now?' asked Maggie.

'We do all that we can. We tell the authorities and make sure Gwen's safe. Then ... Then we go home.'

'Back to the duke's house?'

'No. Home to Evendale.' She held Maggie's gaze, even as heat flushed her face and her chest seemed to constrict. 'Yes?'

Without pausing for thought, Maggie slipped her hand into Verity's, as she'd never done before, and tugged her back the way they'd come. 'Yes.'

***

Gwen's weight was a welcome burden. Ellen cradled her little girl as she drifted into an exhausted sleep. Pressing another kiss to her temple, Ellen settled into the gentleman's armchair by the cold library fire. The low mumble of Maggie's and Verity's voices drifted in through the open door. They were answering questions of a Bow Street Runner.

Ellen pressed her lips tight together. *My brother's dead.* The words swam through her thoughts, never pausing long enough for her to properly catch hold of them. Her brother ... dead. Everything he'd done to Gwen, and to herself, was unforgivable, but he was still her brother. He was still ... She still loved him. At part of her did. A very small part.

The front door opened and closed with the arrival of the doctor for Chakrabarti, while footsteps rattled the ceiling overhead. The ball had resumed. The guests were absolutely riveted by the story of the misunderstood duke who'd saved his fiancée's baby sister from the clutches of their crazed brother.

'...really don't think she should be disturbed.'

The Runner entered the library, notebook in hand. Verity and Maggie charged in after him.

'Do you really have to do this now?' demanded Maggie.

'...running out of champagne.' Lady Faye hurried in the library, two temporary kitchen servants tailing her.

'...asking to see you.' A gentleman dressed as a pierrot tried to cut Calum off as he too strode through the door.

'...such red hair,' murmured Owen, watching Sophy with wonder.

Through the crowd, Ellen watched the duke. Her breathing slowed even as her heartbeat quickened. His shoulders were beginning to fill out again and his cheeks weren't looking so hollow. All the food and attention of the last few weeks were doing him so good.

She felt both calm and exhilarated. Was that even possible? She loved him with every fibre of her being. It wasn't a schoolroom love as she'd felt for Gwen's father; it was love cultivated and matured with understanding and trust. What a fool she'd been refusing his marriage proposal in her desperation to keep from letting her brother control her life. Refusing Calum because of Geoffrey was just as bad as accepting Calum because of Geoffrey. She just hadn't realised that before today. Ironic, almost, now that Geoffrey was dead.

She swallowed, fighting back tears.

From this moment on she was going to start making her own choices. And they would be choices based purely on her own thoughts and feelings and conscience, regardless of what anyone else thought.

And her first choice ... She smiled as Calum ran a hand thought his hair. It was already growing back. She'd have to cut it again for him soon—or Chakrabarti would. She rose to her feet, Gwen still clutched to her chest. 'Will you marry me, Calum Callaghan?'

Nobody heard her speak. Nobody looked her way. Nobody paid her the slightest ounce of attention. Nobody except for Calum. He met her gaze across the crowded room, his month opening in surprise, and then he was at her side, pulling her and Gwen into his arms, bowing his head and burying his face into her shoulder.

'Do ye mean it, lass?' he asked, his voice muffled. 'Don't ask if ye're not completely sure, because if we get married I'm never going to stop loving ye. Not for a second. Not for all of time. It'll be ye and me and Gwen forever.'

She pulled back so she could see his face. His eyes were wide and there was a vulnerability in his gaze, as though he really were wearing his heart on his sleeve. She was going to have to take good care of his heart. It had been beaten and broken too many times before.

She stood up on her tippy toes and kissed him, claiming his mouth with her own. 'Marry me.'

Thanks for reading *The Unworthy Duke*. I hope you enjoyed it.

Sign up to our newsletter romance.com.au/newsletter/ and find out about new releases, must-read series and **ebook deals** at romance.com.au.

Reviews can help readers find books, and I am grateful for all honest reviews. Thank you for taking the time to let others know what you've read, and what you thought.

Share your reading experience on:
Facebook
Instagram
romance.com.au

www.ingramcontent.com/pod-product-compliance
Lightning Source LLC
Chambersburg PA
CBHW011803010726
47498CB00010B/2881